Blocked Out:

Mental Illness is a byproduct of Capitalism .

Mandy Partridge.

1

ISBN-paperback: 978-0-6451209-0-5

ISBN-ebook: 0645120912

ASIN- BO8XZPKY25

Cover design by: Veronica Curties Chen

1. Locked up again.

This is not my bed. These are white sheets, this is a single bed. My sheets are purple. I'm in that place again, aren't I? One of those places.

Shit, what have I done to get taken here this time?

I'm trying to think, I'm trying to think, but my head's feeling really groggy. Did I get drunk?

Oh, my hands are cable tied together. That's a good sign, not.

Still, I can use my teeth to cut through the cable tie. Oh, but my mouth hurts. My teeth, my teeth are all still there. It's my lips. They are all scabby. Have I been in a fight again?

Right, my hands are a bit messed up too. I've lost a fingernail. I've got a cut which has been sewn up. I'm wearing a robe. What was I wearing last night, or whenever?

Oh, my head hurts when I sit up, I think I'll just lie down again. Oh, God.

The cops brought me in. They must have brought me in in handcuffs, then they took them with them, and a nurse or a guard has put the cable ties on me. They must have been scared I'd hurt someone, or hurt myself.

What time is it? Where is my phone?

Oh, they've probably taken my phone away. There are my shoes. So I was wearing the black platform sandals when I was brought in. What would I wear with those? A minidress, or a skirt and top. My denim jacket? Where are those?

OK, I can sit up.

My wallet is in the bedside table. No cash, that's about right. My card is there, and my licence. Did I have some acid in there? Or did I take it? Did I sell it to someone, or give it away?

Did the nurses take it out? Did the cops?

It hurts to stand up. It hurts to walk. It's not far to the little wardrobe. My jacket is in there, but not my other clothes. My jacket smells like smoke. It's got nothing in the pocket except some tissues, and a key. It's a house key. It's my house key. But where is my car key?

That's right, I don't have a car any more.

But that was last time. Last time I was in here. Or not here, exactly. This is a nice place. This must be Carina private hospital or something. Last time I was in the public hospital at the PA. That place where the men kept wandering into my room.

I smashed the car last time, that was how they caught me that time. They pulled me out of the smashed up car. Or something.

This time there was another car. Not my car. I couldn't afford another car after that.

My phone is not here. I need my phone. If I could look at what I posted last night, or yesterday, I could work out what I have done. Maybe.

I feel like shit. My head is thumping. I am sore around the hands and arms, around the neck.

I have done something stupid. Again.

A nurse came in.

"It's seven o'clock, and time for your medication," said the nurse.

"Alright," I said, sounding croaky.

The nurse handed me a small dish of pills.

"What are they?" I asked.

"You've got some anti-psychotics, and some anti-nausea meds. Your chart said that you've a history of nausea reaction to these pills," said the nurse.

"OK," I said, swallowing the pills with a little cup of water.

"Show me inside your mouth," said the nurse.

I opened my mouth.

"Lift up your tongue and move it from side to side," said the nurse.

I did as she said.

"Right then. Rita will be in in a little while to check your vital signs, so don't go back to sleep," said the nurse, as she left.

She made me show her inside my mouth to prove I'd swallowed the pills.

I must have really fucked up this time.

My hand is sore. It's bruised. I've been holding onto something hard with this hand. My first two fingers feel like they are broken. They are all swollen.

I've been holding on to something for dear life.

Rita comes in.

"Hi, I'm Rita, I've just come to take your stats," she says.

Rita put a clip on my finger to take my pulse. She blew up an armband around me to take my blood pressure, and she put a blowtorch in my ear to check my temperature. She wrote it all on my chart.

"Right, that's it then. Breakfast is at eight," said Rita.

"Where do I go?" I asked.

"The dining room is out the door, to your left and down the hall a bit," said Rita.

Then she left too. Busy, these nurses.

How could I tell the time if I don't have my phone?

I want my phone.

They must know that taking someone's phone is a very cruel punishment.

There is a small bathroom next to my room. I look terrible. My face is bruised, a well as my hand. I can clean some of that blood off. It looks like I had a nosebleed, and a split lip.

Ouch. Just gently. God, what has happened to my hair? It's not even. It looks like some is missing from one side. I'll just have to get the hairdresser to fix it up again.

Shit. The blonde is too harsh. The bleach breaks it off. I used to keep it longer, but the bleach made it too thin. Now I'll have to get an even shorter cut, maybe an asymmetric look. Fuck.

I look like I've done ten rounds with Mike Tyson.

My shit is black and watery. My piss smells like energy drink and is dark yellow. It hurts a bit to piss. It hurts a bit to do anything.

There is a clock on the wall above my bed.

It says ten to eight.

If my nails are red, I might have been wearing the red dress. Or the red skirt with a black top. I had that new red underwear that fitted so well.

Breakfast. I don't think I'm very hungry. But I'll go along just in case.

The room is nice, it overlooks some scrubby bushland. There are birds. There are four long tables and lots of chairs. Some other inmates or patients are here already. I'll follow that guy.

Right, I get a plate, a metal and enamel one. The hotbox has got bacon and eggs, sausages and cooked tomatoes. Then there is cereal, muesli, yoghurt, milk, tinned fruit, whole fruit. Plastic knives and forks so we don't cut ourselves. Plastic glasses and metal cups, for the same reason.

I sit at a table by myself. I don't want to talk to anyone here.

They'll all be at least as fucked up as I am. And that's pretty fucked up.

This is not a good place to make friends.

I ate up the hot food, and it was good. Then I ate up the cold food, and it was good too. I didn't realise how hungry I was. I haven't eaten since, I don't know. I vaguely remember a pizza.

That seems like a long time ago.

"You wouldn't have a cigarette, would you love?" asked an older man.

"No, sorry, I don't smoke," I said.

Except I think I do. But I don't have any on me. Not even a lighter. But I suppose they would have taken a lighter off me, if I'd had one. Considering the plastic knives and glasses.

"You eat a lot for someone who is so skinny," said the man.

"Yeah," I said, as I got up and took my plate and bowl and glass back to the counter. I threw away my plastic cutlery, grabbed a couple of napkins and returned to my room.

That's enough conversation for me today.

Back in my room, I realise that I stink. I've got to have a shower. I stink like I haven't had a shower for quite a few days. I smell like I've had sex. But who with, I couldn't say. Mustn't have meant much. Some pickup. That's it, I've got to have a shower to wash off the man smell.

After the breakfast, I can muster the energy to have a shower.

This robe thing ties up at the back, but it's pretty loose.

Oh shit, looks like I've got a few more bruises down there too. My ribs are bruised, and I've got a graze down my back and my bum. I've gone down a wall, and hit the floor. Hard. Someone has hit my face, my arms and my ribs.

The shower feels good. There is soap, but no razor. Looks like I'll just have to be hairy.

The cut on the bottom of my hand has started bleeding again. I'll hold it up, out of the water.

I can't quite count how many stitches there are holding it together.

Right, I'll dry off and get that robe back on. I'll just wrap the hand in toilet paper for the time being.

This robe doesn't really cover much.

What else can I find? There is another robe, and a pair of nanna knickers in a drawer. If I put the second robe back to front over the first robe, people can't see my bum or the pants.

Now my hair. I dry it with the towel, and it looks tragic. I can use a bit of soap to stand it up a bit, give it a bit of body. Fuck I need a hairdresser really badly. Or even just a pair of scissors. But that probably won't happen.

That's the best I can do, I'll just leave it.

I'll leave the mirror alone.

Not much to do in here, without my phone. I wouldn't watch TV for free, so I'm definitely not paying to watch it. There's a brochure about Carina Private Hospital. A floor-plan, a tv and games room, a library. No one will be in the library. I'll go there.

No one is in the library, I have to turn on the light. It's only a small room, a cupboard, but there are books and newspapers. There are lots of self help books. There is a lot of fiction, the common thread seems to be stories of people who have turned their lives around. There are books about politics. I'll pick up a few of them. I've always meant to read more about politics.

Back in my room, I'm reading the back covers, working out which one to read first, when the doctor comes in.

9

2. Doctor Rosenberg.

"Hi, I'm Doctor Rosenberg," said the doctor.

"Hi, I'm Elise," I said, offering my hand, but seeing it is wrapped in toilet paper, pulling it away again.

"I'll just call a nurse to put a proper dressing on that. Rachel! Can you come here with some dressings?" said the doctor to a nurse outside.

Rachel came in and put some cream and a wide band-aid over my stitches. Then she left.

Doctor Rosenberg looked on, and looked at my chart. She wore a peach coloured suit and a patterned silk blouse, big pearls and gold glasses. Her hair was in a dark bob with silver streaks that looked well tended.

"Elise, do you know why you're in here?" asked Rosenberg.

"Ah, I'm guessing I fucked up in a big way, but I can't really remember," I said.

"The police brought you in. You had car-jacked an older man and made him drive to your friend's house," said the doctor.

"Oh shit. I did a car-jacking?" I asked.

"The driver called the cops after he dropped you off, and they came and arrested both you and your friend. You for the car-jacking, and your friend for dealing heroin," said Rosenberg.

"Oh," was all I could say.

"You threatened the driver, and the police, with a replica firearm," said the doctor.

"I did?" I said, holding my right hand. It was a gun that I was holding on to for dear life.

"The police wanted to charge you for a series of offences, but when they realised that you had mental health problems, they knew that no charges would stick to you," said Rosenberg.

"It's a bit of a get-out-of-jail-for-free card, isn't it?" I joked.

"It's no laughing matter, Elise. They could have shot you. If you weren't a pretty white girl, they probably would have," said the doctor.

"Right. I see your point. Did they have to wrestle the gun off me?" I asked.

"You really can't recall, can you? The police took you to the Royal Brisbane, but their psych ward was full. So when they saw that you had private health insurance, they brought you here," said Rosenberg.

"I thought this place looked too nice to be a public hospital. Am I locked in here?" I asked.

"Yes, this is a locked ward. You are under an involuntary assessment order to stay here for a month, while I assess you, then we'll decide what we do with you after that," said the doctor.

"Alright," I said. It was hard to process.

"Are you using very much heroin at the moment?" asked Rosenberg.

"Not as much as I had been before. I was just getting a fifty dollar taste before I went to see a client. I wasn't doing it every day," I said.

"You see, I wanted to proscribe methadone, but I didn't know what sort of a dose you were using. The anti-psychotic will calm you down, but you'll still have cravings for the opioid. I don't want to give you too much, and I only want you to drink it when you really need it. I'd like to see you withdraw from opioids while you're here, or at least transfer your addiction from heroin to methadone," said the doctor.

"How did you know I was using?" I asked.

"You look like a junky. Your friend was arrested with a large quantity of heroin. You car-jacked a man to get to your dealer's house. You have puncture marks and old track marks. You wear a denim jacket in summer to cover up your arms," said Rosenberg.

"I'm really sorry about pulling a gun on the man in the car. I didn't mean to hurt or scare him. I can't even remember doing it. I usually try not to hurt anyone except myself," I said.

"Elise, I want you to try not to hurt yourself either, this time," said the doctor. "You deserve a happy life, a life without drugs. If you carry on like this, you'll kill yourself."

"I want that too," I said, and I couldn't stop myself from crying. The doctor gave me a box of tissues. I wiped my eyes and my nose.

"Have you got your own place?" asked Rosenberg.

"Yes, I've got a flat in Spring Hill," I said.

"Well, that's a good start," said the doctor. "What about work?"

"I get a bit of acting work, but mostly modelling. I just do sex work when I'm waiting to get paid, or if it's a while till the next gig. I usually check my phone every day, my agent calls at short notice, or just sends texts," I said.

"You'll get your phone for half an hour later. Here we use them to reward good behaviour," said Rosenberg.

"Oh, great," I said.

"Just tell your agent you're having an enforced break," joked the doctor.

"She'll think I'm having a boob-job and a butt-lift," I said.

"Do you need surgery to get more work?" asked Rosenberg.

"Really, I thought that the drama degree would lead to solid work. It has meant I get more auditions, for professional companies like QTC and La Boite, but I'm still working as much as when I was a student," I said.

"No discernible difference?" asked the doctor.

"Not like the difference I noticed once I went blonde. That doubled my work. I'll stay blonde now, it really changed everything," I said.

"I'll bet the blonde was a whole lot cheaper than the drama degree too. What about relationships. Have you got someone special?" asked Rosenberg.

"Not really, but I've got a few good friends," I said. Just don't ask me to name them, I thought.

"That's good, we all need friends. Have you got any friends who don't use heroin?" asked the doctor.

"A couple. My neighbour, Judith. She'll keep an eye on my place while I'm not there. She'll tell me if anyone comes around when I'm not there," I said, and I hoped.

"Good. Because you have to distance yourself from your friends who use, if you want to stop using. You've had these psychotic episodes before. They coincide with difficult times in your life, when you feel you're losing control, when you're depressed and can't think of any way out of your situation. I want to help you build a stable life, where you can be in control, and be happy. I'm not judgemental about the sex work. Some women make a fortune and set themselves up for life doing sex work. But if you've got to have a taste before you can visit a client, that's not a good habit to form. If you can't do it straight, you probably shouldn't do it," said Rosenberg.

"Yeah, you're right," I said. "I do my other work straight. If only it was more regular."

"I want you to start thinking about other casual work that could fit in around you modelling and acting. Bar work, sales, market research, cleaning, driving, anything," she said.

"I smashed my car and I can't afford another one," I said.

"Think of things you can do. Make a list. I see you've been to the library, that's good," said the doctor.

"I will make a list. I liked the library, there were lots of political books. I want to understand politics better," I said.

"That's good. Make a list of which books you read too. Use your time here productively. There is a Narcotics Anonymous meeting here on Monday, Wednesday and Fridays. I'd like you to attend, I think it will help you," said Rosenberg.

"OK, I will. What day is it today?" I asked.

13

"It's Sunday, the second of February, 2020. You'll be here until the first of March. Or until we think you're ready to leave," said the doctor.

"Right. Thanks Doctor Rosenberg," I said.

"I'll see you in a few days, Elise," said the doctor.

15

3. Cravings.

Around midday, the cravings started.

I had to go to the Nurse's station, which was half way along a row of twelve rooms, and near the common lounge room.

It hurt to sit up. It hurt to stand up. I was cold. I walked to the wardrobe and got my denim jacket. I put it over my two stylish robes.

I walked slowly down the corridor. I couldn't think. I could hardly keep my balance to walk. My hand was throbbing now. I had to put it under my other arm and hold it to my body.

"Hi, I'm Elise from room twelve," I said.

"Hi, I'm Nurse Wells, but you can call me Jackie," said the nurse who had given me the meds this morning.

"Um, did Doctor Rosenberg leave some other medication for me?" I asked.

"I'll just check your file," said Jackie, as she typed on the computer. Then she checked a folder full of papers.

"I think yours is is the fridge," said the nurse, as she got a key from a keychain on her belt, and unlocked the small fridge. Jackie found a little brown bottle of methadone with a printed label, and brought it up to her bench.

"You have to drink it in front of me," said Jackie.

"No worries," I said. It hurt to hold the bottle and unscrew the lid. I drank the foul stuff, and the nurse gave me a plastic cup of water, to take the taste out of my mouth.

Then my legs just sort of crumpled beneath me, and I was sitting on the floor.

The nurse came around and helped me up, and helped me to a chair near her bench. I took a few minutes to get it back together, then I walked down to my room.

I was in the end room.

Did they put me in there because I was making lots of noise when they brought me in?

I don't know. But I know it seemed like a really long distance to walk.

The walk really tired me out.

Back in my room, I thought I'd lie down for a bit and read. I was out like a light.

I missed lunch.

When I woke up again it was getting dark. I hope I haven't missed dinner.

Where is my phone?

That's right, the clock above my bed. Ten past six. Dinner is from six till seven, I'd better get it together. I'm hot now, I'll take my jacket off.

It doesn't seem so far down the corridor to the dining room now. I can walk faster too.

I'm late. The other patients are all already eating. I'll get my food first, then I'll have to decide where to sit. I'm getting the last of the meat and veg from the hotbox, but it smells good.

I'll sit next to a woman if I can, I don't want to have to sit near men. Though it looks like there are a lot more men in here than women.

I sat next to an older woman, and she didn't even look up at me.

I ate my dinner. I smiled at the older lady, and I put my things away. Some people moved to the lounge room next door, to watch TV. But I went back to my room. I wanted to make a start on 'Capital' by Karl Marx.

A different nurse comes around for the evening meds. He is an African man called John. John gave me pills, but not more methadone. He checked my mouth to make sure I'd swallowed them. And he did my vital signs. There must be less staff on for the night shift.

'Capital' is good so far. I realised I have been using the word 'capitalist' wrongly for ages.

The only capitalist is the man who owns the means of production. The wage-slaves who happily participate in capitalism are not capitalists, even if they think they are.

I go to sleep and dream about workers in factories, and masses of people walking together, marching.

Then I wake up in the night. Where am I?

This is not my bed. Oh, that's right, I'm in one of those places. I'm in the Loony Bin again.

And I'm having the withdrawal symptoms again.

I drag myself down the hallway to the nurses' station. John is there, tall and black in his blue pyjama uniform.

"Oh, Nurse John, I think I need my medication," I manage to say.

"Elise, isn't it? I'll just check your file," says John.

He checked my computer file, and folder, then got the fridge key, unlocked the fridge, and gave me a bottle. The bottle wasn't as full this time. In fact, it was only half full.

I drank it in one gulp, and washed it down with water. Then I did a bit of dry retching, then I got it together.

"Sorry about that," I said.

"You don't have to apologise," said John. "But, girl, you look terrible. What happened to you?"

"Ah, I'm not really sure. The doctor said I car-jacked someone, but I can't really remember what I did," I said.

"It looks like someone beat you really badly. Was it your boyfriend?" asked John.

"I don't have a boyfriend, but it might have been a pick-up, or it might have been the cops," I said.

"Or the person you car-jacked?" asked John.

"I don't know if they'd fight back against a gun," I said.

"Oh, so that's yours, is it?" said John.

"What do you mean?" I said.

"See that safe over there?" asked John. "We put people's possessions in there when they come in. It's mostly phones, wallets and cards, but there is a handgun in a brown paper bag in there at the moment. I was wondering whose it was, heh heh."

"I suppose it must be," I said, looking at my hand.

"Oh, that looks sore. They must have hit your hand, or hit you hand against something hard, until you let it go," said John.

"I think I'll just go back to bed now," I said.

"Sleep well, gun lady," said John.

When I got back to the room, I looked at the clock. It was two fifteen in the morning.

20

4. Group therapy.

I woke up for my meds and vital signs.

It was Nurse Rita again today. They must be rostered over weekends and weekdays as well.

"Don't forget that you've got an NA meeting this morning," said Rita.

"Where do I go for that?" I asked.

"It's in the conference room in the next building. The guard will take you all over there, sit outside, then bring you all back. You have to make sure that you have used the bathroom before you go, as there are no pass-outs from the meeting," said Rita.

"What time is it on?" I asked.

"From nine till eleven," said Rita. "And they mostly wear plain clothes over in the Addiction ward. Laundry have brought back what you were wearing when you came in. You'll get your phone today at midday, so try to ring someone to bring in some plain clothes for you."

"Oh, great, OK," I said.

This would be a hard one to work out. Judith could get some clothes, but she used to rely on me to drive her around. She's a bit old and slow to catch public transport. I'll have to order Ubers for her to get here and back.

Luckily, I gave Judith a key to my flat, as I have locked myself out a few times before. So she can get in. There have to be some clean clothes somewhere in there. I seem to recall the place being a little bit of a mess, but a four room flat can only contain so much mess. Needles, though, there were syringes in the bathroom. I'll have to tell her not to go in there.

Shit.

I've got to ring my agent first, though. Serena will want to know where I am and why and when I'll be available for work again. She'll get the first call. Or maybe text.

Judith will definitely be next.

I check the wardrobe and the red minidress is in there. I suppose it's slightly better than the robe. My underwear is in the drawer.

It hurts to put the bra on. The underwire sticks into my ribs where I have a big bruise. But I can't not wear it. I look slutty enough already.

I go to breakfast and don't talk to anybody. But they look at me, because I'm wearing a red minidress and a black denim jacket.

After breaky, I put on the black platform sandals to go to the next building.

We meet at the door to the ward, near room one. A guard is waiting for us, and ticks our names off a list. Then he used his swipe card to open the first metal door. There is only room for about three people between the first and second doors, so someone holds the first door open while the guard swipes the second door as well.

We walk out into the sunlight, and my eyes are not used to the brightness. I am blinded for a few seconds, then join our group as we walk across a neat garden to another building like ours. These are modern concrete and brick buildings, with closed windows to keep the air conditioning inside. Outside it is fucking hot. The walk to the next building makes me break out in a sweat. The guard chats to the other guard who is stationed outside this building, and opens the two sets of metal doors to let us all in.

This ward is bigger, at least twenty rooms, but otherwise looks exactly the same. Pastel coloured walls and grey carpet, all calming and vaguely cheerful. The guard walks us down the corridor, past the nurses' station and common room, to a door which says 'Conference Room'. Inside more locked doors, there are twenty or so plastic chairs with an armrest for writing.

A man in a dark grey suit and light purple shirt is sitting at one end of the oval of seats.

The patients from the Addiction Ward come in now as well. They are a slightly younger crowd than those of us from Metal Health. They swagger in and take chairs, some chatting with each other.

"Hi, I'm Dave and I'm a recovering alcoholic. I'll be chairing this meeting today. This is a combined Alcoholics and Narcotics Anonymous group. We'll each introduce ourselves, and talk about our addictions, and how we are going in our journey towards sobriety. We'll try to keep it to a few minutes per person. If anyone has anything positive to say, please say it at the end of each person's turn. I might ask questions or try to steer the speech back towards our topic. Please try not to ramble, but keep to the point," said Dave.

"Hi, I'm Anthony and I'm a drug addict. I dealt drugs for the last fifteen years in Sydney, then I got married and tried to straighten out my life. I got a straight job, but I couldn't get away from the social aspect of dealing, seeing my friends, having a joint or passing the bong around. We moved to Brisbane so I could leave my friends behind. But I soon met people through work who smoked or took pills and trips. I got in trouble with the police, and realised I had to stop altogether. I've gone for two weeks without drugs or alcohol in here, and I still crave alcohol every night. I really craved pot for the first few days, but I think I'm ok with that now," said Anthony.

"Thanks Anthony," said Dave. "If you still have alcohol cravings when you are at home, you can try non-alcoholic beer or wine. It tastes the same, and it gives you something to hold on to."

The next guy spoke up. "Hi, I'm Christian, and I'm a recovering heroin addict. I was managing a night club, but I got too wasted and fucked up my booking of bands and DJs. Finding the money and the hammer every day was taking up all of my time and effort, and by the time I got to work, I was past caring. I was using five and six hundred dollars worth of gear per day, and I would do anything for it. I pressured my girlfriend to work as a prostitute to get money for drugs. I went out and worked as a male prostitute. I'm not even gay, but I sucked cocks for money. I knew the only way to get clean was to go to rehab. I've been clean for five weeks and three days, and I'm starting to like myself again now. I don't know if I'll be able to work in the same business, I might have burnt my bridges and ruined my reputation. I'm starting looking at different kinds of work now. I'll need to make new friends too," said Christian.

"Hi, I'm Linda, and I'm a recovering alcoholic," said a pretty dark haired woman of about thirty. "I got so drunk, so often, that I lost custody of my two kids. I wasn't getting them to school on time, or with clean uniforms, so a social worker visited my house, and ended up taking my kids away to foster homes. I got behind on the rent, and lost my house, and ended up living in my car. A lady at the homeless shelter helped me to get in here, so I could stop drinking. I was working behind a bar, but I've got to find another job where I'm not around other alcoholics all the time. Now I'm planning to get a certificate in child-care, so I can look after other people's kids. Then I might be able to get my kids back."

"Hi my name's Steve and I'm a multi-substance abuser. I was ok when I was just smoking the weed and drinking occasionally. But then one of my mates from the building site started getting into speed, and I started taking it too. Soon, my mate Ted was getting into the meth, and I started smoking it too. I stopped sleeping and started thinking crazy thoughts. My mate Ted went totally nuts and robbed a bank, and now he's in jail. I didn't know where else to get meth, and I freaked out a bit. I couldn't go to work. I booked my self in here. Hopefully I've still got a job to go back too. The boss and the other guys didn't realise I was almost as bad a meth-head as Ted. I guess I'm lucky that way. I've nearly done my month now, but I'm going to stay straight. I'm going to save and get out of the boarding house and buy my own place."

Then it was my turn. Shit. What am I going to say?

"Hi, my name is Elise and I'm a heroin addict. I've been using since I used to live in a group home, and I met my first boyfriend. I've been through rehab a couple of times before, and I'm having trouble staying clean out there on my own. My work in modelling is really casual, sometimes I get heaps of gigs, other times, I go for look-sees and auditions and I don't get the jobs. I started hooking to make my rent between gigs. Then I found that I couldn't make myself go to the client's unless I had a fifty bag first. I got into some trouble and the police brought me in. I'm having weird reactions to the methadone, but I'm on anti-psychotics too, so maybe they aren't mixing very well. This is only my second day off illegal drugs," I said.

"Welcome, Elise. You've made the first step. That's brave to admit that you've got a problem and have tried rehab before. Some of us try many times before we finally get sober," said Dave.

"Hi, I'm Russel, and I'm a recovering coke addict", said the redhead guy next to me. He was in a business shirt and trousers, and just looked like an office worker. "I work in investment and wealth management, and I was living the high life with some of my rich clients. My friend who has a chain of hair salons introduced me to cocaine, and we got on really well. Too well. I think I blew about a hundred grand on coke in the last year. My wife left me. Then I was all alone in a big house on Hamilton hill, feeling sorry for myself. The woman who washes my dog found me a blithering mess on the Persian rug. She helped me to book in here and she's looking after my dog. I don't know what would have happened if she hadn't intervened. I was having thoughts about jumping off the Gateway. I thought I had it all, but I was missing something important. Ah, two weeks I've been clean. No more coke for me," said Russel.

"G'day, I'm Jack, and I'm an alcoholic drug addict. I've been drinking since school, and I never really stopped. I'd drink till I was so blind I couldn't remember what happened. Every weekend. Then I broke my leg at work, and took ages healing. I got hooked on painkillers, and I started doctor-shopping to get more and more scripts. I got really messed up between the grog and the pills, and I crashed a work vehicle. I'm an engineer, and I want to get back to work once I sort out my addictions and my head. I've got to find new friends who don't get drunk every weekend. Three weeks sober, the first week was the worst. I'm still getting headaches, but the leg doesn't seem to hurt any more, unless I run on it. I've been going to the gym, that has really helped," said Jack.

After that, a few more people spoke, but I can't really remember their stories. I started thinking about those people who had spoken already, and how we were all going through a similar thing. We were all trying to make sense of our lives, and work out where we'd gone wrong. No one really talked about love, or families, unless they had lost someone special.

We had all alienated ourselves from our families, and many our friends too. Too often our friends had helped enable us to get on and stay on drugs. But we can't blame them. We can only blame ourselves.

Dave gave out some pieces of paper, and pens.

"I want you all to write down three things that you can do to rebuild your lives. It might be big, like finding a new flat or a job, or it might be little, like being kinder to myself, or starting to cook again instead of eating take-away," said Dave.

I tried to think of three things. I tried to think of one thing.

New haircut.

Fuck, what was another thing?

Remember what happened.

One more thing. Shit. New clothes probably won't cut it. New friends? Sounds a bit sad.

Alright, something a bit bigger.

Contact family.

I haven't done that for a very long time. I've never done that. There's got to be someone.

"OK," said Dave, "now I want you to write down one thing that you can do today which will change your life."

Fuck. What can I do today?

Uber for Judith with clothes.

If I get that worked out, I'll be a lot better off.

Dave looked around the room to see if we had all finished writing.

"Don't worry, I won't collect your sheet. What you wrote is for yourselves. I can help, and the group can help, but mostly, we have to help ourselves. Keep thinking about those things, and add to your list when you think of other things that will help in a positive way," said Dave.

Dave said some other stuff, and asked us all some questions, but by now I was starting to get the symptoms again. My hand was throbbing, so I put it under my arm. My head started aching, but I knew I couldn't leave the room till the meeting was over. I tried to listen to what everyone was saying, but I kept tuning out, zoning out, going back to the pain.

When it was finally over, we walked with the uniformed guard back to the mental health wing, through four locked metal doors.

I went straight to the nurses' station. Rita was there.

"Nurse Rita, I really need that methadone," I said, pathetically.

"Right, I'll just open your file and mark it off," said Rita.

She did the computer thing, the file thing, then got the key to the fridge. I saw into it this time. There was milk for coffees, some water bottles, and dozens of little bottles and packets of meds. Everyone in here must be on something. Or a couple of things.

My bottle was only half full again. At least I wasn't as bad as the last time I was locked up. I think I started on two bottles that time. I was really fucked up then. I'm only half as bad this time. A quarter as bad.

My hand stopped hurting. My head stopped aching. I could stand up straight and I didn't feel like falling down or spewing. I thanked the nurse.

"Oh, Elise, you might as well have this now. I usually unlock the phones at twelve, but it's past eleven now. You can hand it back in on your way to lunch," said Rita.

She handed over my phone.

I could hardly believe it.

I almost floated back to my room.

29

5. My phone, at last.

Right, I had to check my messages first.

Serena has left a few texts of the "Where the hell are you?" type. I missed a job. Damn.

"Dear Serena, I am so sorry to have missed that job. I had another psychotic episode, and have been involuntarily hospitalised until the first of March. So sorry, Elise."

I checked the other messages, but they could wait. They would be clients or my 'friends' looking for drugs. I deleted both the messages and the contacts. I don't need these friends any more.

I had to call Judith, my neighbour. She was old and didn't really know how to do texts.

Either that, or her glasses weren't strong enough to read the little writing on the phone.

I would have to phone her.

Her handset phone rang about ten times before she answered it.

"Hello," said Judith.

"Hello Judith, it's me, Elise from next door," I said.

"Elise, dear, why did you phone? You should have just come over," said Judith.

"Judith, I'm in the hospital again, and I need to ask you a big favour," I said.

"Oh, you poor thing. Are you alright?" said Judith.

"I've had another episode. I'll have to stay here for a month. I'm out at the Carina private hospital. Judith, could you possibly go across to my flat and pack a bag with clothes and underwear? I can call Uber cars to pick you up and take you home. Visiting hours here are from four till six in the afternoon," I said.

"Oh, oh, oh you poor dear. Yes, I can find you a bag of clothes. Have you got slippers?" asked Judith.

"No, I don't have any slippers. I usually just wear thick socks if it's cold. I need socks and undies, and a pair of shoes, and a toothbrush and hairbrush would be good too," I said.

"Do you want your make-up, dear?" asked Judith.

"No, oh wait, yes, you'd better find the foundation and powder. I'm a bit bruised and I'd like to cover it up," I said.

"Bruised? Oh, are you really alright. Did someone beat you?" asked Judith.

"I just got involved in an altercation, but it's nothing serious. Actually, Judith, can you grab my short blond wig as well?" I asked.

"Yes, yes, I'll have a look around and find you some nice things to wear. Now, how will I know when the Uber car is here?" said Judith.

"I'll order one for four thirty. It will stop just outside near the stairwell. I'll pay for it in advance, so you don't have to worry about money. The car will have a sign on the window, a white square with Uber on it," I said.

"Alright. I've never caught an Uber car before. It will be an adventure," said Judith.

"When you get here, I'm in the mental health ward, room 12. My last name is Forsyth, if you don't know, Elise Forsyth," I said.

"Right, I've written all that down. Four thirty. Carina Private Hospital. Mental Health, room twelve. Elise Forsyth. I'll see you then, dear," said Judith.

"Thanks, Judith, I'll see you this arvo," I said.

I hoped she'd come. She's getting a little forgetful in her old age, but if she's written it down, she'll hopefully remember.

Now I'll go online and book an Uber for her, while I've got it together.

I've just got to look at facebook.

Good. No incriminating photos or video. Just a few 'where are you?'s and 'Call me!'s on my page and in my personal messages.

What about my performer page? Yeah, much the same. There's a link to that band video clip that I danced in a couple of months ago. It's finally up, so the song must have been released. I'll watch it with the sound right down. Oh yeah, not that bad. The song is pretty crap, but the band look good, and I look good too.

Right, I've probably got time to check my other website too, before lunch. What is the password again? Right. Oh, these men are all so revolting. Demanding. Where am I? As if any of you of you dicks could give a toss. These guys don't even warrant a message. They can just wait. I'll just head back to facebook and check Karen's page. She hasn't put up anything recently. I wonder where she is? I'll just send her a private message. Oh, she hasn't responded to my last two private messages either. I'll just write "Thinking of you".

Who are these other people who've written on my page?

Now I'll just quickly check my bank, and see if I've paid the rent. Password? Yep. Great, the rent is paid for this fortnight, and I've got enough to pay next fortnight's when it's due.

Thank God for that.

Now it's lunch time and I'll have to hand the phone back. Things aren't too bad.

Just averagely bad.

I had lunch and had a little nap, but at five o'clock I was looking out the window, wondering when and if Judith was going to show up.

Then a nurse brought her in to the nurses' station. They checked the green shopping bags that she carried.

"We're just checking for razors or scissors or sharp things. Is it just clothes?" asked Rita.

"Oh, I brought a little make-up bag, and shoes too, and a brush," said Judith, looking confused.

"That's alright dear, you can give those things to Elise. We just have to check for alcohol and dangerous things. Here is Elise now," said Rita.

"Hello Judith, I'm so glad you came," I said.

"Oh, Elise, just look at you," said Judith, and she gave me an awkward hug.

Judith would be about five foot two, dumpy and with her grey hair dyed a bright henna red, and I am five eleven. She wears button through floral dresses and flat slip-on shoes, but coifs her hair into a beehive with tendrils.

"I'm ok, but you can see why I asked for the make-up. You look great, Judith," I said.

"Thank you, dear," said Judith.

"My room is down this way," I said, ushering her along.

I let her sit on the one chair, and I sat on the bed.

"Oh, I'm so glad you brought me a pair of jeans," I said, emptying the clothes on to the bed.

"I know it's hot, but I thought there would be air-conditioning," said Judith.

"Great, tops, undies, my make-up bag," I said, as I folded things and stuffed them into my drawers. I tipped out the make-up bag on the bed. I found the powder compact with it's own little mirror, and automatically stared putting some on my face.

"How did you get those bruises, dear?" asked Judith.

"I know this sounds terrible, but I don't really know. I got really drunk at my friend's place, and got into a fight. I don't even remember what about. Or who I was fighting with. The police brought me here," I said.

"The police came around to your place as well," said Judith. "I had to let them in, or they would have broken down your door. But they just looked around for a few minutes. I don't think they took anything. But it was hard to tell, they made me wait outside. Your place is a bit messier than you usually keep it," said Judith.

"Oh, Judith, what have I done?" I said.

"I don't know dear, what have you done?" said Judith.

"I wish I knew. But I'm going to find out. I have stopped drinking, and there is an Alcoholics Anonymous group in here that I can go to. And a nice lady doctor who is a psychiatrist," I said.

33

"That's the way, Elise, you've got to be strong," said Judith. "My husband Crispin used to drink, he liked Scotch. He only gave up when it was too late, when the cancer made it too painful for him to drink. If he'd stopped earlier, I might have had him for longer," said Judith.

"I'm going to stay sober," I said, "and I'm going to sort out my life. I'm going to stay away from my scuzzy friends and make new ones."

"Speaking of scuzzy friends, that Damien came around to see you, and wanted me to let him in. But I wouldn't. I don't like him. He was insistent, so I shut my door in his face," said Judith.

"Oh, I'm so sorry. You did the right thing. He is a creep," I said.

"I thought it was all finished with him?" asked Judith.

"Oh, totally. He was probably coming around to borrow money, or to take my tv to the pawn shop or something," I said.

"Rotten sod," said Judith.

"Remember how he used to borrow my car, and disappear for a week?" I said.

"It was good when you had the car," said Judith.

I used to take her out for grocery trips, and she'd buy a whole week's worth of food. Now she was back to walking to the convenience store, and just buying food for the day. Her walking was slow, and she couldn't carry much up the stairs.

"I'm going to get more work, and buy another car," I said. "It might take a while, but I'll do it."

"I'm sure you will, dear," said Judith.

"I have ordered you another Uber car, for five thirty. I only get my phone for an hour, so I did it all then," I said.

"Thank you, dear, I've had quite a day," said Judith.

I walked Judith as far as the metal doors. She waved goodbye as the nurse let her out.

I had to try and remember about the car. And about Damien. There was a connection, and I wasn't letting myself remember it for some reason.

Damien was my ex-boyfriend. Well, not so much boyfriend, as ex-fuck.

He was a heroin addict, and got me back on the heroin too. And he was the one who first got me selling myself. He would wait on Brunswick St with me, and tell the John to bring me straight back afterwards. A tall skinny punk with black spiky hair, he'd wear band t-shirts and tight black jeans, and a leather jacket when it wasn't in the hock shop.

The car. What the fuck happened to the car?

It was such a nice little car.

36

6. Remembering the time before.

I had dinner and read a bit more Marx.

When I couldn't concentrate any more, I turned out the light.

I decided to think about my car and what happened to it.

It was a cherry red Chrysler Crystal Pearl, 2011 model. The Pearl had black upholstery, and it had a great stereo system. People would take their photo standing next to it. I used to drive it to work, and the other girls would ask for a lift home.

How did I get it again?

I remember driving it on the Gold Coast highway a lot. It's about a hundred kays or an hour's drive away. I was driving to uni. I was living down at the Goldy, but driving up to Brisbane to go to uni at Kelvin Grove QUT. So I was often thinking about the various plays we had to read. We mostly did modern Australian plays, some English and American, but we also had to do Shakespeare. I was dressed in a medieval style dress, acting as Viola from the Twelfth Night.

I was reciting my lines in the car, fucking Shakespeare, so hard to remember, word for word.

I remember finishing the show, a student show, but in front of a real audience. Such a feeling of relief came over me as I said my last lines.

We went front of house to see the audience still in costume. My friend Karen, who played Olivia, was with me. She's a hot brunette with a big rack, and had played one of my love interests in the show. I had spent most of the show in drag, dressed as Cezario, and was in lurve with Duke Orsino, my master. But I got to wear a dress at the end.

We got down to the foyer to see our family and friends. Ray was there. He smiled and waved, and I waved back.

"Is he your dad?" asked Karen.

"No, he's my sugar-daddy," I said.

"What the fuck?" said Karen.

"You know that nice car I drive?" I said.

"Fuck, you're kidding!" said Karen.

"And he pays for my flat in Spring Hill, he's got a big place down in Broadbeach," I said.

"So he bought you the car so you could drive back and forth," said Karen.

We got to the bottom of the stairs and Karen's boyfriend was there along with Ray. Ray could have been his dad. Tall and grey, in a grey suit and light blue shirt, Ray looked happy. He handed me a champagne, and clinked his own glass on mine.

"You didn't tell me you had the lead role," said Ray.

"One of the leads, my friend Karen and that guy Andrew had lead roles too," I said.

"You did a great job. This uni course has really made an actor out of you," said Ray.

"Thanks so much," I said.

Ray had bought me the car. I had met him online. When I was thinking about doing the drama degree, I had googled something like - "How do I support myself through uni?"

I followed the links to the sugar-daddy website.

And I signed up.

Ray contacted me. He liked the fact that I had light brown hair and natural blonde streaks. He'd had enough of bleach blondes. He seemed like a decent guy. But then, what would I know?

He was a forty-five year old man picking up an eighteen year old high school graduate.

Ray asked me if I'd had a boyfriend before, and I said no. It was so funny, because then he thought I was a virgin.

I wasn't a virgin. I had moved out of my foster home because the "brother" molested me.

Then at the group home, the House Parent groomed me and raped me repeatedly. Another girl and I both complained to the social worker, and we got a new House Parent.

But at eighteen, I aged out of the group home.

I got a job at KFC and a small flat in Annerley. The group home had been in Yeronga, so I was inching towards the city. That life there was lonely and boring.

Then Toby from the modelling agency saw me in Ric's Bar, and told me to come in to his office. He gave me his card, he was such a tall sweet handsome gay boy. He helped me get photos and work, and life became more interesting. I used to ride a bicycle around to go-sees, to work at KFC, to nightclubs and bars, everywhere.

The modelling work led to some acting work, just TV ads and video clips, but it was fun work, and interesting. Chatting to the other actors made me want to study acting, to see if I could make a real career out of it.

When Ray came along, it seemed like the easy way out.

He wasn't too bad at first. But he often ordered for me in restaurants, like I was a child or something. I had to read the menu quickly, and decide before he decided for me.

It was Ray who decided that I needed a flat in town, so I didn't have to do the Gold Coast Highway twice a day. Fridays, that road is a carpark for kilometres. After the flat, I only drove the highway on Friday nights and Monday mornings.

But the car bought me another sort of freedom as well.

Through the drama students and my modelling mates, I took to smoking weed and scoffing ecstasies. Unlike a lot of my friends, I could drive around to people's places at all hours of the day or night. I became useful to my drug dealing mates.

I was off my trolley when it happened. The accident.

I wasn't driving to the coast. I was driving my friend out to her drug dealer's house. Karen was just going to pick up ten or twenty pills for her group of friends. But we had been up all the Wednesday night, and it was Thursday night when we did the drive. I thought I had come down, but really, I was in that speedy afterburner from a night on four or five pills. My body was still awake, but my brain has ceased functioning properly quite some time before.

We were on our way to Ipswich, going to Darra, I think. But we got confused about which exit to take, I attempted one which was too early, and Karen said to get back on the highway. I was going too fast, and I smashed into a big concrete road divider. I totalled the car. I was fucked up but Karen was worse. They let me out of hospital, but Karen had to stay. They took me to the mental health ward of the Princess Alexandra hospital and locked me in Rehab for a month.

After that, Ray wouldn't buy me another car. But he did make sure I got private health insurance.

The relationship didn't last that long after that.

I had gone blonde half way through my final year. He dumped me after I graduated.

He said, "You're just another dumb bottle blonde like all the rest of them now, anyway."

41

7. The public hospital.

At first, I was in a normal ward. I had broken my collarbone and had lots of cuts and abrasions. They bandaged me up and put me in a room with Karen. She was much worse off than I, she had broken limbs and she was attached to a ventilator. I kept trying to talk to her, but she wouldn't answer me. The nurse told me she was in a coma and might not wake up for days. I cried a lot and screamed a lot, I felt so guilty.

So two big guys took me down to the addictions ward, down the elevator and out to the carpark, a newer building built next to the big one.

In through the metal doors to the foyer, then more metal doors to the ward. I had to share a room with a man, with only a shower curtain between us.

"Hey pretty," said the man, "What's your name?"

"I don't want to talk right now, I just want to rest," I said.

"Would you like to suck my cock?" asked the man. "I've got a nice big cock. You'd really like it. You look like the kind of girl who likes cock. Do you like to be fucked? Do you like it in the arse?"

"If you don't shut up about your cock, I'm going to start screaming," I said.

"I've got a nice, big wide cock, with a big head on it. I'll show it to you. I'll just pull back this curtain," said the man.

"Get the fuck away from me! You disgusting pervert! Shut the fuck up about your fucking cock! I don't want to see it! I don't want to touch it! Cover it up!" I screamed.

A nurse came running in.

"What's wrong Elise?" asked the nurse.

"This fucking pervert won't shut up about his cock and telling me what he wants me to do to it. You can't put me in here with him. I'll share with another woman, but not with this man, or any man. Are there any private rooms?" I said.

"I'll ask the head nurse if we can swap you with someone. It might take a while," she said.

Then she left me in the room with the pervert.

I grabbed my pillow and blanket and locked myself in our tiny bathroom.

I dried the floor with toilet paper, and I lay down on the floor.

That's where I spent my first night.

Next day I refused to leave the bathroom until I got my own room.

So they made Nathan give up his private room for me. He was by himself because he's beaten up too many other patients already. Carl the creep would get him as a new room-mate.

The new room was tiny, but I had privacy.

I slept a lot. I was on methadone and anti-depressants, like a rollercoaster.

I couldn't even visit Karen, across the lawn one building away. In a coma.

And the other men wouldn't leave me alone. At meal times, they'd all try to sit next to me and talk to me. There were twenty men in that ward, and only two other women, and one trans woman.

As I drifted off to sleep, I hoped I wouldn't dream of the public ward.

44

8. Withdrawals again.

It's four oh five this time.

Dark and cold, I'm all cramped up in a ball on my bed. It's hard to straighten out. It hurts to lie down. It hurts to sit up.

I'm wearing a big t-shirt, so I need to put a cardigan on. My hand hurts as it goes through the sleeve.

The hall is endlessly long. I'm tip-toeing so I don't wake up the other patients.

John is the nurse at the station again.

"Elise, isn't it?" asks John.

I nod. He knows why I'm there.

John goes through the computer file, then the folder. Then he gets the key to the fridge and gets my bottle.

"Thank you, John," I manage, as I chug it down.

Still half a bottle. This must be what my dose is, for now.

"You're looking better now you've got your own clothes," said John.

His dark brown face is unlined, but I reckon he's about twenty. I feel infinitely older than him at twenty-six.

I wanted to say more to him, but another patient with withdrawal symptoms drags themselves to the nurses' station, a pitiful sight. So I walk back to my room, and try to get back to sleep.

I feel so bad about hurting Karen. I hope she's alright. I hope she will forgive me for causing the accident.

But that was last time I lost it.

What happened this time?

Who have I been scoring off? How did I meet them? Where have I been hanging out? What have I been doing?

I'm drawing a bit of a blank.

I can see myself dancing at a club at the Valley. Is it the Family bar, or Cloudland, or maybe the Empire?

It must be Cloudland, because we're going up to the rooftop garden for a smoke. That guy, Ben has got a joint, what a relief.

It's been a long day shooting that video. We started at dawn and didn't finish till it got dark.

They ordered pizzas for lunch. Afterwards, Ben and his business partner said they'd put on a bar tab for the actors, and we all rode in band vans to the Valley. A couple of quick cocktails hit the spot, but I could really do with a smoke, or something else.

"Thanks for the smoke, Ben, it's been a long day," I said.

"I was just talking to Simeon from the band about doing some blow," said Ben.

"Sounds good," I said, "Count me in".

So Ben led me to the loos on the floor below us. They were unisex cubicles, all marble and mirrors. Ben, Simeon and I squashed into one cubicle together.

There was a tiny shelf, made out of mirror, above the toilet roll holder. Ben tipped out a little pile of coke onto the shelf, and carved up some lines with a credit card.

"Nice shelf!" I said.

"It's supposed to be a place to put your phone," said Simeon.

"Yeah, right," said Ben.

"And it's made of mirror so the phone can look at itself," said Simeon.

"Ladies first," said Ben, as he offered me a rolled up banknote.

I took the plastic fifty and snorted a line. I did half through each nostril, so I could have a break, and not burn my nose.

We shuffled around so Simeon could go next, then Ben did the last line. He cleaned up the little shelf with his finger, and licked it.

"Nice blow," said Simeon.

"Yeah, thanks Ben," I said.

"No worries, plenty more where that came from. Ready for a dance?" said Ben.

We spilled out into the corridor, and found our way to the dance floor. A few of the other musicians and extras from the video clip were there, and we had a big dance. It was good to hear different songs, as we'd heard the video clip song about a hundred times that day.

Later that night I went back to Ben's place for more coke, and of course I ended up in bed with him. I didn't really fancy him or anything, he was a bit ugly, but I was so high on blow that I would have fucked anyone.

"Are you doing anything next weekend?" asked Ben.

"I'll have to check my phone. My agent sends me texts about work, often at short notice," I said.

"Well, I'm shooting another film clip for a different band next Saturday, so if you'd like to be in it, I could arrange that," said Ben.

"Cool," I said. I was thinking "work, sex and blow."

"But maybe you'll need a different look. Have you got a red wig?" asked Ben.

"You can't have the same blonde dancing in every video," I said.

"We've got some good wigs at our studio. We shoot some clips there, they're not all on location like yesterday's," said Ben.

So I've appeared in quite a few of Ben's productions, in a red wig, a blue wig, a long blonde wig. Ben's obviously a big coke fiend, and his production house works for the three big record companies who have offices in Brisbane. They compete with a few other producers to make video clips for all of them.

They work with the modelling and talent agencies to find the beautiful people, or the goths, or whoever they are looking for this week.

Though I fucked Ben a few times, I clearly didn't mean much to him. I saw him flirting with other girls, and other girls flirting with him.

When he invited a couple of busty burlesque dancers into the toilet cubicle after a day's shooting, I knew I was no longer 'flavour of the month.'

But I had met Ben's dealer, Pete.

Pete had come by the studio to drop off a bag for Ben one day. While Ben was 'working' in his office, I got Pete's number on his way out.

Pete lived in a little worker's cottage in the back streets of Spring Hill. I could ride my bike to his place in about five minutes. He was not far from Centenary Pool, so I'd often drop in to his place to score, then go for a swim.

Pete was also not the most handsome of guys. He was a little overweight, and white and pasty from being indoors all the time. He'd wear black trousers, and band t-shirts or paisley shirts, and shiny black shoes.

"I'm off to the pool. You should come with me for a swim one day," I said.

"I dunno, I'm pretty busy," said Pete.

"I only ever go for half an hour," I said. "I swim some laps, and then I just sun myself till I'm dry, then hop on my bike."

"Half an hour?" asked Pete. "I could handle that."

"You just need to get yourself a rashie, so you don't get burnt," I said.

"A rashie?" asked Pete.

"You know, a rash vest, like the surfers wear," I said.

"Oh yeah, that's a good idea. I'd much rather wear board shorts than speedos," said Pete.

"Only the gay guys wear speedos," I said.

"Are there many fags at the pool?" asked Pete.

"Oh, it's a bit of a body parade, but not terrible. At least the gays are only looking at each other, and not at me," I said.

"I'll definitely get a rashie," said Pete.

I honestly didn't think he would.

But the next time I went around to Pete's, he asked if I was going to the pool afterwards.

"Of course, Pete. It's thirty fucking five degrees today. If I don't get in the pool, I'll melt," I said.

"Just wait till I get changed," said Pete, as he disappeared into his bedroom.

He came out in a pair of big floral boardies and a navy rashie, all brand new. He grabbed a towel and a pair of thongs, and came out into the sun with me. He walked up the hill, and I pushed my bike along, and we hit the pool at that great early afternoon hour before the swimming squads get there.

I swam my ten laps, and he swam a couple, then lazed around in the shallow end. I dried out on a deck chair while Pete hung around in the empty kiddy pool, a bit circular pool under the funky gym building, with a view of the diving towers.

"Pete, I'm heading home now. You know I'm just up in the pink palace," I said.

"Thanks heaps for bringing me here, Elise. I can't believe I live like two hundred metres away, and have never been here before," said Pete.

"Sometimes, you just need a friend to introduce you to a place," I said.

"Hey, I know the pink palace. My friend Tim lived on the ground floor," said Pete.

"I'm up on the top floor. I think I know that Tim guy," I said. "I'm in the back right flat, next to an old lady who has lived there for thirty years."

"We are practically neighbours", said Pete.

"You shouldn't stay out too long, Pete. The sun is harsh, and you're pretty white," I said.

"Yeah, I'm not far behind you," said Pete, waving from the shallow pool.

I wasn't sure if he was checking out girls or guys, or both. It didn't really bother me, either way. I don't think he was trying to hit on me. I think that like many dealers, he had a lot of customers, but not a lot of friends. Not many people who'd suggest going to the pool, or any place other than clubs and parties where he could do drugs. I was probably a 'straight friend' for Pete.

And I wasn't anywhere close to straight, but probably a lot straighter than him.

He wouldn't stay long because he'd need another line soon. So would I, or at least, a smoke.

It was Pete who got me started on the hammer in a real way. He couldn't always get the coke. The supply was irregular. But he always seemed to be able to get the heroin. He sold speed too, and meth, acid and pills, and pot. But he wouldn't smoke pot at his house, because he was so close to the neighbours on both sides, and didn't want them to smell it.

This is how I met my contacts, through work, though friends and fucks.

Soon it was medication time, then breakfast.

51

9. The Shrink again.

Today I had to see the psychiatrist again.

I put on my jeans and a light pink polo shirt, and flat sandals. I found my piece of paper from the NA meeting. I thought I was making progress.

"Good morning Elise," said Doctor Rosenberg.

"Good morning, Doctor," I said.

The nurse had brought another chair in to my room, so the doctor and I could both sit down properly.

"The nurse said you'd had some bad reactions to the methadone," said the doctor.

"Only the first couple of times," I said. "I can keep it down well now, but the craving is still hitting me at weird times."

"Your body might be reacting differently with the anti-psychotics. But I'll keep you on the same dose for a week, and see how you go," said Doctor Rosenberg. "So, how are you going?"

"I'm doing much better. I went to the NA meeting, and I made this list," I said, handing her the piece of paper.

New haircut.

Remember what happened.

Contact family.

Uber for Judith with clothes.

Doctor Rosenberg read the list, took some notes in her book, then looked at me again.

"Have you remembered what happened?" she said.

"Not this time. But I remembered what happened last time I got taken away," I said.

"You must be blocking it out," said Rosenberg.

"I had to really think about what happened last time too," I said. "I asked my friend Judith to bring me some clothes, and I had to order Ubers for her. She reminded me how nice my old car was, so I concentrated on thinking about the car. Last time I had an episode, I smashed my car, and hurt my friend Karen. I was driving us out to Ipswich to score, I hadn't slept, and I lost control at a freeway exit."

The doctor looked at me, and said, "Go on."

"I remembered driving to the Gold Coast a lot. Then I remembered my sugar-daddy, Ray, who bought the car for me. It was a cherry red Chrysler Crystal Pearl, and he bought it so I could get myself to lectures at QUT. Karen was my friend from Drama, we acted in the Twelfth Night together. But we were also taking heaps of ecstasies, drinking and smoking weed. Karen didn't have a car, so I'd drive her places to score. I partied through the week nights, then drove to Broadbeach for quiet weekends of restaurants and walks on the beach. But Ray was heaps older than me," I said.

"Did you love him?" asked Rosenberg.

"Of course not. It was a purely financial arrangement," I said.

"He paid for your expenses while you studied?" asked the doctor.

"I met him through a sugar-daddy website," I said. "I couldn't have afforded the uni fees, let alone rent while I studied, or a car. He was the kind of guy who liked being in control of a relationship, in control of the money. He would order for me in restaurants, until I learned to read the menu and order quickly. He didn't like me having friends. He didn't like me bleaching my hair. He dumped me when I had the accident."

"He didn't mind you living in the city Monday to Friday?" asked Rosenberg.

"He'd ring me every night, and every morning. He wouldn't come to see me in modern plays, but he came to see me do a Shakespeare. I hid my partying and drug taking from him. He hated me going blonde, like all the other sluts, but it definitely got me more work, and I started banking my payments, putting money away for the first time in my life," I said.

"Sounds like he didn't like you maturing and finding your independence," said the doctor.

"No, I think I was dreading graduating. He wanted me to move in with him full time after that. I would have died of boredom. He lived off his investments, and only went to see his accountant occasionally. Otherwise, he was like a retiree, staying at home and trying different restaurants. If he liked one, he'd go all the time, but he'd drive up and down the coast checking out different places, and walking on different beaches."

"I wanted to work in the city, this is where most of the theatre and modelling work is. There is a bit of film production work on the coast, but it's sporadic. Even here, it's always a struggle to get a gig," I said.

"Have you had any other serious relationships?" asked Doctor Rosenberg.

"Not really, no," I said.

"Have you ever told someone that you loved them? Or had someone tell you that they love you?" asked the doctor.

"No," I said, "and don't judge me either. Not all of us get that. Only the lucky ones."

"I'm not judging you Elise. I want you to have love in your life and friendships. We all deserve that. You've put 'Contact family' on your list. Have you had any thoughts about that?" asked Rosenberg.

"Ah, I can remember living in the group home in Yeronga. I had my first episode when I lived there. And I remember living with a foster family. My foster parents used to tell me that they loved me. I felt pressured to say it back to them. But I never really meant it. My foster brother used to say that to me too, and he couldn't keep his hands off me whenever his parents weren't around. Bernard. That was his name. Revolting creature. I had to go to the same school he went to, though he was three years ahead of me."

"His mates were revolting too. The disgusting things they used to say to me at school. And I was only a little kid. God I hated Bernard. I hated his parents too, Anne and Howard. They pretended to be so caring. But they didn't give a shit about me. Anne taught me all about housework. She was such a doormat. Howard sat on his lounge chair like he was the king of the fucking world, while she brought him drinks, and his dinner on a tray. The rest of us would eat at the shabby veneer table. She'd cook steaks for Howard and Bernard, but she and I would eat sausages. Her kitchen smelled like cheap cooking oil. She deep fried a lot of foods. Her hands and arms had heaps of tiny burns from splattering oil."

"I honestly can't remember what happened before I moved in with them. I must have been about ten," I said.

"You can't remember your birth family at all?" asked Rosenberg.

"It's just like a brick wall. I can't remember people or places or feelings or sounds or anything. And I can't remember much about this most recent fuck-up either. It's like missing episodes of a soap opera, but it's my own fucking life," I said.

"You've been trying really hard, Elise", said Doctor Rosenberg. "You've remembered about your study and your car and a couple of friends. That is good. Don't try to force it. And you don't have to make stuff up to fill in the gaps. I've found your records from the Princess Alexandra, but I'm having trouble finding medical records previous to that. These records are from since we started filing them online, about thirteen years ago. Records before that are still kept in filing cabinets. I have requested a search for those files, and it might take a few days for them to arrive by courier."

"It might be at the children's hospital. That's the first place I got taken too. I know I've been in there, but I don't know why. I remember looking down on Southbank parklands, but not being allowed to go. I don't know when or why, it's just like a haze of different faces, nurses, other kids. Fucked up kids. And I was the most fucked up. The other kids felt sorry for me, so I hated them.

The green carpet. The windows that didn't open. The balcony with the high metal grate that you could never climb up. That's all I'm getting," I said.

"That's OK," said the doctor. "What about the NA meeting. Did that help to talk with the other patients?"

"Oh, it was weird. I felt like I had done everything that all of them had done. Except having kids, I can't relate to that, or being a parent. But the drugs things, I had done all of those things. Having friends who drink too much. Starting taking pills or speed just for fun, then wanting to have them all the time. Heroin. Having heroin because I couldn't score speed, and then thinking like I had won some sort of prize. Like I knew all the answers. Like I had discovered the meaning of life. Sad, isn't it? That heroin should be the meaning of life. But that's what it feels like. I had a blast, and I felt happy, content, like I could sleep easy, but awake. When I had heroin, nobody could hurt me. Nothing they said would bother me. I could do anything, and not feel guilty or as if it were my fault. It makes hard things easy," I said.

"So you don't get the same thing from methadone?" asked the Doctor.

"Methadone just takes the pain away. It helps me to sleep. It makes me a bit fuzzy. On heroin, everything is sharp, clear. You can see through the bullshit. But not enough heroin is a bit like methadone. It just takes the edge off, but you know you'll need some more in a few hours. Methadone seems to work for longer. But I'm on those other pills too, so it's hard to know what effects are from what," I said.

"The anti-psychotics should calm you down, but can keep you awake. The anti-depressants can help you to sleep. People often notice side-effects, and the drugs can work differently on different people," said Rosenberg.

"Would the drugs be stopping me from remembering?" I asked.

"The human mind is a very complex thing," said Rosenberg. "It is most likely that you have blocked out a very traumatic experience, to save your own sanity. You've had trouble remembering both some things which just happened, and things which happened in the past, your childhood. Your file warns that you have been very violent in the past, but you seem to be calm, and in control now. That alone shows a distinct improvement. But your file is by no means complete. It only goes back five years, to when you were twenty one. I think your problems might have started a long time before that, very possibly during the time that you can't remember, the history that is so painful that you have blocked it out. I can search medical records, but I want you to search your memory. You've been right to think about sounds, smells, the feel of driving, the music in the car. These sensory memories can trigger deeper memories. You're old enough to deal with your past now, Elise. I think the memories want to come back, and you're still not sure that you can deal with them. But you are more mature now, and much stronger. You can deal with whatever comes up. I will help you," said Doctor Rosenberg.

"Thanks Doctor Rosenberg," I said. "Um, what is your first name?"

"My name is Natalie," said the doctor.

"Oh, so you have a Christian name and a Jewish name?" I asked.

"I come from a non-practising Jewish and Christian background," said Natalie.

"I remembered that Natalie meant that your were born at Christmas," I said.

"Can you remember who told you that?" Natalie asked.

"No," I said.

58

10. Another NA meeting.

I thought about who my Natalie was.

I think she was a school friend, but from which school, I couldn't say.

I remembered lazy days at Centenary Pool and Spring Hill Baths with Pete. If there was a swimming carnival at the big pool, Pete and I would go to the smaller indoor style pool instead. The Baths were about twenty five yards long, and surrounded by the pastel coloured doors of the old change rooms. The small grandstands and balconies enclosed all but the rectangle of space above the pool.

We would meet at his place and do some coke, then go for a slow swim and lounge around on deck chairs. Sometimes I'd go back to Pete's place for more coke and a fuck. But we weren't officially 'going out' or anything, In fact, we hardly ever spoke about our relationship.

I had actually thought that Pete was gay, and I think he may very well have been bi. He would sometimes ring me up, then come around to my flat quite late at night. Sometimes, I'd buy my own coke. Other times, he'd give me some of his. We always used condoms.

Pete was pretty quiet, but liked listening to loud music. We tried going to clubs or concerts, but he always wanted to leave before the band played.

If I'd been taking Karen to buy drugs, why wasn't I taking her to Pete's place?

Who was I scoring off, and why?

When I get my phone, I'll check Pete's facebook. And Karen's.

I was scoring somewhere else. And I was going out with someone else.

I've got to get it together to go to another NA meeting.

I can wear my pink jeans and a nice white jumper. Judith sure did pack lots of nice pastel clothes. And the wig. She packed my short blonde bob wig, it's perfect. I used to have my hair just like this, and I'd wear it if I had visible regrowth between dye jobs.

The other psych and drugs patients and myself wait for the guard to unlock the conference room.

"You look just like the girl in the Pepsi ad," said Russel.

"Yeah, I did a Pepsi ad," I said.

"Really? That looked like heaps of fun," said Russel.

"They paid us well. It took three days to film that little ad. The clouds kept blowing over the sun, and we sat around waiting for clear skies. And the wind blew those big inflatables all over the place too," I said.

"Sounds like nice work if you can get it," said Russel.

The other guard came with his keycard, which worked where our guard's card had malfunctioned. The air-conditioning needed to be turned on hard in this locked up room. It was hot outside.

No one said much because Dave waited with us out in the corridor, until the room became cool enough to sit down in. We appreciated the air-conditioning, and seated ourselves in silence, until Dave started the meeting.

"Hi, I'm Dave, and I'm a recovering alcoholic. I'll be chairing the meeting today. If you have any questions, you can direct them towards myself or the whole group. I knew I had to stop drinking when my wife said she'd have to leave and take the kids if I didn't stop. Drinking kept me thinking about myself, and stopped me from thinking about them. I used to kid myself that I was socialising, but really, all of my mates were fellow alcoholics who hung out at the same bar. Now when I go out, I go out with my wife, or with the kids. And at home, I make sure I give them my attention too. I hope I am becoming a better person, and going back to being the kind of person I was before I started drinking to excess. Five years clean," said Dave.

"Hi, I'm Christian, and I'm a recovering Heroin addict. I've been contacting my friends for the last few days, to see if anybody needs a worker. I might have got myself work as a Roadie with a band. I just have to make sure I can get my Rigger's Ticket, and I've got a job. I am so grateful, I had almost given up hope. It's been six weeks since I've stopped using, and the cravings are getting less and further between now. I've got the money to do the Rigger's course, and get the Ticket, then I've got steady work. And the band are ok as well, no having to listen to shit music every night. I'm so lucky, but I've been really working hard as well. I knew that someone would believe in me. Six and a half weeks clean," said Christian.

Christian was lucky that he was a handsome guy. If he had been ugly, none of his music industry mates would have given him a gig. But he was rocking that sort of rockabilly style, with the gelled hair, the white t-shirt and the leather jacket, with black jeans. Like he was trying to be the Fonz from Happy Days or something. God, I'm a bitch. I can't exactly criticise anyone else's appearance at the moment. I guess I'm a bit brain-washed by working in the fashion industry. It has made me judge people by their clothes, rather than what is inside. I have to work on that. This is one of the reasons that I usually pick the wrong kind of man.

"Hi I'm Russel, and I'm a recovering coke addict. Two and a half weeks, and I'm still craving it quite a lot. Songs on the radio make me want to snort coke. Looking at nice cars makes me want to snort coke. I have to sell my house, as my wife is suing me for divorce, and she'll get a big percentage. I think I can sell and still afford a small place with a view in Hamilton. My dog park friends are my only friends who don't do drugs. I've got to keep my dog park friends. Martha the dog groomer is still looking after my dog, Floss. My work has taken my time away really well, and once they got the doctor's report, they stopped hassling me at all. I'm trying the gym, but I just don't know. I think I injured my Achilles tendon. Oh, and by the way, Elise is the girl in the Pepsi commercial, for those who were wondering," said Russel.

The dick. They must have been gossiping about me over in the drugs ward. Fuck a duck.

"Hi, I'm Anthony and I'm a drug addict. I hoped I'd left the drugs behind in Sydney, and now I'm leaving the drugs and my druggie friends in Brisbane. I'm still really craving alcohol, after two and a half weeks. I think I'm over the pot now. Two and a half weeks, and I'm doing ok. I'm having really good conversations with my wife, Lauretta. She is amazing, she has a job in an office, and she goes to Latin American dancing a couple of times a week, and looks after our sons. She organises a babysitter if I can't look after the kids when she goes out. She'd even get one when I was in, but was going to be so drunk and stoned, I might not look after the kids properly. But no more. I can look after our kids. Hell, I can even go out and do salsa dancing. I'm still young. I have lost half a stone since I've been in here, not drinking, and just doing pushups, sit-ups and squats every morning. I'm into that kind of music. I'm into many different kinds of music," said Anthony.

"Hi I'm Linda, and I'm a recovering alcoholic. I've been clean for one week, and I'm still craving alcohol. I know I have to never drink again ever, because I want to get my kids back. I have got some crisis accomodation lined up for when I get out of here. Then, as soon as I can save bond and rent money, I'll get my own place again. I'm going to get my certificate in child care, and I can work waiting tables until I get that. I have made myself so physically sick from drinking alcohol. I feel much healthier not drinking, and food tastes better again. Even hospital food. I like cooking, and making good meals for my kids. I really miss them. I'm not even allowed to see them. I suppose it's for there own good. My social worker thinks I've got a good chance of getting them back again," said Linda.

"Hi I'm Jack and I'm a recovering drug addict. Three and a half weeks clean, so I'm almost through my month here. I'm feeling heaps healthier and fitter, I've been getting right into the gym. I'm not touching the pills again, or anything, no drinking either. I'm going to join a fitness class when I get out, meet new friends, maybe even a woman. A non-drinking woman. I've never had a relationship with a woman who wasn't also a heavy drinker. But I'm going to break that pattern. Work are cool with me going back, so I guess I'm very lucky. Yeah, I told you guys I thought it was Elise on that ad," said Jack.

"Ah, can we keep our stories about ourselves and shut up about Elise and the Pespsi ad? People seem to be working on their plans for making better lives, so that's great," said Dave.

I shot Dave a quick smile for shutting them up.

A new girl was sitting next to me. Small, and dark, she looked about nineteen.

"Hi I'm Everley and I'm a drug addict. I've got addicted to speed and smack again, so I'm back for another month. I thought I was on top of it last time, but I just got desperate again. I had a job at a sushi train, and I had learnt all the procedures, and thought I was doing really well. But I got sacked, and then got put on a three month waiting period to get the dole, because I couldn't provide an employment separation certificate. But the rent doesn't just stop, I needed money for bills, so I took up soliciting at the casino again. I still know a few of the girls who work there, and the set-up is good. It's close to cheaper hotels like the Ibis, only a short walk away. But I picked up an undercover cop, and I had some hammer and a syringe in the hotels bathroom, so I got charged for soliciting, drugs and an implement. Two days clean, I really want to stay clean. But it's easy in here, and much harder out there. And it's hard to work all week for a few hundred dollars, when you know you can make that in a couple of hours doing sex-work," said Everley.

"Hi, I'm Elise and I'm a recovering psychotic heroin addict. I've been clean for four days and I'm going to stay clean. Yes that was me in the Pepsi ad, but I don't like watching it. I can see how high on coke I was that day. The producer had just invited about six of us into his trailer, and carved up some lines. The sun had come out, and he wanted the money shot, soon, because the shoot had dragged on for a couple of days of shit weather. We were all so plastered we could hardly see all those inflatable balls and shit blowing everywhere. I froze my tits off in that bikini. What I got paid for that shoot, I probably spent on drugs in the next two weeks. If I'd been smart and saved it up, I could have lived off the modelling and acting work. But because I got addicted to drugs, I had to do sex-work as well. My psychiatrist told me that she knew women who set themselves up for life with what they mad from sex-work. I couldn't even afford to buy myself a new car when I smashed my last one. But I can't make myself do a call-out unless I have some skag first. So I can't do sex-work because I can't do drugs. I'll have to stick to modelling or take on other legal work like waiting tables or something too. I've been trying to contact my non-drug using friends, and a friend who I hurt when I was wasted," I said.

"I'm glad that Elise mentioned friends, and I'm glad that she cleared that up about the Pepsi ad too. I've brought some paper and pens for you all to make a short list today, of people who will support you, friends and family. Now not everyone will have family who are clean and can help, but we all must have at least one friend who is clean. When you're out, I encourage you to join your local AA or NA meetings, as fellow recovering addicts understand what you're going through. I want you to write down the name of one straight friend who can help you, and who you can help," said Dave.

I thought about it, and wrote down 'Judith.'

"Now, I want you to write down the names of three other friends who are straight. They don't have to be able to help, just being a friend is all they have to do. These can be work-mates or old friends who you've lost contact with, but want to communicate with again," said Dave.

I wrote down 'Serena' as I was pretty sure that she was straight. Who else?

I wrote down 'Karen,' because, even though she used to take drugs, she might not now, and I'd love to make contact with her again.

Did I have any other straight friends?

'Daniel.' Daniel wasn't heterosexual straight, but he was drugs straight. I hung out with Daniel at Centenary pool, when I went there with Pete. Daniel had recognised me from QUT. He was also studying the Drama course, but he was in first year when I was in third year. I wasn't sure if Daniel was on facebook, but I knew where he hung out at uni and the pool, and I knew his last name. So I could find him on facebook.

I did have some straight friends.

And I'll get my phone today, so I should be able to contact them.

The meeting finished and the guard took the other nuts and I back to the psych ward. I kind of hoped that Everley would be in my ward, but she was with the druggies.

66

11. The phone is a window.

The nurses know we've been good, and they smile when they hand out our phones. I suppose it's like teachers handing them out to students at the end of the day.

We all scurry off to check our phones in private.

Serena has sent a text. "So sorry to hear you're not well, Elise. Wishing you a speedy recovery. You'll have plenty of work waiting for you when you get out. Don't change your hair from how it was in the pepsi ad."

Ok, I should reply.

Um.

"Thanks Serena, for being so understanding. I'll definitely stay blonde, but can't get my roots done till I get out. But I've got a great wig. That ad's made me popular in here too, unfortunately, E."

No other texts that aren't begging letters from charities. Or creepy men.

There is a voice mail too. Who the fuck would that be?

"Hey Elise, it's Damien here. Why aren't you at home? I've been looking for you. You're supposed to tell me if you're going anywhere."

Who the fuck is Damien?

Why the fuck should I tell him anything?

Shit. I can see that the Video Pimp is going to be a hard one to shake to the side. He seems very persistent. Too persistent. Persistent in a desperate-junky kind of a way. How the hell am I going to get him to stop targeting me? He's a creepy, stalking extortionist. I sure can pick them. I wonder how many women he is draining money from? Is he the kind of guy who would follow me down a quiet bike-track, or break in to my home and attack me?

He's got a nice voice though. The voice sounded familiar. I'm always sucked in by the good looks or the nice voice. I've got to be a better judge of character.

I'll quickly check facebook.

Daniel. What was his last name? Daniel Charles. Is he on there? Oh, there are three of them.

Let's look at their photos. Oh, it's definitely that one, I'll send a friend request. I'll check his public photos. Right, he still goes to the pool. Oh, here are some acting shots, very nice.

Now I'll see if Karen answered my messages. Still no. I'll just check the front of her page.

Fuck.

"Thinking of you on the anniversary of your passing. Heart. Cathy."

It can't be true. I'll scroll along further.

"So sorry to learn that you have died. I always hoped you would wake up from your coma."

Fuck. Not only is she dead, but she never left the hospital after the accident.

Her facebook page is a tribute page now. She's been dead for more than a year.

No wonder she didn't write back to me.

She's dead and I killed her.

It was an accident.

I feel terrible. Karen was so beautiful. She was an excellent actress, and could remember tricky lines and do all sorts of accents.

I'll just check on Daniel. Ok, he posted last week, so he is still alive.

Now what about Damien. What is his last name? No idea.

I'll just search his first name. Damien Ellis. He is not a friend, but he has written a message.

"Where is it, bitch. I've been to your place, and it's not fucking there. I'll be waiting."

Who the fuck is this guy?

I'm not his friend, but I can see his friends and some photos. His friends all look like whores. He's a big swarthy gentleman in a suit with a Hawaiian shirt. There's a photo of him with the Candyman, a famous 'businessman' from the Gold Coast.

What would I possibly have of his? Today is the fifth and he wrote this on the third. He's been through my place?

I'll have to ring Judith. She'll know if anyone has been through.

Her dialup phone rings a lot of times.

"Hello," says Judith.

"Hi Judith, it's Elise here," I said.

"Oh Elise, I'm glad you rang. Your boyfriend has been around. When I came back from the hospital the other day, he was just letting himself in. He had a copy of your key. I stood at the door and watched him. I didn't see him take anything," said Judith.

"Oh Judith. I don't have a boyfriend. How did this guy get my key. Did you catch his name?" I said.

"He said his name was Damien. He was sure you had something of his. He didn't know that you were in hospital," said Judith.

"You didn't tell him which hospital, did you Judith?" I asked.

"I wasn't born yesterday. I told him that the police had already been through your flat, and he stopped searching after that," said Judith.

"Thank you Judith, you're a lifesaver. I don't know what he was looking for, but if he thinks the police have it, he might not come after me," I said.

"You should get the lock changed," said Judith.

"My thoughts exactly. Could you possibly get it done, and I'll put the money into your account for it?" I asked.

I talked Judith through finding her bank account details for me, then said goodbye.

Then I checked the pay-per-view site. Five or six regular customers have had a whinge. Only one guy called Roger actually sounded concerned, the others just sounded annoyed. And there's a message from Damien, too He's threatening to shut down my site.

What is he? My video pimp?

Then my half hour with my phone was up.

I handed it back to Nurse Jackie, and she chucked it in the safe with everyone else's.

At least I've sorted out a few things.

I can't believe Karen is dead. Or rather, I didn't want to believe it.

71

12. Visiting Hours.

I had lunch and didn't really talk to anyone.

Steve was there, but he hadn't been to the NA meeting, but he is still in here. He looks fucked up. I guess he has more problems than he was mentioning at NA meetings. I get that. I definitely self-censor at the NA meetings. We can't exactly talk about any criminal activity which we might be doing at present, or planning in the future. There is something he's not telling us at the NA meeting, maybe many things. I think he's more intelligent than he's letting on. I think that Steve acts like the dumb hunk who's into art, but really, he's a bit deeper, more intellectual, but he thinks he would appear gay to show that side of himself. He's clearly been brought up in the kind of environment where masculinity was valued, but underplayed. I wonder what he has done to be in the Psych Ward, rather than the Drugs Ward?

We got some sort of stir fry today. It tastes alright, but I'm not sure what it's meant to be.

What could Damien be looking for that was his, that wasn't there?

Was it the gun?

But it's not even a real gun, its a replica. So he wouldn't be shooting anyone with it. Maybe just threatening them.

But I've got a feeling that it's my gun. That I paid for it.

Think about it in my hand. The feel of it.

I feel like I've used it as a prop, but I haven't threatened anybody with it.

Except that I did a car-jacking. Fucking hell.

It was thrown in. As part payment. It was a music video set in a bar, or some sort of underworld club house. The pay wasn't equity rates, and it was cash, but they could chuck in an expensive prop as part payment. I was acting as some sort of gangster's moll. A short black wig and short black clothes. A short black gun. Some shitty hiphop track using the same sample over and over.

God I've done some lame gigs.

What else could belong to this Damien guy?

If he is my video pimp, did he set up the website? Is it his computer and video camera?

This could be more like it.

Did I have the computer skills to set up a pay-per-view site?

No. Someone else must have done it for me.

But surely, I would have just paid them to set it up, not keep paying them over and over?

Or was it drugs?

Was he a dealer, and he has given me drugs on credit?

Was I setting up deals between him and other people?

Was I being a Go-between?

Fuck, this amnesia shit is really fucking annoying. Why can't I remember any of the recent details of my day-to-day life? Why can't I remember my childhood? I'm getting the middle bits now, but why is it so patchy? Was it so boring, or so terrible? What's wrong with me?

After lunch, I read some more Marx and got into the Means of Production, and the Industrial Revolution. With the ruling class setting up the means of production, the workers were exploited for their labour. Unlike when they laboured on their own farms, in the factory, they were alienated from their finished product, and from the means of production itself. They were also alienated from the capitalist, and from their fellow workers, with whom they were seen to compete.

The capitalist, and the worker start to be viewed as autonomous selves, rather than part of a network of individuals, a society. Marx calls this 'Gattungswesen' or species-essence.

I feel that.

I feel alienated from all of those things. And more. I feel alienated from my sanity as well.

So capitalism is psychological warfare, as well as class warfare.

This is what Margaret Thatcher meant when she said, "There is no society."

I can totally understand why workers would feel hopeless if stuck in a boring, underpaid job for their whole lives. Especially if they feel lucky to even get a job, and know that with their wage, they could never afford to buy their own place. If they've applied for dozens, or hundreds of jobs, lowering their expectations all the way.

I'll never be able to afford my own place. I'll have trouble scraping it together for a new car. I didn't realise that Marx looked into the worker's wellbeing, their psyche, as well as their financial position. I guess that under feudalism, the workers really were much better off, than under Capital.

I'll probably have an unstable career as a performer, and then hope for a wage-slave job when I am too old and nobody wants to look at me any more.

Fuck. Is that all there is?

Visiting hours roll around, but I'm not expecting anybody.

Nurse Jackie came into my room.

"Were you expecting a visitor?" asked Jackie.

"No," I said.

"There is some guy here who says he is your boyfriend," said Jackie.

"I don't have a boyfriend. Is his name Damien?" I asked.

"Yes," said Jackie.

"Can you please not let him in?" I asked.

"He's not in. He's out at the outer entrance with the Security Guard," said Jackie. "Who is this guy?"

"I'm not sure, but I think he's some kind of Pimp. I definitely don't want to see him. Does he know I'm here?" I asked.

"I don't think so. We don't give out a lot of information about patients," said Jackie.

"Good. Keep him away from me. He has left threatening messages on my phone and social media," I said.

"Right, he's out of here then, and I'll put his name on the Exclusion list," said Jackie, and she went back to her station.

Thank God they can't see in from the outside.

An exclusion list, hey? It sounds like quite a few people are hiding in here, or staying away from the wrong sort of people. If someone's abuse drove you in here, you definitely need protecting from them, while you are recovering. And afterwards.

I suppose we are safe enough in here. Metal doors, guards, windows that don't open. But what about when we get back outside?

I really have to remember the car-jacking.

Where was I going? What was I doing? Who did I hold up? Why couldn't I have just taken an Uber?

Why is this Damien person trying to track me down?

I've discovered that I can listen to the radio through the TV set, for free. The set is credit-card operated for TV, but the radio service is free.

I can listen to Nova or B105, and hear the latest commercial music. Or I can listen to triple zed and hear local bands and DJs.

I decide to try and bring back my earliest memories.

I can remember playing on a beach with a little blonde boy. Is he my brother? We are in shallow water, with no waves. Is it Tallebudgera creek? Are those blonde adults my parents? It's pretty hazy. At home, we've made a castle out of cardboard boxes. But we aren't just playing in them. We are hiding in them.

The boy and I are afraid. We are trying to stay really quiet. It's ok to wet your pants in the back yard. It's not bad like wetting them inside in the lounge room.

I had a brother. I might still have a brother.

What is his name?

Is Elise Forsyth my real name?

Next memory is the hospital.

The other kids are looking at me.

I won't stop screaming.

The doctors drug me up to shut me up.

The foster home. Bernard the brother. Anne the mother. Howard the dad. There's not much love there. Bernard in the swimming pool, calling me in. I've got my togs on, but I can't make myself jump in the water. It's hot. I go and have a shower instead. Lock myself in. I don't take my togs off.

At the school, Bernard tells his friends that I'm scared of the water.

I wasn't scared of the water.

I was scared of him.

At school, we have to do swimming lessons. I wear a racing suit and a long rashie which is too old and has stretched down nearly to my knees.

The boys are looking at me. I just look at the concrete. I look at the line on the bottom of the pool. I don't look at anybody.

I'm not a great swimmer, but I can swim. I'm not scared of the water.

The mother Anne makes fish and chips. It's yucky. It's not what I'm used to. It makes me feel a bit sick. It leaves an oily aftertaste in my mouth.

I'm screaming again. I have attacked someone.

I'm in that place again.

In the Seclusion Room.

The humiliation room.

Held face down on a padded mattress is a padded room, getting a needle stuck involuntarily in my bum.

There are two Seclusion rooms. One in emergency, and one upstairs in the psych ward. I've been in both. A few times. Plenty of times.

"A frequent flyer," the nurses laugh.

Natalie comes to visit me. My Natalie. She's in school uniform, she's come after school. State High is pretty close to the hospital.

"I don't blame you for doing it to him," says Natalie.

"I thought I did it to myself," I said, indicating the cuts on my arm and my leg.

"You had a big go at Bernard, before you tried killing yourself," says Natalie. "Don't you remember?" She looks confused.

"I can't remember Natalie. I'm fucked in the head. Why am I so fucked up?" I said.

"You're not fucked up. He just pushed you too far. He was saying nasty things about you at school, ruining your reputation. He deserved to be beaten up. I was just surprised it was you who did it. A few of the boys in our class had been talking about having a go at him for weeks. When I saw Bernard at school with his arm in plaster, and bandaids on his face, I thought the boys had done it. Not you," said Natalie.

"I beat him up?" I asked.

"You broke his arm. You're a fucking legend. I asked Miss McGuckin where you were, and she said you were in hospital. I figured they'd take you here. Do you want a musky mint?" asked Natalie.

She handed me a small pink mint. We bought these at the shop near the train station. They were the cheapest lollies to buy, lots of little pink disks in a plastic packet. We used to eat them at the train station, waiting for the train and checking out school-boys and men. Musky mints smelled like musky deodorant and mint tea.

Mint tea.

I don't think I was drinking that in the house of deep fry.

"Thanks so much for visiting me. You have been my only visitor," I said to Natalie. "Besides the cops, and the Social Worker. But they don't count. They have to visit me as part of their job."

Natalie came because she was my friend.

Natalie Pasquale, that was her whole name.

"My name means Christmas and Easter," said Natalie.

"Presents and easter eggs!" I said.

We weren't very old.

Natalie had to go to catch a train back home before her mum got home from work.

Next time I get my phone, I'll look for her on facebook too.

I need all the friends I can get.

79

13. Remembering the group home.

Natalie came to visit me in the group home too.

I had to change schools, because Yeronga High was just down the road. And I didn't want to go back to State High if Bernard was still there. State High is too big a school too, like over 2000 students. Yeronga only has 750, so it seems smaller and more friendly.

All the kids in the group home went to Yeronga, except for Paul the ballet dancer. He went to Kelvin Grove in the mornings and dance school in the afternoons, or maybe the other way around.

The other kids all gave him shit for being a poof.

I didn't call him a poof. They called me a head-case.

"Don't call him a poof, and don't call me a head-case," I said.

"Or what?" the boy said.

"Or I'll fuck you up like I did to that boy at my old school, before I got expelled," I said.

That shut him up.

"Thanks for standing up for me," said Paul.

"They can go and fuck themselves," I said, with a smile for Paul.

"Did you really beat someone up?" asked Paul.

"Um, yeah. But he'd been touching me and trying to feel me up at home and he was supposed to be my brother," I said.

"Fucking creep," said Paul.

"So I'm not going to take any shit here either, and neither are you," I said.

"Damned straight," said Paul.

Paul was my first ally at the group home. There were eight of us. The Aboriginal kids sort of kept to themselves, and the Maori kid, Tana hung out with them. Glen and Susan and Greg were the Murri kids. Two were brother and sister, but I don't know which two. Tom and Arnold were the two big white boys who had done the name calling.

If they wanted to get the other white kids onside, they were going the wrong way about it.

As the nut and the fag, Paul and I would identify more with the Indigenous kids, than the bullies.

Yeronga High has a big percentage of African and Middle Eastern immigrant kids. Their families came to the area, close to the TAFE college where they could learn English and trades.

So our mixed up crowd fitted right in to the high school.

Peter was the House Parent. He was a divorced father of one son, about thirty, and he liked to play guitar. Sometimes he'd have his mates come around for 'band practice'. Except that they all played guitar, there was no drummer, and none of them could really sing either.

It was more like guitar practise club. Peter's mates would sort of leer at Susan and Tana and I, so we would go off to one of our rooms and hang out there. They had 'Band practice' in our only living space. The boys would stay in there, because that was where the video games were being played, though they had to turn their sound down for the 'Music.'

Paul would just hang out with us girls. He had more in common with us, anyway. Tana had an ipad, and she would find cool songs on youtube. We would watch, or we might sing and dance along.

Other times, we would just read books or magazines, or do homework. There were two computers and one printer in the office room which we could use to do homework and assignments in there. But we had to book in on the roster by the hour, so we all got a turn.

Peter tried making a move on Susan when she was in the computer room. She got away before he could take her clothes off, and she didn't tell us about it for ages.

Peter had a friend called Rick, also a guitarist, who would bring beers over to 'practice', and offer them to us girls if we would listen to them play.

One night, Rick invited Tana to a "party."

"I'll go if Elise goes," said Tana.

Rick lived in a run-down house in Yerongapilly, with a few other guys. The "party" was the flatmates, their girlfriends and a few mates, all drinking beer and cask wine and smoking bongs. Tana was shocked that people would be "breaking the law."

Rick said, "Smoking pot is harmless. Here, I'll show you what to do."

He packed a cone of chopped up weed, and showed us how to put a finger on the shot-gun hole, then light and inhale. Tana and I had a smoke, then sat around watching and listening for a while.

Then we decided to walk home. Rick didn't want to drive us home yet, so we walked a couple of kilometres home. We didn't want to get into trouble.

Paul had an end of term dance concert, so we three girls bought tickets. We had to ration our pocket money, and catch a train and a bus to get there, but it was excellent. They did a classical piece before interval, then some short modern pieces afterwards. It was at the Ballet School in West End, and Paul introduced us to heaps of the girl dancers after the show. We walked down to the Three Monkeys cafe to have hot chocolates afterwards. Then we all took the train home together, we felt so grown up.

Natalie didn't think much of my group home friends, except for Paul. She was in the netball team, and played mathletics, and did debating, so she was always busy. But she'd make time to come and visit, especially if she was on this side of town for sport or something. Natalie thought that Paul would have a career, but didn't think that the rest of us had much going for us. She tried to get me into netball, but conceded that I didn't have fast enough reflexes, or enough muscles to throw the ball hard enough.

"What were your parents good at?" asked Natalie.

"Mum and dad used to go kayaking," I said.

"Oh, it's a pity your school doesn't have rowing," said Natalie.

"Did they take you?" asked Paul.

"They'd take us for short paddles, on top of their boards, but often they'd just leave my brother and I on the beach, and they'd take off for a big paddle," I said.

"Weren't you scared?" asked

"No, we'd have our little camp set up on the beach, with food and drinks and towels, even a little tent if it was windy or rainy," I said.

"I'll bet it was them who drank the mint tea," said Natalie. "They sound like health nuts."

"Mum was vegetarian, but she still cooked meat for dad," I said.

"Where did you live? Was it full of hippy shit?" asked Natalie, a bit of a detective.

"We lived out of town, but it wasn't far to the beach, or it didn't seem far," I said. "My brother had a hippy name".

"You mean like Saffron or Summer?" asked Paul.

"No, I think it was Storm or Skye, it was Skye," I said.

"Skye Forsyth, let's look for him on facebook," said Natalie. State High had a program which gave every student a laptop, so Natalie checked on hers.

"No, he's not there. I'll just check Storm Forsyth too," said Natalie.

"Not everyone's parent's let them use facebook," said Paul.

"Not everyone's got parents," I said.

"There's no Storm Forsyth either. Maybe he had to change his last name too. Or he's just not on there," said Natalie.

Not everyone's got parents.

What happened to mine?

84

14. Fitting the jigsaw.

I'm piecing it together now, like pieces of a jigsaw puzzle.

I have this amnesia about certain things, which I've been trying to work on for a long time.

At school, I'd ask friends like Paul and Natalie to help, tell them the clues.

But it's progressive. Whenever I do something stupid, I forget the whole episode. And the episodes keep happening. I don't really know how many episodes I've had. Psychotic episodes. I suffer from Psychosis. I am psychotic. Fuck.

I had blocked out fighting with Bernard and breaking his arm. I blocked out the car crash where I injured and later killed Karen. And I have blocked out this car-jacking episode as well.

In fact, the recent stuff is all a bit blurry. The high school and uni stuff seems pretty clear now, but the years since graduation are patchy, there are scenes here and there – the pool with Pete, vid clips with Ben, lots of sitting at the hairdresser's and getting my make-up done, photo and video shoots, waiting around in theatres and studios.

When I checked my facebook photos, it's all just work stuff. Parades, ads, clips, the other people often have their names tagged, but I don't feel like any of them are my friends, just work associates.

That other site is more dodgy – how on earth did I get into that?

I can't really think about it now, I've got to get ready for my psych appointment.

I do feel better after a shower, and the bruising is fading now. I've worked out a way to tease my hair and brush it over to the shorter side, so it looks like an asymmetric style growing out. A bit of soap holds it in place.

Judith had packed me a good selection of clothes – jeans and slacks and a few t-shirts and jumpers which could all match. I put on the black slacks and light purple shirt with the pink cardy.

Natalie Rosenburg came in wearing a maroon skirt suit with a silk blouse died in jewel-coloured swirls. She was probably wearing about fifty thousand dollars worth of gold jewellery, but it was all very understated. Solid, but understated.

"How are you feeling today, dear?" asked the doctor.

"Much better thanks, Doctor Rosenberg," I said. "My cravings are lining up with medication times now, so I'm not waking in the night, and I'm getting good sleep," I said.

"That's good, Elise. I'll keep you on that dosage for now, but next week I'll cut the dose a bit, so you might go back to having irregular cravings for the methadone. Your face looks much better. Are you healing up physically?" asked Rosenburg.

"Yes, my bruises are fading and it doesn't hurt to put my bra on now," I said.

"What about the remembering?" asked the doctor.

"I remembered my Natalie, Natalie Pasquale. She was my friend from State High, who visited me in hospital after my first episode. She helped me to remember things and told me the gossip from my 'old' school. She told me that I'd beaten my foster brother, Bernard, and broken his arm. Natalie thought that some other boys from our class had done it. She came to visit me at the group home in Yeronga. Natalie thought my friend Paul had a career in dance, but wasn't sure what I'd be good at. I told her that my parents were keen kayakers. She remembered my memory of the mint tea, and I remembered the hippy house near Noosa, which backed right on to the river. My parents would go on long kayak trips and leave us in the house, or in a tent, right by the river," I said.

"Is that all you remember about your parents?" asked Doctor Natalie.

"Yeah, that bit's still pretty patchy, but I remembered a lot of later stuff too," I said.

"Let's stay on this topic for a bit. I ordered a search of the archives, and I was sent a folder on your first admission," said Rosenburg.

"Is that the time I broke Bernard's arm?" I asked.

"No, Elise, it was the time before. The first time you were in hospital, you were in shock. You had witnessed something terrible, and you had shut down to a non-communicative state. You were in the psych ward for a month, then they moved you to a regular ward for two months. You wouldn't speak or feed yourself, and you slept a lot of the time. The doctors considered you harmless to other patients, so let you in a general ward. It was 2002 and you were only eight," said Natalie.

"I had witnessed something terrible?" I asked.

I needed to know this.

Doctor Natalie had a manilla folder in her hands, it was thick with computer print outs. She leafed through it.

"Perhaps it would be best to show you a newspaper clipping from the time. Somebody had cut this out of the Courier Mail and put it in your file," said the doctor.

She handed me the yellowed clipping, in a plastic jacket with holes for a foolscap binder.

I saw the photo first, and I took the paper out of the plastic thing.

It was mum and dad. He was in a pair of togs, soaking wet, with a big medal on a ribbon around his neck. Mum was in a sundress, his arm was around her.

The title of the article was "Ironman and wife both dead."

I looked up at Natalie, and looked down at the article. It read -

"Iron Man John Forsyth and his wife Heather were both found dead at their Noosa River property on Saturday. Both John and Heather had died from multiple knife wounds. The couple's son, Skye notified the police about the tragedy, and was first on the scene.

John Forsyth was The Nutri Grain Iron Man for five years running from 1993 to 1997, and won numerous National titles in Surf Life-saving events. He has been an active member of the Sunshine Coast's Surf Life-Savers Association for many years, actively recruiting nippers and adults alike.

Heather Forsyth has been a professional surfer for three years in her youth, when she was Heather Clifton. She has designed 'Surf Dog' sportswear, and raised a sporting family.

They are survived by their son Skye, 10, and daughter Elise, 8, who have both been members of the Noosa Nippers. Investigations are continuing."

"Someone killed my mum and dad, and I saw it.

"Dad killed mum, and I saw it.

"Dad killed himself and I saw it.

"Skye and I saw it.

"We couldn't do anything to stop it," I said.

Natalie put her hand on my hand.

"I'm sorry Elise," she said. "It must have been very hard for you and your brother to live through."

"What happened to him?" I asked.

"I don't know. Only you were admitted to the hospital," said Natalie.

"So Child Services put me in that foster home, without my brother?" I asked.

"They often try to keep siblings together. I'll see if I can do a search for him. Family Services must have placed him too, if you were both orphaned," said the doctor.

"I'd really like to talk to him again," I said.

"It would be good for you too," said the doctor.

"I saw it. I saw it and I ran down the path to our little beach, our beach on the river, and I hid in the tent. Skye found me there. I wouldn't go back to the house until they took them away," I said.

"They must have looked really terrible," said Natalie.

"There was blood everywhere. Like a horror movie. I couldn't stop looking. I ran away," I said.

"You were eight and Skye was ten. It was eighteen years ago, so Skye would be twenty-eight now," said the doctor.

"We looked for him on facebook, the other Natalie and I. When I was at Yeronga. We couldn't find him," I said.

"Not everybody is on facebook," said Dr Rosenburg. "Especially not minors. And no-one is in the telephone book anymore."

"I might even have grandparents and everything. Uncles and aunts and cousins and stuff. But mostly I just want to see Skye again. But if I'm really fucked up, he might be really fucked up too. Twenty-eight. He could be married and a dad himself by now. Anyway, I'll look for him. I've remembered a few friends who I wanted to keep in touch with. And I remembered that my friend Karen died. I caused the car accident, and she was injured, and died after being in a coma. I feel really guilty about that. I had blocked that out too. It was almost like it had never happened. I can't remember this last episode yet, the car-jacking. But I'm working on it," I said.

"You've done very well, Elise. I can see you've really been working on it. Have you been getting something out of the NA meetings too?" asked the doctor.

"Yes," I said. "I've really recognised patterns in my behaviour, in all of our behaviour, about how we get in to these habits, these opportunities, then how we change our lives so the addiction becomes a more important thing. More important than work, or relationships. We justify these changes to ourselves in different ways."

"It's like Marx's theory of alienation. We are alienated from our products, and the means of production, and our co-workers. As junkies, or addicts, we are alienated from our families and friends, from our work, from everything except our drugs. My closest relationship was with my dealer. Not that I can even remember who my dealer is. All my past sexual partners have been dealers. Or clients. Maybe I am the dealer?" I said.

"Well, think about it more, and I'll see you next week. You're doing really well. Once you find out all about yourself, and accept all of the things that you have done, or have been done to you, you will know yourself, and understand yourself," said the doctor.

"But will I be ready to find these things out?" I asked.

"You will remember these incidents when you are ready to deal with them. You must be mature enough now to handle the things that you buried when you were a little girl. You have survived a very traumatic experience, and you have developed your own coping mechanism for that. Your task now is to unlock that coping mechanism. Drugs have been part of your coping mechanism. They help you to forget. You have selectively forgotten traumatic experiences in your life, as a way to survive. Now, you are learning to survive without those things. Be gentle with yourself, Elise," said the doctor.

Doctor Rosenburg moved on to her next patient.

I thought about what she had told me. I had remembered Skye, and I had looked for him before, but I hadn't remembered my parents at all. Besides the herb tea and the kayaking, that was all I was getting.

Now I'm getting mum doing yoga on the deck, her long hair loose except for a couple of thin plaits holding the front bits back from her face. Mum picking through swatches of lycra and stretch fabrics, choosing matching bits for rashies and togs. She had a sewing machine at home, and would make up test garments, but got the industrial sewing done in India. Mum spent a lot of time with us at home, and only went out to her office and shop when she had to.

Dad got up really early for training every day. He'd sometimes drag us along, but only if it was Nippers training day. He would run for kilometres. He reckoned it was a skill retained from when our ancestors were hunters. God he was full of bullshit.

He also worked as a personal trainer, and made fun of many of his unfit clients. But he bought Skye and I paddle-boards, and showed us safe places to paddle to by ourselves. We couldn't make the distances that he and mum would paddle to.

I stayed in that tent because it was my safe place. I ran down there when I saw all the blood.

How could he do such a thing?

And why?

I remember watching him compete in events, swimming, running, kayaking. He would get that really determined and sort of mean look on his face, and he'd just focus on speed or whatever. He did look, sort of ruthless. He did fight with mum sometimes, but it was usually over small things like food, or money, which was maybe a bigger thing.

Mum just usually talked her way out of it.

No wonder I hated having to move to Brisbane. Living on the Noosa River was great. We were close to the beach, and Noosaville state school was fun, and included 'water safety' as a class.

This must be why it felt so much like retirement to just walk on the beach with Ray. I was used to running on the beach, swimming fast, "walking was for sissies."

Mum had that long, wavy golden hair. If I grew mine long, or got a long wig, I could look a lot like her.

Recent stuff. Who is Damien Ellis, and how did I meet him? What is he trying to get back off me? I get the feeling that he's kind of dangerous. He hangs out in strip clubs, and picks up strippers and sex-workers to do online sex-work. He buys you a computer and cameras, and sets you up online at peepshow dot com. But he makes you sign a contract, that you'll repay him five hundred dollars a fortnight, he'll come by for the cash. That way there's no online evidence of the transactions. So you never pay off the computer and the video cameras, you just keep paying the Video Pimp. How do I meet these people?

15. Friday night NA.

Friday's NA meeting was in the afternoon just after work hours, so that some ex-patients who wanted to attend, but were working, could get there.

In the afternoon, we met at the nurses' station, and the guard walked the head-cases over to the druggies' ward. Some of the visitors were waiting outside, but they would be admitted separately from us.

In the meeting room, I sat down, and Russel sat next to me.

"Sorry if I embarrassed you last time," said Russel.

"It's alright," I said. "I get recognition a little bit, mostly for video clips, someone will start singing the song at me. I sometimes don't even remember the songs, if I didn't like them," I said.

"Yeah, well the pepsi ad is on TV at the moment, pretty frequently," said Russel.

"Oh, really? I don't really watch TV much," I said.

"You don't?" asked Russel.

"Well, it's all crap isn't it? From the rightwing propaganda fake news, to the vacuous soap operas and quiz shows. I prefer listening to music or the radio."

Russel looked at me like I came from another planet.

"On Fridays, we often have a cigarette out on the deck after the meeting," said Russel.

The visitors came in and took their seats. Dave took his place and looked around the circle.

"Good evening, I'm Dave and I'm a recovering alcoholic. I'll be chairing this meeting today. This is a combined Alcoholics and Narcotics Anonymous group. As inpatients and outpatients of Carina Private, we can support each other in our journeys towards sobriety. We can admit to failures and forgive, and we can celebrate each other's successes. I have been sober for six years, and hope to stay this way. My kids are growing up knowing a sober dad, and a mum who will have an occasional social drink, but never at home. That's too tempting for me, and my wife understands," said Dave.

"Hi I'm Steve, I'm a recovering drug addict. I've just started back at work, and my work-mates have been good about my time off. No-one has mentioned my mate Ted the meth-head at all. We get regular breaks, and if it's really hot, the boss turns on the big fans which we use to dry concrete in wet weather. I'm so tired at the end of the day, but I make sure I make myself a healthy dinner. I'm feeling heaps stronger, and I can keep going for longer, without drugs. It's hard not having a beer, but I'm drinking soda water. I've booked myself in to life drawing class, one night a week, starting next week. I'm good at art and it's something I've always wanted to try. I've been clean for a month and two days," said Steve.

"Hi, I'm Russel and I'm a recovering drug addict. I've been off the coke for three weeks. I spoke to my boss about changing which clients I'm in charge of, and why. He took it really well, after I had explained exactly why. He even asked me who I thought we should give those clients to, which of my colleagues wouldn't mind working for coke-fiends. He is shuffling our portfolios around, so a few of us will get new clients. He would never give up a client because they liked to party, but he didn't want them being a bad influence on his staff. I miss my dog. It's nice to get away from the phone too. At first, I couldn't cope, the loss of the phone hit me hardest, but now, I find it gives me a feeling of freedom," said Russel.

"Hello, I'm Elise and I'm a recovering drug addict. I'm really glad I'm talking to Doctor Rosenburg, because she is helping me to remember important things. I remembered my parents, and what happened to them. I've been blocking that out for my entire life. The doctor said my taking drugs was part of my coping mechanism to forget traumatic events. She called it trauma-fueled Psychosis. But I have to remember those events and deal with them or accept them, if I'm going to get better. I've done every drug that there is, but I've stopped now. I want to remember and reconnect with friends and stop being completely antisocial. I do have friends who don't do drugs, but I had to really think about who they were. My boss at the agency, and many of my casual work associates are straight. Most of my friends in recent years have been druggy friends, people who I score with and from. I'm going to keep away from these people, if I'm not scoring, they're not interested in me anyway. I deleted their messages, and them, from my phone. I've been clean for six days," I said.

"Hi, I'm Everley. I'm a heroin addict and Ive been clean for four days. I really want to stay clean this time. I've worked out that I want to have a proper relationship with a man, and that won't ever happen if I'm doing sex-work. I have to ditch my hooker friends, even though they are a great bunch of girls. Hanging out with them will only lead me to the casino again. I've also gone out with dealers, or just traded sex for drugs, too many times. I'm twenty and I have overdosed on heroin five times. If my friends hadn't resuscitated me, I would be dead. And that's a heavy trip to lay on your friends. I want to study something and get a well paying job. Maybe social work or something helping others, I don't know. I'm on two bottles of methadone, and the cravings hit me at all hours. I get lonely at night with no phone and nobody to talk to. It's hard, and it's supposed to be easier each time, but it's not. It's always hard," said Everley.

Dave said, "Social work and Counselling are great jobs to train for, Everley. You can start with short courses online. If you can overcome your addiction, you can help others to do it too."

"Hi, I'm Christian and I'm a recovering drug addict. I'm feeling good about knowing I've got a job to go to when I get out of here. But I'm feeling bad about my Hep B and C diagnosis. I'm supposed to tell all my sexual partners from the last few months, but my ex-girlfriend won't answer my calls or texts and I don't even know the other people's full names, let alone phone numbers. I've got to take anti-virals, but the drugs aren't guaranteed to get rid of the infection. I might have it for life. I feel like I've been really stupid, and now I'm paying the price. I've been clean for six weeks and two days," said Christian.

Next in the circle was a tall woman with short hair and sensible clothes. "Hi, I'm Carolyn, and I'm a recovering alcoholic, drug addict and self harmer. I've been clean for two years now, and I don't want to or feel like hurting myself any more. I was a victim of incest as a child, and I blocked out my memories with alcohol and drugs. Because of my religious upbringing, I was ashamed to admit to myself that I was a lesbian, and didn't come out until I was twenty. Now I love myself, and I have a girlfriend who I love, and who loves me. I never thought this would happen, I didn't think I deserved it. I'm working as a Psych Nurse in Ipswich, but I come to this group, because this is where I got clean. If I can do it, you can all do it too," said Carolyn.

"Hi, I'm Linda, and I'm an alcoholic. I feel shame for all the stupid things I did for alcohol. I drank the money that should have been feeding my kids better, I drank the rent money. I got drunk and brought home strange men to fuck in the room next to my kids. I just stopped thinking about them, and only thought about me. Nine days clean, and I'm never going to drink again. I've got to find another job, away from alcohol altogether. Child care or aged care, whichever has the shortest course to start working. I'm so lucky to have a social worker from a charity to pay for a study course, as well as my stay in here. I just couldn't have managed on my own. My own mother won't even talk to me. But my ex's mother will, and said she is glad I'm here, if only my ex could do it too. She has offered me their old car, which still has registration on it. She said she knew I'd need one. My old car was unroadworthy and the rego had expired. I found out that my kids are at one foster home, together, and they've been asking about me. I'll do whatever it takes to get them back again," said Linda.

"Hi I'm Jack and I'm a drug addict and alcoholic. Three weeks and five days clean. I was thinking that I have nearly made it, I'll be good again. Then I started remembering some of the bullshit stories I've been telling doctors all around my area, and at the local hospitals too. I was doctor shopping for codeine or any painkillers I could get, I faked injuries and back-aches and migraines, I really lied my head off to heaps of different doctors and pharmacists. I will be too ashamed to go to any doctor on the south side. If I ever do get sick or injured, no-one will believe a word I say. And worse than that, I robbed people's letterboxes for bills so I could get fake ID made up and see doctors under their names. The police got on to me, and if I wasn't in the Psych Ward, I would have heaps of fraud charges against me. I'm a fucking idiot. I was picking up chicks using this other guy's name, because I thought it sounded more sexy than my name. What's wrong with me? Doctor Rosenburg told me she didn't think I was a schizophrenic, that I just made up the IDs to still get drugs, after the Doctors wouldn't proscribe them for 'Jack' anymore. But I even got my last job as 'Alex White', so lots of people in South Brisbane know me by that name. I'm fucked. I had been thinking that Jack Tanzi didn't have many problems, but really, I've got all of Alex White's problems too. And the real Alex White must hate my guts. I got a driver's licence in his name, and I lost nine points for speeding. I think I'll probably stay in for a bit longer than the month to sort out some of the stuff I've been in denial about," said Jack.

"Hi, I'm Danny, and I'm a recovering heroin addict. I was the worst junky and smack dealer there ever was. I hung out with a motorbike gang and ran smack up and down the coast as far as Sydney and Melbourne. I OD'ed and dropped heaps of times, I did rehab five times before I got it right. I got Hep B and C and HIV, so I'll take retrovirals now for the rest of my life. My wife died from an overdose. We didn't have kids, thank God. I still ride my bike, just for fun, no drug-running. I've got a nice dog, Sheena, a Staffy, who I take for a walk every day, and she sits on the back of the bike for short runs too. I've got a job fixing bikes, I was always quite mechanical, now I'm a mechanic. I still have other bikers ask me occasionally if I can score. But I just say 'I'm never doing that again,' and they get the picture. Two and a half years clean, and I'm going to stay clean," said Danny.

Then Dave said, "Thanks everyone for your honesty. Being a Friday night meeting, we will forgo the exercises, and go for a smoke and a chat out onto the recreation deck. If people don't want to smoke, they can stay in here, or smokers can use half the deck, and non-smokers the other half. The deck's pretty big."

So we filed out the other door from the meeting room, on to a large wooden deck. The rails were only waist high, but about three floors up, as the hill below us dropped away. There could be no jumping off this deck unless you broke your legs, then you wouldn't be running very far. But it gave the nice feeling of being outside. We were amongst the gum trees, and the odd pine tree and flowering trees.

There was some gym equipment at one end of the deck. The healthy end. The other end had some outdoor chair and a couple of ash-tray stands which looked pretty solid. The smokers headed for the chairs.

I hung back, because if I'd gone this long without a cigarette, I could probably go longer.

"It's nice to meet you, Elise," said Carolyn.

"Hi, was it Carolyn?" I said.

"Yeah, Carolyn. I've been coming along to Friday nights for years, when I'm not rostered on at work. Otherwise I want to hit the Valley and Spring Hill and check out the gay bars," said Carolyn.

"I probably saw you at The Beat when I worked there," said Linda. "I used to dye my hair really red back then."

"Oh, the Beat? Sure, I've been out dancing there a million times," said Carolyn.

"I remember smoking joints in the courtyard out the back of the Beat," I said.

"Oh my God, I took so many e's at The Beat, dancing on that dance-floor that lights up," said Everley.

"We're not really supposed to talk about partying at NA meetings," said Carolyn.

"That's OK, Dave's over there with the smokers. This meeting is just like an Aussie barbecue," said Everley.

"It's probably an economic thing. I actually gave up the smokes when I had to decide between buying ciggies or wine. If I could only afford one vice, it was going to be alcohol," said Linda.

"Yeah, I can't believe that fags are thirty five dollars a pack now. Fuck. That's nearly as much as a point of hammer," I said.

"I'd rather take a pill than smoke a packet of cigs," said Everley. "Cheaper, too."

"Really, all substances fuck with your head, just to a greater or lesser extent," said Carolyn.

"What I'll miss is the fun of taking party drugs," said Everley. "I really enjoyed that feeling of anticipation, going to a club or a festival, scoffling the pills while you're waiting to get in, just in case there are police with dogs further down the line. Having a drink as you're waiting for it to come on. Dancing like a maniac for hours. Finding a quiet place outside to blow a spliff, or going home afterwards to chill around the bucket bong. I'll miss that. My friends will still do that, and I'd be too tempted to do it too if I went out with them."

"Yeah, I got into the party scene when I was a student," I said. "But for the last few years, I've only partied after gigs, otherwise I'd just stay home and have a drink or a smoke. I was mostly using hammer to go and meet clients. I've got to stop doing that."

"It's hard, though, isn't it?" said Everley. "Hard to give up the easy money of hooking. I'll have to give up my flat in town, and move to somewhere cheaper in the suburbs."

"You weren't working from home, were you?" I asked.

"I've been renting a two bedroom flat, The front room I work in, the back room I live in. It's cheaper than paying for hotels all the time," said Everley.

"I just don't see how you girls can do it with so many dirty men", said Carolyn, sounding a bit disgusted.

"Oh, I always make them have a shower first," I said. "And they wear condoms for everything."

We all laughed, and saw that Dave was walking over to our group. Time to change the subject.

"My girlfriend always says that I shouldn't mix with the ex-druggies because it will make me want to take more. But it's the exact opposite. Hearing everybody talk reminds me of how far I've come, and how I never want to go back there, no matter how glamorous it seems," said Carolyn.

"It's good to see that at least the ladies are trying not to smoke at meetings," said Dave.

"I'm so old I can remember when people smoked in bars. I smoked at work behind the bar. But I'm glad the government stopped it. All of my clothes used to reek of smoke," said Linda.

"At high school, the look used to be a tight white t-shirt with a pack of Winfields stuffed in the shoulder," said Carolyn.

"My friends are younger, and hardly anyone smokes ciggies because they are too expensive," said Everley.

"People call marijuana the gateway drug. But when I talk to addicts, the first drug used was most commonly cigarettes. They are the real gateway drug," said Dave.

"Someone described drug taking as ritualised self comforting. I can totally relate to that," said Linda.

"Yes, I'd definitely use drugs to calm myself down, or to help myself stop crying," I said.

"AA tells us that no person is an island, that we all seek friendship and community. We often take drugs alone, but many of us start drinking or using in a social group. Taking drugs can stop us from feeling that we are part of a community. That's why reaching out to others is so important on our road to sobriety," said Dave.

I thought about that as we walked back to the Psych Ward. Though I felt that I didn't have a lot in common with Linda, Steve and Jack, really they were my peer group. What Jack said about his doctor shopping and fake identity, I feel like that. I feel like I'm the Pepsi girl or the girl from the Regurgitator clip, or the Tones and I clip, or the Myer parade. I'm a different girl for every appearance, my job is sort of schizophrenic. And I don't really retain friends from job to job. My life is like a series of appearances, with a different cast of characters each time.
I've got to make an effort to maintain my friendships, to have a group of people around me that I can talk to.

16. A quiet weekend.

The hospital definitely has a quieter vibe on the weekend. The doctors only come in for emergencies, and I don't know if they had many admin staff on either. But the food was still good. I'm quite getting in to having a cooked breakfast every day. I have definitely been on the too skinny side, and I could afford to put on a couple of kilos and still look good.

I got a few more books, and camped out in my room for the duration. Between reading politics and psychology, I thought about things.

My early life was filled in for me now. That part of the jigsaw as nearly complete. The foster family and the group home, at least I had some sort of structure there.

It was when I moved into that flat in Annerley that it all started to come apart, and unravel. I didn't have to answer to anyone, except the boss at work. So I didn't. My place was a total pigsty. I hardly ever washed up or went to the laundromat. I'd wash clothes in the shower if I was desperate. Without housemates to be embarrassed in front of, I brought home so many different men for sex. Some of them I saw a few times, but none of them grew into relationships. I think I kind of wanted it, but didn't know how to make it happen. Or maybe I knew how to make that happen, but didn't want that to happen. Or not with any of those guys anyway.

Once I had brought some of those guys home, I couldn't wait to get rid of them. Men seemed like such a bunch of dickheads, all so sure of themselves. I'd tell them my phone number, and hoped they'd call. Or I'd tell them the wrong number if I didn't want them to call back. At least I learnt to enjoy sex. I don't think I got it at all for the first few times.

The next time I had friends was when I was at uni. I remember the first day, thinking how I had met the beautiful people. I guess the lecturers at QUT saw so many auditions, and most people got the basics of acting, so they could afford to just pick the attractive ones, who would have a natural advantage in the industry anyway.

The best looking of the guys was Justin, with his gelled blonde hair and gym-toned body. He loved himself a lot, but you need self-confidence in this industry. Barnaby was another big guy, but not so handsome. Our lecturer said that the agencies tell them what kind of actors they need, and they needed big guys for all the action movies they were making on the Gold Coast. They didn't say, but it must have been the same for boobs.

Roberta had the biggest natural boobs I've ever seen, and long dark hair all the way down to her bum. She walked like a ballet dancer, and could really light up the stage with her smile. Karen also had a big rack, but not as big as Roberta. When I stood next to them, I looked like the small boob chick, and I've got decent sized boobs. Helen was a tiny blonde, we joked that she could work child roles for the rest of her life. Her brother and sister were also actors, but she was the baby of the family.

Dustin was a pretty gay boy in our class, bleach blonde and athletic, he looked straight, but sounded very gay. I think that he had a brief thing with Daniel, my pool friend, who was the year behind us. Though we competed to get the lead roles, we worked together well, and we all got a turn to shine.

I liked how we'd read the texts first, and discuss them, the characters, their motivations, all before rehearsals started. It gave us a good understanding of the group dynamics before we had to get up and read the lines, then block the moves across the stage.

I've got to look for all of these people. Only Karen and I got into taking the drugs. The others were happy to have a few champagnes after the show, or maybe some shots of spirits on closing night. We'd do a play every term, so four terms a year, three years, I did twelve productions with these guys, from Butoh to Dada to a musical, a Brecht political musical, that boring Shakespeare and some Australian dramas like Williamson.

Between rehearsals and shows, we did a lot of sitting around and waiting. So we'd chat, and get to know each other. I think I got on best with Karen because she didn't take herself too seriously. Roberta was a farm girl who had come in to the city from Theodore. She stayed with a great aunt in an apartment on the river at Kangaroo Point. She wasn't allowed to have any friends over. Karen lived in a rundown share-house in Paddington. Her flatmates all studied at different unis, and they would often have parties, with a bathtub full of beer and ice. I remember a party of a very hot night, where Karen and I ended up sitting in the bath in our undies, with the remains of the ice floating in the chilly water. Suddenly the whole party was in the bathroom, pelting each other with ice-cubes.

Helen was a relationships girl. For the first year or so, she went out with Justin, a perfect blonde couple. Then they split up over something, and she started going out with Barnaby.

Barnaby's real name was David, but there was already a well known actor with the same first and last name as him, so he used his daggy middle name, which was definitely a name that no-one else had. He was a pretty rugged guy, he drove a ute and worked as a labourer when he wasn't studying. I think he worked solidly over the holidays, so he lived on his savings through the term.

He was tight with money, and never bought drinks to a party.

He didn't seem like Helen's type at all, and she had dumped him by the time we got to third year. I was seeing Ray, so I didn't really look around at other men much. One was bad enough, was how I looked at it. Karen also went out with Barnaby, in our final year.

Dustin was a triple threat – a singer, dancer, actor, who had an endless supply of jokes, both clean and dirty. He hung out at the Beat, and the other gay bars in the Valley. I'd sometimes go out to the clubs with him, especially on Tuesday night. On Tuesdays, there was no cover charge at the Wickham or the Beat, and we'd have drinks at my place first, then walk down the hill to the Valley clubs. Dustin was so scared of getting gay-bashed, he told me he'd never walk in that area after dark alone. A friend of his, who was a fashion designer, had been gay-bashed to death on his way home from a club one night.

I think that Dustin went to London after he graduated, he wanted to work in London's West End. I'll have to find him online. And the others. I had gone to see Helen in the Tempest at La Boite. She was ideal for Miranda, small and pretty, and could do the iambic pentameter verse and almost sound understandable. As much as you can in a Shakespeare show. I've auditioned with La Boite a few times, but haven't got a part yet. Same with QT, our state theatre company. Justin got a QT show straight after graduating. He played a young hero in a modern Aus drama, I can't even remember the name of the show. But I remember being jealous that he'd got in to the company.

Roberta got offers to work in porno films, but I don't know if she went there. Roberta told us that her family lived on a huge farm, and owned a whole lot of others. At lunch hours, she would walk around the refectory checking out the business students. I walked with her one day, and she would stop and pick at her salad.

"See that guy over there in the grey suit," said Roberta.

"Which one?" I asked, they were all wearing them.

"The Armani suit. The tall guy with the natural looking blonde streaks," said Roberta.

I checked out the business students. The tall blonde guy did have a better cut suit on than his mates. They all wore black shiny shoes and collared shirts, but no ties.

"I see the one you mean," I said. We were leaning against some waist high pot plants with palms in them.

"Just wait till he makes a gesture, and check out his watch," said Roberta.

"I like his mate with the dark hair, in the blue shirt," I said.

"His suit is a cheap readymade, and it doesn't fit him properly," said Roberta.

That was enough to turn her off this guy, who was by far the most handsome in the group. After a while, the blond waved his arm, and his jacket revealed a square gold watch with Roman Numerals.

"That's a Cartier, it's worth forty grand," said Roberta.

"How do you know?" I asked.

"I've got a weekend job at Myers, and I work in men's apparel."

"So you check out all the expensive gear?" I asked

"We don't sell those watches that cost over five thousand very often. And when we do, I get a bonus," said Roberta.

"Your boss probably put you in that department because the men like looking at attractive women," I said.

"Yeah, but they often take their wives or girlfriends shopping. They're not out to impress the sales assistant," said Roberta.

"So, are you going to talk to this guy?" I asked.

"Maybe," said Roberta.

"It's hard when they're in a group. I'll tell you what – I'll wait here, and you walk over to that drinks fridge to get another mineral water, and hang around like you can't decide," I said.

"Terrific idea," said Roberta, as she binned the salad container. She walked over to the drinks fridge and flicked her hair back. Grey suit was at the fridge about twenty seconds later. But I had to get walking, because blue shirt had gotten up, and was walking over my way. I'd get back to our friends, who hung out on the lawn, because most of us couldn't afford to buy food here.

The lawn near the Drama building was were all the povo students hung out. Creative Industries as a faculty was training up artistic young people to fit into the corporate world. The 'Creatives' stood out with their colourful clothes and trendy hairstyles. Most of QUT was very grey suit wearing.

I wonder if Roberta found herself a Rolex man?

I wonder if she would still talk to me?

At least I never screwed any of the uni guys, or any of my friend's boyfriends. At least I don't think I did. But they might be pretty pissed off about Karen.

Now I've got to think about Damien a bit.

If he didn't come around for the gun, he might have come around for the computer or drugs. If it was the computer, maybe he did set up my pay-per-view site, the computer and cameras.

Wouldn't I have already paid him for that? Or was I paying him off over time?

Couldn't I pay him off electronically? Or was it about leaving a paper trail with the banks and stuff?

How did I meet him again?

I'm not getting much, I'll have to check his webpage to see if anything there jogs my memory.

109

17. All Sunday with the phone.

On Sunday, I actually got my phone for the whole day. It must be some reward for good behaviour or something.

There is a text from Serena.

"Oh, Elise, I could get you so much work right now, so you'd better get better. How was the gig in Fiji? Did you really get to sail back here in the yacht? Flying first class is always the best way to get to a gig. Haven't seen the ad yet. Pepsi is still on high rotation. Love, Serena."

Fiji? Must have been a memorable gig. I'll just write a quick reply.

"Hi Serena. Everyone's mad for the coke ad. What was the Fiji ad for again? I'm on strong sedatives and my memory is playing up a bit. Cheers, Elise."

I'll have a look on facebook. There is a message from Daniel Charles.

"Hi Darling, haven't seen you at the pool for a bit. Are you OK? I'm doing an Oscar Wilde show for QTC this year, they must have needed someone unafraid to be totally faggy. Saw the pepsi ad, looking good Elise. Heart emoji, Daniel."

God he's sweet. I'll message him back.

"Daniel, my beautiful friend. I'm in hospital for a bit, no, it's not plastic surgery. I'm at the Betty Ford clinic. Congrats on the show, you will be fab. Elise."

Right, I've got a list of people to look for and send friend's requests to.

Natalie Pasquale.

Wow. It looks like Natalie has it all going on. Handsome husband, she dresses well, like someone with a professional job. It doesn't say what she does. I'll send a friend's request and a brief message.

"Hi Natalie, I'm finally remembering. Dad killed mum, then himself, and I had blocked it all out. You were the first one who helped me to remember, so I hope you will be my friend again, Elise."

Right. Next.

Paul Corrigan.

Whoa. Paul is a professional dancer now, at the Casino in Melbourne. There are lots of photos of him in costume, and others of him and pretty girl dancers drinking cocktails in plush bars.

And he has Tana Tutaki in his friends list.

"Dear Paul, I'm in therapy, trying to remember my past and reconnect with friends. Glad you survived the group home, and have done so well with your dancing. Elise."

Now I'll check out Tana.

Oh my God, she's on a women's rugby team. She's looking fit, and she has grown a lot.

She's got tribal tattoos. I'll just send her a short message.

"Dear Tana, do you remember me from Group Home? I'm much better now, and reconnecting with friends. Hope you are well and happy, Elise."

Ok, now the uni crowd.

Justin Ford was in Sydney, and had gone completely blonde, not just streaks any more. It looks like he has been working for Sydney Theatre Company. I'll just send a friends request and not send a message.

Barnaby Jones, his profile pic is in full costume, with a very fake moustache and beard. He's doing some Gilbert and Sullivan show. A friend has posted an ad for cough lollies that he acted in, dated a few months ago. He doesn't use this page very often, or he only looks, seldom posts. I'll just send a friend request.

Dustin Black. Dustin was living in London now, and working in a West End musical. He also appeared in late night cabarets. His page was a busy mix of ads for his shows, cute animal pictures, political cartoons and memes, and youtube clips of unusual songs. I'll send him a friends request and a message.

"Dustin, how dare you be so famous? You're a West End Star, and I'm still only doing Pepsi commercials. Cheers big ears, Elise." I typed.

Next on the list was Roberta. Roberta Campari? No, that was our nickname for her. It was Roberta Campagna. I looked for that name, but no-one. When I typed just 'Campagna', up came a list of people, and one was her handsome brother, Marco. I looked at his friend's list, and there was Roberta Campari. She has used her nickname as a stage name or whatever.

Her page included a lot of glamour photos of Roberta, with her finest assets on display in some low cut gowns and blouses. She looked like she was running a business, but what kind of business? I don't know. I wrote her a friend's request.

Helen Dennison was living in LA. She had toned down to about a size six, and her features all looked very sharp. She still had her long blonde hair, artfully styled in every photo. In her profile pic, she was wearing one of those super skinny suits, in pale pink, with a white silk camisole under it. I just sent a friend request.

Suddenly, I felt exhausted at being sociable, and I hadn't even left my room. I put down the phone, and got up. I went for a walk to the library. I took back a couple of books, and found a few new ones. There was also a ream of paper, and some envelopes on the desk. I grabbed a few pieces, as I wanted to write on something other than my lists from NA meetings.

Back in my room, I tried to concentrate on reading, but something from the phone messages was stuck in my mind. What was it?

Fiji.

I've been there. Just recently. I had to get my passport in order to go there.

I remember taking pictures on my phone.

Why didn't I look here before?

Right, here are an odd collection of snaps. The reverse order they appear in makes no sense, so I'll go from the start of this series.

Toby driving me to the airport in a big company car. He's the older model who had recruited me to the agency.

Next I'm on the plane, by myself, in a big first class compartment. No, not alone. Evan Harrison from Harrison Hair was sitting in the compartment next to me.

Next snaps are in a salon.

Then I'm on a beach with Crimson, the stylist, and a pile of clothes and accessories. Nice beach. Lots of big old palm trees, black rocks and white sand, azure water.

There are some restaurant snaps. Evan, Crimson, some islander guys and some white guys who I don't know.

There are some jungle snaps. Then there is a Tiki bar. There are some blurry night time snaps.

Next are some yacht snaps.

Well it's not really a yacht, it's a cruiser, and it's pretty big. I'm sharing a cabin with Crimson, the stylist. I take some selfies of us, all made up and styled. There is a mountain of blow on the shelf under the mirror, surrounded by makeup and hair products. Better not be uploading that particular snap to the internet.

The next ones are a bit of a mystery.

The fuel station at the Manly harbour. One of the crew is filling up the boat.

A backyard party with the same crew.

A garden shed in a neighbour's garden, a couple of fences away.

Then it's night. There are a couple of blurry ones. Something that looks like a fishing buoy?

A cemetery. Old graves which have crumbled away. A name on a black marble tomb. Samios.

A main road, three lanes each way, lots of headlights, low-rise building lights, blurry.

What the fuck was I doing?

I must have been off my chops.

I can't remember taking these, any of these.

Was I trying to leave myself some clues? Some evidence of what I was doing? Was I so off my face that I thought I would forget what I was doing?

If I've just been on this Fiji trip, this could be the time leading up to the car-jacking.

Why didn't I just call an Uber? Or hail a taxi? Maybe I did.

I can check that.

If I came here on Sunday the second of February, then Saturday the first must have been the night I lost it.

I'll check my Uber account.

Yes, I did order one to Cleveland cemetery at eight thirty at night. A driver came but refused me because I was intoxicated.

OK.

I was desperate to get away, the Uber refused me, so I car-jacked somebody. I was intoxicated. I'd just been on a private boat cruise and a party near the harbour. And I smelled like I'd had sex with somebody.

I left myself a bunch of blurry photos hoping that they'd mean something.

Did I know that I wouldn't remember because it was a bit traumatic?

Where did I car-jack the driver to take me too?

Rosenburg said my heroin dealer's place.

Was I scoring off Damien? Did I lead the police to his house?

No wonder he was shitty with me.

Or was I scoring off someone else, and Damien is shitty for another reason?

Why did I need heroin if I was so off my trolley on coke that I couldn't remember what was happening?

Why was I carrying a replica handgun if I had just been on an international flight and boat trip?

Am I sure it's mine? Did I steal it from someone at the party, or on the boat?

No, it was mine, it was part payment for doing that video clip, the gangster hiphop song.

And where was all that nice gear that I'd been wearing on the cruise? Those nice swimsuits,

I had one of those Camilla caftans and a really nice pair of Jimmy Choo shoes which were mine, not the stylist's.

Where the fuck are those?

Now I'm pissed off. I spent a lot on those clothes and I want them back.

Fuck.

I flicked back through the photos, and found a selfie in the caftan, at the stern of the boat, moored in front of a Fijian beach. No piles of coke anywhere. I'll send this one to Serena.

"Hi Serena. I remember now the hair shoot in Fiji, here is a selfie. Unfortunately I think I lost my bag with this Camilla number and a pair of Jimmies in it. Glad I finished the shoot before I lost the plot. Elise."

I was looking at the photo, when Serena emailed back.

"Dear Elise, glad you are remembering, and great selfie! Evan Harrison was happy with the results. Check out this shot which is going up on a billboard. Love, Serena." Attached was a photo of myself on a stand-up paddle-board, in white togs with a yellow and white floaty thing over the top, close to shore, the photographer looking down from a cliff. I'm looking up at them, and my hair is illuminated by the sun behind me, all golden waves. I must have a weave in because it looks a bit longer than it is now. It looks like paradise.

Being totally honest, I do look a bit coked up. But I don't think other people would notice. It's just that 'I don't have a care in the world' look that rock stars aim for.

Funny how I look so great but am so fucked up on the inside.

117

18. More questions than answers.

Before I handed the phone in, I had to check on the pay-per-view site.

"Come on, Sally, where are you?" said one dude.

"Sally, we want you to show us your new hair," said another.

"When I paid for the month, I was supposed to be getting at least one show per week. It's been a week and a half, and no show! Why should I resubscribe?" said a third one.

So Sally was my stage name on this site.

Right, what does 'Sally' look like then? In my profile picture, I'm wearing a leather mask and false eyelashes long enough to protrude from it. I've got the bright red lipstick and lots of black around the eyes. Then there's a black leather lace-up corset, and a pair of long patent leather or PVC gloves. I'm in my bedroom at home, but I have re-arranged a little bit. I have taken down my necklaces from their nails on the wall, and hung up a whip and some furry leather handcuffs, a dildo and an ostrich feather fan. How cheesy.

I don't see how I usually run this site. The phone version of the program is not the same as the computer version. The computer version has a lot more options, and one camera is on that computer, another two are wired up to it.

Do I really need the money from this?

This is revolting.

"Hey Sally, I see that you're online. Are you going to do a show for me? Is that you on the Pepsi ad?" says the text from whoever.

I quickly shut down the program. I've got to shut down that website.

But I think I might need my computer at home for that.

I don't want anyone linking Elise Forsyth, the Pepsi girl, to Sally at Peepshow dot com.

I've written a list of the photos.

Toby in company car.

Flying first class.

With Evan Harrison.

Salon with Crimson.

Beach with Crimson.

Restaurant group, Evan, Crimson, others.

Jungle.

Tiki bar.

Yacht.

Cabin with Crimson and coke.

Fuel station Manly harbour.

Backyard party with crew.

Neighbours shed.

clothes on floor, blurry.

Cemetery.

fishing buoy.

Samios grave.

six lane road – Old Cleveland Rd.

What am I trying to tell myself here?

Toby drove me to the airport, so it was an agency gig.

Flying first class means I was flying with the client, who must be Evan Harrison. He owns a chain of hairdressers, sells beauty products and drives flash cars. I'm surprised that a hair client would book me, who has short hair, for a model. I know Crimson, the stylist, I've worked with her before. She's a big coke fiend. She knew I liked to party, maybe that is why I got the job.

So Crimson's doing make-up and styling. She has brought bags and bags of clothes. She shows them to me as I sit in the hairdresser's chair, getting my roots done. Philip is the young gay hairdresser, who bleaches my roots and ties in the hair weave. He matched it to my hair colour after the dye, then tied it to tiny clumps of my own hair. It takes hours. We have breaks every so often to have a line.

I tried on a million outfits, and chose the best looking ones for the different shoots. The photographer, Louis Primo, had flown in from Sydney. He was a hot looking Argentinian, who you couldn't help but smile at. Though I wore a swimsuit at the beach, I got to wear a long skirt and light cotton shirt, over a little camisole, for the jungle shoot. A lot of Harrison's customers were older ladies, so more modest clothes would appeal to them. I got to climb a big tree, and because I was well covered, the angle looking up the tree at me, didn't look obscene.

Evan and his other staff weren't on the shoots with us, I think they had more important business to attend to. On the boat, we'd all have lines before or after meals. The boat had a Galley Master to cook all the meals.

The selfie that I took lying on the deck, there were these big white oval floats which hung over the sides, to stop the boat from hitting the jetty, or other boats. There were also some lying around in the hold downstairs.

I kicked one, when I was stumbling around in those high heels, and it was hard as a rock. The ones upstairs were soft and light, you could use one like a pillow, when you were lying on the deck. Theses ones were hard, and when I went to pick it up, weighed about ten kilos. This wasn't a fishing float. This was a stack of cocaine compacted and disguised to look like a fishing float. This wasn't a pleasure cruise, it was a drug smuggling run.

I could get into a lot of trouble.

Or, I could get really rich. If I was smart enough. And if I had enough guts.

19. Monday means the shrink and NA.

Monday morning, and there is less methadone in my bottle today. But I'm going to try to make it through to the 7pm medication delivery.

I've got Doctor Rosenberg coming in, then the NA meeting. I feel bad because I'm going to have to lie to the doctor, but I can't tell her everything.

"Good morning Elise," said Natalie.

"Good morning, Doctor Rosenberg," I said.

"How is the healing up going?" asked the doctor.

"My face is heaps better, the hand is coming along and my other bruising is starting to fade," I said.

"That's good," said Natalie, "I'm altering your dosage this week, for both the methadone and the anti-depressants. The antipsychotic drug, we'll keep the same. It's one which must build up in your system to a certain level, to be effective. How is the remembering going?"

"Having the phone for a while yesterday really helped. I found my recent photographs, which gave me a clue as to what I've been doing. It's like I gave myself clues, in case I forgot, or thought that I was likely to forget," I said.

"That in itself is interesting, but go on," said Dr Rosenberg.

"Before this episode, I did a gig in Fiji for Evan Harrison," I said.

"That man who owns Harrison Hair?" asked the doctor.

"Yes. We flew to Fiji and I got styled up with a hair weave, and posed on his boat and at the beach, then we sailed back to Brisbane on his cruiser. We snorted a lot of coke on the trip. After we moored the boat at Manly, I was invited to a crew party at a house near the harbour. I'm pretty sure he raped me, then I stole a neighbour's bicycle to get away. I called an Uber, when I recognised where I was, but the Uber wouldn't take me because I was intoxicated, and maybe bleeding from the face."

"So I jumped in a car waiting at the traffic lights, pulled out my gun and asked him to drive me to Damien's house. I must have been so high on coke, that I thought I'd need heroin to come down. Damien was the one who got me working at Peepshow dot com, and I think he bought and set up my big computer at home for me. He tried to visit me here, I think he wants either the computer or money, or both. At least I am safe from him while I am in here," I said.

"Do you want to keep doing internet porn acting?" asked Dr Rosenberg.

"Not really, no, I'd rather not. And I don't want anything more to do with Damien either. I'll have to shut all that down, but I'm pretty sure I need the computer at home to do that. I got the gun as part payment for a video clip for a metal band. They had overspent their production budget on guns for props, and couldn't pay the talent properly. Sometimes, we take whatever we can get. I was going to sell the gun, but I actually felt a bit safer when I carried it with me," I said.

"Did you think you could use it to stop Evan Harrison from raping you?" asked the doctor.

"Uurgh! He was so revolting. I had to wait until he was asleep, then I crept out of there. I stole the bicycle so I wouldn't make noise and wake anyone up. Then I just dumped it somewhere. I'm a terrible person," I said.

"You were on drugs, you had just been raped, and you were having a psychotic episode. So you did things you wouldn't ordinarily do. You were desperate to get away. At least you can admit these things to yourself now, that is a step forward," said Natalie.

"The photos, some of them weren't very good or clear, the sort of photo I'd usually delete. But I took them not to be a great picture, or to go on the internet, but as a memory prompt for myself, for later. Did I know I was going to black it all out after a drug binge?" I asked.

"Did you? Is this one of your coping strategies for your memory issues? Do you just forget traumatic incidents, or do you forget day to day things too?" asked the doctor.

"I think that I have a bit of a problem with binging on drugs and alcohol, to the point when I wake up wondering what happened, or how did I get here. I'll often check my social media to make sure that people haven't taken my photo when I'm wasted, and put it up online. All I could do was detag myself. If I see myself wearing sunglasses at night, I know I've been trashed. Then, it's as if my memories of the night stem from these pictures, I can check who I was out with, where I went, what I was wearing. I had forgotten the Fiji trip until my agent Serena mentioned it. I remembered it with the photos, and thinking about the Camilla Kaftan. I'm really pissed off that I lost that kaftan, it was gorgeous, and so comfortable."

"But I went directly from the Fiji job to the party at Manly, then to Damien's place, then hospital. I haven't been home to drop anything off, so I lost the bag with my clothes and a pair of Jimmy Choos as well. Spewing!" I said.

"So you're not just losing your memory, but losing your valued possessions as well. Do you think you've lost many things?" asked Dr Rosenberg.

"I've never really thought about it. I guess I have often called friends the day after, looking for clothes and umbrellas and things. If I don't find them, they are sort of collateral damage. But I usually buy cheap things, except for my phone, and the occasional luxury item like the Kaftan. I've hardly ever lost my phone," I said.

"Have the NA meetings been helping you?" asked Natalie.

"Yes. Something that Jack said really resonated with me. He said he had been 'in denial' about what he had done. My memory problems are also about being in denial. I can't feel guilty about having done something bad, if I can't remember doing it. So I use my amnesia to facilitate myself doing bad things, things that I know are wrong. I stole a bike, and car-jacked a man, to get to where I thought I needed to be. I let my addiction over-ride my moral compass, to score drugs. And

I was already so trashed that I couldn't remember what I was doing. I am ashamed of myself, and the behaviours I have been exhibiting, time and again. I don't want to live like this. I can't go on living like this. I have to change, and be a decent person again," I said.

"This is very good, Elise. You have worked hard to stop denying these truths to yourself. You have done bad things, but you have admitted them to yourself. We don't practise the classic 'twelve step program' because of the religious aspects to it, but the next step that we do practise is thinking about how you can apologise or make reparations for the bad things you have done," said Dr Rosenberg.

"That's given me something to think about," I said. "It's too late to apologise to Karen, whose death I caused. I don't know how to contact the man I car-jacked. But I can mend other bridges that I have broken. I can try to always be a good person, and not rob or injure others. I'm going to stay straight, and not socialise with friends who I know are fellow drug addicts. I am reaching out to old friends, to rekindle friendships with people who aren't addicts. If I have a relationship, I want it to be with someone who isn't an addict. That would be a first. Even my sugar-daddy was an alcoholic, though he only drank at dinner every night, then after dinner. Even that is addiction. I can see it now. I never could before."

"You're making a lot of progress, Elise. You've been through a lot, and you've survived however you could. I'm glad you have recalled what you have blocked out. Changing yourself is hard work. It is like you have torn down your old house, your fortress which you constructed to stop yourself feeling guilt and pain. From now on, you'll be building a new structure for yourself, where you can have truth and self-acceptance. You're not a bad person. You have lived through some very bad experiences, and your coping mechanisms have been helping you to destroy yourself. Now you're going to survive and be strong, and not have to do things that you'd rather forget. I'll see you on Thursday, and I want you to keep up the good work," said the doctor.

I did well. I managed to tell the doctor most of what I remembered, without the really incriminating stuff.

Now I've got to try and suss out who from the group has any useful connections. If I want to shift ten kilos of coke, it's got to be to someone who has enough money to buy it.

I don't know why I went to Damien's place, he just isn't that big time. He'd been buying hammer by the gram bag for about two grand, or by the ten gram bag for fifteen grand. He couldn't get his hands on the money to buy a big quantity like Evan could.

But someone must know someone who would. Evan Harrison wasn't the only coke dealer in Brisbane. I'm in here with twenty other junkies, all from different drug networks. Someone will know a big buyer. I just have to find out who, at a meeting where we're not supposed to glorify drug use. But bragging about how many drugs we used to use seems to be a feature of these meetings.

I'll have to sit at the beginning of the circle, so I can stimulate the others to brag about their dealing connections.

That's not a bad strategy.

"Hi, I'm Dave and I'm a recovering alcoholic. I'll be chairing this meeting today. This is a combined Alcoholics and Narcotics Anonymous group. We follow the twelve steps to sobriety, but without the religious bits. So we don't have to believe in God. But we do have to believe in ourselves, and each other. We have made the decision to turn our lives around, and to lead good lives, without addiction. We should make a list of all the persons we have harmed during our addictions. And we should make amends to those people. So our exercise today will be to list all of the people who you have harmed, and then write how you will make amends. I will start. When I was drinking, I neglected my wife and children, both with my presence and with my pay. I spent all of my money on myself, and my wife spent everything she had on the children and household bills.

I made amends by spending my time with my family, and sharing my wage with my wife, so our kids can have everything they need. It took me a long time to realise how selfish I was being. Six years sober," said Dave.

"Hi I'm Elise, and I'm a psychotic drug addict. I have realised this week that I suffered from amnesia after traumatic events, but that I also have a habit of binging on drugs to the point of memory loss. On my list of people I've harmed and want to make amends with are my brother Skye, and my friends from school, Natalie and Paul, and my uni friends Justin, Barnaby, Dustin, Roberta and Helen. I feel I must apologise for causing the death of our classmate, Karen. I was driving her to our dealer's house, and I hadn't slept, but was coming down from ecstasy and coke, and I smashed my car, and Karen was injured, and later died. It was my fault, but I blocked it out and forgot that she had even died. We had been scoring off a friend at Spring Hill, who was a big-time dealer, but he got busted with multiple kilos off coke, and went to jail. So the only other person who we knew how to score from lived right out at Ipswich. I smashed my car on the big highway to Ipswich, it was my fault, but I can't make amends to a dead person. I also remembered my recent trauma, but I don't think I have to make amends to any-one there except for the man who I car-jacked. And I would't know how to contact him. Anyway, eight days clean, remembering what I've done, and determined to build a better life," I said.

"Hi, I'm Everley, and I'm a recovering heroin addict. This is my seventh day clean. Writing this list was very hard for me, because I've done a lot of property crime. I have stolen food from my local shops for years, since I was at school. Not only that, but I would also steal clothes and bedsheets and towels and anything else I needed. I will have to stop stealing, and apologise to the shop owners who I have ripped off. I stole from my family, and I should make amends with my mum, who kicked me out for stealing her rent money. I even stole from my fellow strippers when I worked at the strip club. I'd steal other girl's cash tips while they were on stage, how fucked is that? I'm going to stay away from stripping, sex-work and all drugs. I'll get a straight job and be a straight person," said Everley.

"Hi, I'm Russel, and I'm a recovering drug addict. I've been clean for three and a half weeks, and I'm not craving the high or the social life now. On my list is my ex-wife Michaela, who I lied to so many times about drugs and money. She stopped trusting me, and I kept lying to her until I drove her away. I also lied to my parents about taking drugs, and I will have to face them once I get out. I'll make sure that Michaela is well taken care of in our divorce settlement. I was such a bad coke fiend, and I was a cheap bastard too. I used to get my hair cut at Joe Palazzo's, and my hairdresser would sell me a point of coke. When I started to buy it by the gram, he introduced me to Joe, and I would go around to his West End salon. Joe invited me to a party, and I invited him to a party at my place. I talked him in to using my firm to do his bookwork. Because I did blow with him, I knew that he laundered his drug money through his hair businesses. So I cultivated my friendship with Joe, just so I could get free blow when I was with him, and cheap blow when I wasn't. I've been making amends with my boss and workmates, and I won't manage Joe's accounts now, so I'm not tempted to go back there," said Russel.

Bingo. Russel knows Joe Palazzo. He is Evan Harrison's main rival in hairdressing, and in dealing too, it seems.

"Hi, I'm Anthony, and I'm a recovering drug addict. Three weeks clean today, and nearly ready to face up to all my responsibilities. My list is my wife Lauretta and my two sons Matteo and George. I'm going to be a good dad, a straight dad, and I'm only going to mix with straight people.

When I was in Sydney, I started dealing when I worked at the fruit markets. We did early days, long hours, and I sold a bit of goey to my mates at the market. Then I got a job for a bigger fruit vender called Franco Panetone. Franco knew I was dealing, and he said that if I was going to deal using his van, then I had to buy my drugs from him as well. So I started driving bags of weed and speed and hammer around in the truck, as well as fruit and veg. After a few years, I was unloading shipping containers full of all sorts of stuff, and sending it all over Sydney. It was after I saw some of my rival dealers being taken out by hitmen, that I realised I had to change my life in a real way. That's what made me leave Sydney. I wanted to stay alive long enough to enjoy the money. Anyway, I can say on my CV that I've got experience in transport and logistics, and managing distribution networks. Of Fruit, of course," said Anthony.

Holy shit. Anthony was working for the Mafia in Sydney. He'd definitely have the connections to sell a mountain of coke.

"Hi, I'm Linda and I'm a recovering alcoholic. Two weeks clean. I've been able to look at just how stupid I've been really clearly in the last week. Listening to other people being really honest has let me be really honest with myself. I lost my husband John, because I drank too much and always relied on him to be the responsible parent. And I must make amends with my children, Damon and Flora, who I have disappointed. I've been looking at lots of other jobs I can apply for, and courses to study for better jobs. My social worker, Maxine, has told me that I could get a government payment to study a lot of different courses, which actually lead to well-paid work. I'd be a much better mum with a bigger paycheque. And I am capable of a better paid job. I've always been good with numbers, so maybe I'd be good at accounting. They always need accountants." said Linda.

"Hi, I'm Jack. I'm a schizophrenic and recovering drug addict. I've got quite a long list, starting with my parents. I've been deceitful to all my local doctors, to my landlord, my former boss. Worst is that I did identity fraud, and I really damaged the good name of Alex White. I hope that he can forgive me. I have blamed my friends for encouraging me to drink and do drugs, but it was always me saying 'yes' to the grog and the drugs. It was never my friends' fault. I'm four weeks clean now, and I might stay an extra week in rehab, then get back our there. I've found out where my local AA and NA groups meet in Caboolture. So I'll join up there when I'm out," said Jack.

"Thanks everyone for being so honest. Right, I want you to have a look at your lists, and I want you to think about who you are going to make amends with first. Now write a big number one next to their name. Your project for this week is to at least contact that person. Then write a two next to the person who you will next approach. I'd like to number your list to at least three, and hopefully five or more. We all have people around us, we just need to reach out to them. It can be a text, a phone call, a letter or an email. You might ask the person to visit you. This week, try to make that connection. This person is important to you, so it's worth the effort. They might even be worried about you, and glad you called to tell them how you are. They might not be, they might swear at you or hang up on you. But you have made an effort. Next time we meet, or next week, you might like to reach out to the second person on your list. It's a good exercise to think about what that person might say to you; and what you might then say back to them. These feelings are difficult to express in words, so it helps to practise what you will say. We all know that you don't have a lot of time with your phones, or on the pay-phone, so use that time wisely," said Dave.

132

20. A lot to think about.

I was really hanging out before medication time last night. But I wanted to hold out till 7am this morning. If I ask for it early, I'll get all out of kilter with my meds again.

I lay awake this morning thinking about everything I'd learned yesterday. Anthony knows some very big time dealers in Sydney. Russel knows a big time dealer in Brisbane. One or the other of them should be able to help me out when I'm outside.

The trouble is that both Anthony and Russel are across in the Drug ward, while I'm in the Psych ward. That means I only get to speak to them at NA meetings. So the only time I can speak in person is after that Friday evening NA meeting, when we chat on the deck.

Right. I might need some help from my Psych ward gang.

Who is in my crew? I've got Linda the alco, Steve the meth-head, Jack the schizo, and that older woman who doesn't speak at all. There are also two older men who don't attend meetings, but do talk a little. Then there are the outsiders, Carolyn the dyke and Danny the biker.

Between us, we should be able to break up the male female divide of the post NA meeting chat.

One of those older guys asked me for a cigarette, so there must be a smoker's deck or yard attached to this ward too. The smokers will hang out there numerous times per day. I reckon I'm most likely to find any sympathy with Jack the schizo, but Linda and Steve might come onside with me. But there's got to be something in it for them.

Cigarettes are the obvious answer. They probably serve as currency in this place just like at the PA. But I can't get out to buy any because I'm an involuntary patient. But a voluntary patient could walk down to Carindale and buy whatever they want. So which of us are the involuntary patients?

From what I've listened to at NA meetings, Russel might be the only voluntary patient, and he's in the Drug ward. That leaves the oldies, whose names I don't even know. Yet.

Actually, a cigarette could just get me through to seven o'clock.

I'll put on the pink things and the jeans today. They are clean. The laundry service is actually really good here. My face is looking better and my hand is healing up. My hair still looks like shit, and getting worse daily.

On the far side of the TV room, a sliding door leads to a small balcony. From here, steps lead down to our "recreation area," an enclosed garden with a high metal fence and perspex panels so we can see the trees. There is some exercise equipment on the far side of the yard. Most of our ward are standing on the near side of the yard, smoking. Jack and Steve were smoking with one of the older men and the older lady.

"Hello Sunshine. I was wondering when you'd crack," said Steve.

"I've just got to hold out until medication time," I said.

"Isn't someone going to offer the young lady a cigarette?" asked the older man, who clearly didn't have any.

The older woman held out a packet of Alpines towards me, and I gratefully took one. Jack passed me a lighter, and I lit up.

"Thank you so much, I'm afraid I don't know your name," I said.

"This is Majorie, and I'm Clement," said the older man. He spoke like a school teacher or a public speaker.

"Pleased to meet you, Clement and Marjorie. I'm Elise," I said.

"Were you trying to give up everything at once, cold turkey?" asked Jack.

"Well, I tend to go so hard on everything, that maybe I was trying to go hard on sobriety too," I joked.

"Maybe she didn't remember that she smoked," said Steve, who obviously paid attention at meetings.

"Back when I was young, everybody smoked," said Clement.

"Was that during the Old Testament?" asked Jack.

"Not quite, my son, but it does seem like that sometimes. Back when people were decent." said Clement.

"So how do I buy cigarettes if I can't get down to the shops?" I asked.

"You have to ask someone who is allowed down there to buy some for you," said Steve, looking at Clement.

"Oh Clement, if I gave you my bankcard, could you possibly buy me a packet of cigarettes?" I asked.

"Of course," said Clement. "But if you'd like another item too, it would sound better if my journey was primarily for some other purpose," said Clement.

"Oh, I really need some hair dye as well. Any box with a picture of a light blonde on it," I said.

"The nurses will probably work out who that's for," said Clement.

"Thanks so much, Clement," I said.

"It's arranged then. I'll see you at breakfast," said Clement, as he headed upstairs.

I drew on my menthol flavoured smoke and it was actually quite good. But I just wanted plain cigs. I'd tell him when I gave him my card.

"Marjorie is allowed to have a packet of smokes, but no lighter," said Steve.

"Oh, why is that?" I asked.

"It's because she burns things," said Jack.

Marjorie let out a laugh.

It was the first time I'd heard her make any noise at all.

On the way up the stairs, Steve said to me, "Oh, by the way, Clement is a priest who's in here for molesting young boys. He's trying to break the habit."

"Should I trust him with my credit card?" I asked.

"Well, I do," said Steve.

It was a relief to get my medication. It hit the spot for the first couple of hours. After that, I got that slightly on edge feeling of wanting more. All the time, or at least, whenever I thought about it. So I read my politics books, and thought about my plan for when I get out.

What I really need is contact details for Russel and Anthony. At least I can talk about social media, and suggest being friends on one of those platforms. Then we could have a channel of communication, anyway.

Clement delivered the ciggies and the hair dye to my room. I checked my hair. If this was my second week in here, I might leave the dying until my third or fourth week. My regrowth wasn't that bad yet. Normally, I'd do it every two to three weeks, but no-one is really going to see me in here. I'll dye it just before I go back out into the real world. Clement brought me Schwartzkopf dye, which is a good brand. I should have asked for a conditioning treatment too.

I wanted to think about other people that I knew too.

When I first started doing coke, I had bludged it off Ben, then bought it off Pete. Let me think about Pete. He lived in that tiny house in Spring Hill, where he didn't smoke joints because he thought the neighbours could smell it. So I'd have a smoke at my place before I rode my bike to his place. I still had my car at that stage, but there was no room to park it anywhere near Love St. So funny that his place was on Love Street. We did drugs and sex there, but there wasn't really much love. Taking Pete to the pool was a revelation. He hadn't been doing any outside activities for a long time. He told me the last time he'd been outdoors, was to go to a rave or a festival.

I remembered lounging around at Centenary.

"Right. I'm going to swim my laps now," I said.

"How do you know how many laps to swim?" asked Pete.

"I just make myself do ten. Five hundred metres seems like a fair distance. More than that just seems unachievable," I said.

"I had trouble doing one lap," said Pete.

"What stroke were you doing?" I asked.

"Freestyle," said Pete.

"Well, try breaststroke. Freestyle tires you out. Breaststroke is slower and doesn't make you puffed. I usually just swim breaststroke, with a bit of freestyle at the end. Notice how only the really buff swimmers do butterfly? That's cos it's hard as fuck," I said.

"Oh, okay, I'll give it a go," said Pete. "Are you sure they're not just all here to perve?"

"I'm sure that people are also here to perve, but I think that they are primarily here to swim, or at least, cool off. I can see that there are nice looking men here, but I can also see that heaps of them are gay and not interested in looking at me. That actually makes me feel more comfortable being here," I said.

"You're not worried about all the fags?" asked Pete.

"To me, they're a bit like other women. I don't look at other women in a competitive way, and I don't look at gays that way either. It's way more frightening to be around heaps of predatory heterosexual men," I said.

"Really? I thought that women liked a lot of attention?" said Pete.

"Only to a certain extent. In limited doses. I'd hate to be really famous, and have that attention all the time. I've only had that to a limited extent when I've done videos and tv ads, and it is short lasting. Anonymity comes back, and it is a blessing," I said.

"You know, when Ben first introduced you to me, he said 'Elise is a famous actor, and she studied drama, you'll like her,' and you said 'I'm not famous, I'm just the chick on the trampoline ad.' I thought you had a good perspective on it. I had seen that ad, so I immediately felt like I had known you for longer, and I thought about other ads I might have seen you in. I knew that I'd only seen single images of you, dressed up and tarted up, when the real you goes to the pool with no makeup on, some old togs and cut-off jeans. That stuff is just work for you," said Pete.

So Pete's image of me was a mixture of meeting me in person, and his memory of seeing pictures or film of me, usually used to sell some random product. Usually with hair dyed and styled, false eyelashes, covered in makeup, posed and lit and filmed fifty times until it was exactly perfect.

"Yeah, this is the backstage me," I think I said.

"Well, you've made me feel at home at the pool. And I only really felt at home at my house. People smile at me here, because they know that I'm the fat friend of the hottest girl here," said Pete.

That was probably about as close as Pete ever got to telling me how he felt about me.

Normally, we would just do coke and fuck. He was good at it, actually made an effort. Made sure that I enjoyed it as much as he did. That's pretty unusual for a man, in my experience. Most couldn't be bothered, or simply don't know how.

We had a casual thing going for about six months. Then one morning, all his friends started ringing me up, asking where he was. I had no idea.

I rode around to his house, which was locked, and he wasn't answering his phone. His neighbour spoke to me over the fence, and told me that the police had been around at his house early that morning, and had taken him away.

He didn't call me that day.

The next day, he called, and told me that he'd been arrested. He had used his one phone call the day before to call his lawyer. Pete had been done with fifty grammes of coke, and some other drugs too, and implements for using and dealing. Queensland's Drugs Misuse Act is particularly draconian, and Pete went from the watch-house to court to jail.

I thought that, because of my criminal record, I couldn't visit him in jail. But now that I think about it, if all my charges have been dropped because I am mentally unstable, I shouldn't really have any convictions for anything. Only charges which couldn't stick.

I could visit Pete Sheffield in jail. And I would. He'd probably appreciate a visitor. I have been a bad friend.

Would Pete know anyone who could buy a kilo of coke? I don't think so, but you never know.

It's also unlikely that Damien would know anyone that big time either.

I'm better off to focus on those two over at the drugs ward.

I've got to penetrate the men's bragging circle after the Friday NA meeting. I'll take another woman with me. I don't know if Linda would be up for the task. Linda looks like she has probably heard too many sad stories from too many bad men.

Unlike myself, who has only heard a few sad stories from a few bad guys. I'm still up for it.

And I think Everley is too. Everley might be even more up for it than I am.

Anyway, if I offer her a cigarette, she'll come over to the blokes' circle and smoke a ciggy with me. Safety in numbers.

140

21. Friday's relaxed meeting.

Through the week, I had sat next to Everley at Wednesday's meeting, and asked her if she smoked.

"Cigarettes?" had been Everley's answer.

"Yeah, ciggies, because I managed to score a packet if you're interested," I said.

"Yeah, I'd love one. I didn't want to ask any of the guys for one in case they'd expect something in return," said Everley.

So I slipped her some. Clement had bought me a packet of Peter Jacksons, which he liked to scab off me, and a packet of Sobranie coloured cocktail cigarettes, which he must have thought were young lady's smokes. I slipped her a couple of Sobranies.

By Friday, I was feeling alright with my methadone dose. I'd checked on my social media, and quite a few of the people I'd reached out to had written back. Only Barnaby brought up the whole Karen issue. I wrote back telling him I still felt incredibly sorry and guilty about that. I told him I was changing my life, and trying to make amends with people for the bad things I had done.

I am becoming a better person, but I'm not quite perfect yet.

My plans were coming together.

Friday's NA meeting was hilarious. Everley had also cottoned on to the fact that if you sit next to Dave, the conversation always goes in a clockwise direction, so if you want to direct the tone of what people say, you go first.

"Hi, I'm Dave, and I'm a recovering alcoholic. I'll be chairing the meeting today. If you have any questions, you can direct them towards myself or the whole group. Being a Friday, we've got some members who have been through Rehab, but keep coming to our group to keep themselves and us on the straight and narrow. Also, we've been working on making amends, so if people want to comment on that, we can see how we are progressing. I've been working hard to be a better husband and father, and I've also tried to be a good son and son-in-law. Since I've stopped drinking, my in-laws have been very accepting of me, and my parents have forgiven me, though I lost my dad. I realise that at my age, I have to support my elders as well as my kids, so no more spending all my money and time on grog. I've been clean for six years and one month," said Dave.

"Hi, I'm Everley, and I'm a recovering drug addict. Eleven days clean, and trying to make amends with my family and friends. Talking and texting with friends, I have become aware of what incredible lies I have told everyone. I've told people that I inherited money, that I acted in porno films, that I was straight when I was high, and that I was high when I was straight. I've tried to borrow money off people to buy drugs, but told them all sorts of lies, the worst of which was that I was paying for a friend's funeral. When I worked as a stripper, I'd always slip a John my number when he was having a lap dance, so we could meet later and I'd get more money off him. I used to get pissed off if Johns didn't carry cash and only had a credit card in their wallet, because I was never stupid enough to steal credit cards. I know now that that was wrong, and I'll never do it again. I guess that growing up in a household of poverty and petty crime made thieving seem quite normal. My mum used to send me out with enough money for milk and bread, but asked me to slip a block of chocolate under my jacket as well. I'm going to pay for all my groceries from now on," said Everley.

Right, so Everley want to make it a brag session about lies today. I can go to that party. Will the others pick up on it?

"Hi, I'm Elise, and I'm a recovering drug addict with Psychosis. I've been straight for thirteen days, and I am working at making amends with my brother, my school friends and my uni friends. I think the person I've lied to the most is myself. My whole life. I knew that my dad killed my mum, then himself, but I told myself that my parents just had to give me up for adoption. I was thinking about contacting an old boyfriend, and told myself that we had just drifted apart, when I knew that he had been busted with mountains off coke, and had gone to jail. I told myself that I couldn't visit him in jail because of my criminal record, but when I thought about it, I realised that I didn't have any convictions for all my charges, because I'm mentally unwell and not legally responsible for myself. I could have visited him, and I will, when I get out. He would have to have cleaned up his act, after a few years in jail. But mostly I told myself that I didn't have any problems, when my life lurched from one disaster to the next, and my ways of coping were just as bad as the trauma. This is the first time that I can actually think about my whole life, and assemble all the episodes into one narrative. And I was just plodding along as if it was all normal," I said.

"Hi, I'm Anthony and I'm a recovering drug addict. Three and a half weeks clean, and the end is in sight for me now. My wife has been visiting me, and she is so happy that I'm finally doing it this time. Lauretta watched me try to change when we moved to Brisbane, but I soon slipped back in to my Sydney habits. I lied to her more than any-one. I lied to her about working for the Mafia, but then, I didn't used to think about them like that. They were just the Italian guys that I worked for, who just happened to deal a lot of drugs as well as fruit. So I suppose I lied to myself about it too. But they were crazy times. I went to a big wedding where the groom and bride both flew in in helicopters. I stayed in a luxury chalet on Perisher, and got flown to a twenty-first party on Whitsunday island. They weren't making that kind of money selling fruit. But I told Lauretta they did. I practised some salsa dancing with Lauretta. She said I was good at it. She said she wants to learn the tango, but doesn't want to dance it with anybody but me. I feel like the luckiest guy in the world," said Anthony.

"Hi, I'm Linda, and I'm a recovering alcoholic, two and a half weeks clean. I used to lie to my husband John a lot. He would work during the day, and I'd often do split shifts for lunch, then evenings. He'd have a couple of beers at dinner, then go to sleep. I'd often stay out drinking with the punters after I'd knocked off, and we'd go to other clubs which opened late. I had lots of flings with different men, and I never told him about any of them. I've tried making amends with him, but he's got a new woman now, and won't even take my call unless it's about a custody visit. He will look after her children, and their children, but not our children. They had to go to a foster home. I'll make amends with my kids when I get them back. I've started an online accounting course, and I'm really good at it. I'm going to focus on that for the rest of my time here," said Linda.

"Hi, I'm Steve and I'm a recovering drug addict. I've booked myself in for an extra two weeks, because when I was out, Ted's mates kept calling me and asking me around to their places for parties. I know they only wanted me there for my money, so they could scab drugs off me. But I couldn't handle the pressure. I was so tempted just to go around there and party with them. I'm better off in here where there is no temptation, until I am stronger. I've used up my sick leave but I could take unpaid leave and still not lose my job. Five weeks clean," said Steve.

"Hi, I'm Carolyn, and I'm a recovering addict and self harmer. Two years clean, and I've certainly told a lot of lies to a lot of people, including myself. But I learned from the best. My reverend used to molest me and my sister. Then dad would also abuse me, and pass me around to his friends so they could also abuse me. Dad insisted that I lie to mum and tell her nothing ever happened. I had to lie to the teacher at school if she asked about my home life. No wonder I learned to distrust and dislike men. I never had an honest relationship with a man. I didn't admit to myself that I was a lesbian until I was well grown up, and I didn't actually find a girlfriend for quite some time after that. I used to take acid and ecstasy and get so messed up, but I thought I was having a great time. And being an ugly dyke, I'd get into fights with men. I was so self-destructive. I went from cutting myself up to letting men beat me up. But I know I don't deserve that now, that I deserve respect from others and myself. Getting drunk and fighting are two things that I'll never do again, and wish that I never had done. Meeting Tracy really helped me to grow as a person, and to be able to laugh at who I was before. I wouldn't have met her unless I'd been sober. Her father was a violent alcoholic, so she certainly doesn't want her girlfriend to be a violent alcoholic. If I can do it, you can all do it, my friends," said Carolyn.

"Hi, I'm Russel, and I'm a recovering drug addict. Four weeks clean now, and I think I'll be moving out pretty soon. I've been making amends with my boss at work, which has been great, and my ex-wife Michaela, which hasn't been great. I told her some pretty massive lies. I told her I didn't do drugs, and that my clients didn't do drugs. I told her I never did drugs at home or at work. I told her I didn't do drugs when I visited my clients, and really that was the only reason I visited my clients. All other clients I saw at work. She was so suspicious of me, she even trailed me down to the dog park, to make sure I was really going there. I totally blew her trust in a real way. So much so that she aborted our baby. Her dad had been an alcoholic, and she didn't want the father of her child to be a druggie. I was so devastated, I'd always wanted to be a dad. I really miss my dog, Flossy. And my dog park friends, who are all straight, as far as I know," said Russel.

"Hi, I'm Jack, and I'm a recovering addict and schizophrenic. Four and a half weeks clean. I don't even want to think about all the lies I've told, and to how many different people. If I had to make amends with every person I've lied to or ripped off, it would take me the rest of my life. I have pretended to be a pharmacist, and a doctor, and even a cop. I don't know what I was thinking, I was just so wasted and desperate. But I'm moving back up to the north side to be near my parents, I really want to mend that relationship first. I think I have ruined my reputation around South

Brisbane. There's also a woman I had a relationship with, called Rose. I think about her a lot, and want to get back in contact with her, even though it's been over a year since we broke up. I'd like to apologise to her, and pay back the money I borrowed from her. If she'd be my friend again, I'd be so happy. But she'd be an idiot to take me back. She took out a protection order against me. I know that my parents will want to take me to their church, but I don't want to go. Fuck that," said Jack.

"Hi, I'm Danny and I'm a recovering addict. Two and a half years clean, never touching heroin again. I have made amends with a lot of people in my life, but those who I know are still drug abusers, I steer clear of. I feel sorry for them. But I'll tell them about NA or AA if they want to hear it. Having been a heroin addict, I told a lot of lies. I had one girlfriend in Brisbane, and one on the Gold Coast, at the same time, for about a year. I sold people drugs and really ripped them off, and justified it to myself. I even ripped my friends off. I sold people 'speed' and 'coke' which was really heroin. I did a short stint at Arthur Gorrie, and all I learned was how to smuggle drugs and share home made syringes. They call it the university of crime, and they are right. All the crims talk about is crime and how to do it. That should have taught me to stop. But it was only when I lost my wife Gladys, that I finally stopped. Be smarter than me, and stop before you lose someone special," said Danny.

"Being a Friday," said Dave, "we'll move outside to the deck for informal discussion. Thanks for sharing, everyone. Sometimes, when we hear about what our peers have done, it gives us the courage to admit what we have done. Remember that we are all moving forward, just by being here," said Dave.

So, we filed outside, and I was armed with both packets of cigarettes. Everley still had one of her cigarettes. She wanted to infiltrate the smokers group too. I wondered why? Was she keen to talk to one of the guys in the psych ward? It could only be Jack or Steve. Both of them were alright looking, Jack was actually quite good looking, but he was totally fucked up. But I can't exactly point the finger.

We lit up our smokes with the blokes.

"Oh, I've been hanging out for a dart," said Steve.

"God, me too," said Anthony.

"I'll miss having a fag with all you druggies," said Russel.

"We'll miss you too, Russel," said Everley.

"I'll be gone too in three days," said Anthony.

"Oh, we won't miss you," I said, joking.

"Yes we will," said Everley. "We could always be Fakebook friends."

"We could start a group called 'fucked up junkies anonymous,' everyone would want to join," said Jack.

"I hope that Christian is alright out there, being a roadie. At least he had work to go to," said Anthony.

"You'll find something mate," said Russel. "I feel so lucky that I've a job to go back to."

"Is anyone on Insta, or is it only shallow people like me?" I asked.

"I can't stand Instagram, and Twitter is for wankers," said Anthony.

"I've got an Insta account," said Russel, "but it's mostly for dog photos."

"I've got an Insta page, but it's mostly for pictures of high heels," said Everley.

"Do you mean, like, you wearing high heels?" asked Steve, looking interested.

"Ah, some photos are me, and others are friends or just girls I see wearing great shoes," said Everley.

"I'd like to see that," said Carolyn. "Do you include boots?"

"Stripper heels?" asked Steve. He was keen.

"Just whatever takes my fancy, that day," said Everley.

"What's your insta handle, Elise?" asked Russel.

"EliseReleaseTheBeast," I said.

"Elise the beast, oh, that's a classic," said Carolyn.

"It's mostly work shots, and some behind the scenes stuff," I said.

"Cool, we'll join your fan club," said Jack.

This had gone well.

149

22. Insanity is a bi-product of Capitalism.

Rod Tweedy wrote this - "Mental illness is now recognised as one of the biggest causes of individual distress and misery in our societies and cities, comparable to poverty and unemployment. One in four adults in the UK today has been diagnosed with a mental illness, and four million people take antidepressants every year. 'What greater indictment of a system could there be,' George Monbiot asked, 'than an epidemic of mental illness?'"

One in four of us has a mental illness? I didn't realise it was so common.

I'd like to apply Tweedy's theory to my peer group of substance abusers.

The most successful capitalist amongst us is Russel. He manages the investments and business strategies for an array of high-end clients. So Russel spends his time making sure that the rich stay rich and hopefully get even more rich. But a client has introduced him to coke, as a fun high end consumable, like champagne and caviar. These wealthy people, I've noticed, like to indulge themselves and show off to others about how much money they spend on their clothes, jewellery, cars and houses. It's the same with coke. Russel and his hairdresser mate, Joe Palazzo, would view coke as a status symbol. They'd look down on other junkies who did speed or smack, because they thought their drug was the best, superior to the others. The ruling class think they are superior to others, but the fact that many are so dependent on alcohol or drugs demonstrates that even though they have accumulated wealth, they are not happy.

More working class druggies and alcos seem to turn to drugs more as a support because their working lives don't give them what they need. They slave their guts out in various jobs, for just enough money to live on. They don't get the kind of choices about where to live, what to drive and wear, they live in the cheapest place they can find, drive what they can afford, and buy rich people's cast-offs at the op shop.

Workers like Anthony work hard for their boss, and if the boss encourages illegal activity hidden behind legal work, well that's just a secret, something to get away with. Workers like Steve get into drugs through their peer group, and the boss is not happy about it, because it decreases productivity. Small business people like Christian try to make a living catering to those with enough money to spend going out, seeing bands, listening to music, having a drink and a smoke. But running small businesses is a bit like gambling – you have to be just the right type of cool, the band has to be popular enough to draw a crowd, you've got to follow the trends. If you're a promoter who has a spliff after a gig, you're cool, but if you're a junky shooting up before a gig, you're poison. Linda had the working class dream – married, two jobs, two kids, but she had lost her joy in life. She started finding excitement hanging around the clubs after her work finished, looking for that thrill that her working drone life was not providing. She hadn't even dreamt about fulfilling work until she spoke to her counsellor. So downtrodden, she couldn't even imagine a fun job.

Then there's your criminal underclass. Like Everley, you grow up thinking that shoplifting is just how you get the more expensive items on your grocery list. Everley knows that she can work a legal job, and get paid chickenfeed, or she can sell her body, and earn enough to be comfortable. But neither of these work choices make her happy, both are just to be endured for the money. Drugs for Everley are an escape from an existence where there are only shades of endurability, not much actual enjoyment. So the escape becomes the enjoyment.

On a tangent from the classes are the crazies like Jack and Clement and myself. We know there are rules about how to behave within the capitalist scheme of production, but we either can't work them out, try our best but just can't do it, or enjoy breaking the rules. With our insanity, as opposed to just substance abuse, we don't see the point of the rules of behaviour to start with.

Jack got addicted to painkillers, so he started seeing different doctors and chemists, and telling different stories. He didn't go looking for heroin like a pot smoker would, he acted out different personas to different doctors, who along with the pharmacists, were his dealers. Jack stole someone else's identity, and found he liked being the other guy better than himself. Is this a reaction to having such narrow rules around identity, to protect individual's all important financial credit? Did he feel trapped by his identity, and was seeking a way out? Was he enacting his own 'Witness protection scheme', or is he doing that now, in therapy?

Society certainly sends us mixed messages on this one. No, you can't change your name and be a different person, you have to use your original name. Unless you get married. Or you are a transgendered person, or you're in Show Business. Then it's quite acceptable, a good business decision, even. Regular Jacks aren't allowed to become Alex Whites, especially if there is already an Alex White living in that place. We must maintain that identity, from the birth certificate to the electoral roll, to the tax office, to the criminal record. Identity must be controlled, because capitalism is all about control. If you want to control the means of production, you've got to control the workers as well. In order for Jack to become a legal drug addict, he had to become a schizophrenic. And it will be much easier to get off the drugs than to untangle the personalities he has developed.

Clement might have become a priest because he didn't want to be gay, or a paedophile. He got up in the pulpit and preached to a church full of people about how to live your life right according to God. But he obviously couldn't stop himself from acting out his gay and paedophilic tendencies. But he's in here because he wants to be here, or maybe because his church wants him in here, not because the police or a court have ordered him to be in here. But if he's been a priest for his whole life, he's probably made heaps of money for the church, so the church provides for him when he has 'broken down.'

And then there is me. I'm a product of a Domestic Violence relationship, who has never had a proper relationship at all. I can cash in on my looks to live quite comfortably, but I'm a drug addict too. But my looks will fade, so I'd better cash in now while I'm still young, and plan for something different in the future. I don't understand the rules at all, and I guess that legal types give up on people like me and just label us 'crazy.' But I'm not any more crazy than the society who created me, and created my psych ward peers. We psychotics and schizos and self harmers and druggies are all a bi-product of capitalism, not fitting into the structures of the means of production. Our various mental disorders, whether addiction, psychosis, paedophilia, schizophrenia, are all inextricably tied up with our jobs, what we produce and consume, and how we fit in to the capitalist means of production. The class system offers us different forms of employment, and different drugs to use. But the wealthy are not immune from mental illness, despite 'winning' at capitalism.

I wonder what Marjorie is in here for?

It will be hard to find out unless she talks to me, and she doesn't seem to talk.

Thinking about the outpatients, Carolyn had a lot of her problems, because she was the victim of men like Clement. So if the paedophile expresses their 'love' and abuses a child, they are reinforcing their own illness, and producing mental illness in their victim too.

I wonder if Clement was abused as a child himself? Is paedophilia a self-perpetuating cycle?

We certainly feel like the bi-products of a sick system.

When I think about Danny, he is the one who lost the most to his addiction. He had a wife who he was happy with, but she was also an addict. He lost her to her addiction, the same that he had. But he seems happy, and he wants to help us from fucking up our lives like he did.

Even the worst of us are humans, and can change, and deserve respect and self-respect.

Our stories are all the same story, only the details are different.

154

23. A weekend with social media.

My plans are taking shape, and my shrink Natalie thinks I'm improving too. She seems to think that remembering something is somehow equivalent to accepting it. I have remembered some heavy stuff, and I'm not really accepting it at all. But at least I am remembering it.

I might have some friends when I get back out, as well. I've got my phone for both days of this weekend.

First, I'd better check if Serena has texted.

"Hi Elise, I've got a contract here for you to sign for the next Pepsi ad. It's not filming for a while, but it shows that they like your work. Also Evan Harrison wants you to do a hair fashion show coming up in April. Hope you're improving, Serena."

I'll have to write back to her. But I'm so not keen to see Evan Harrison again.

"Hi Serena, Wow that's great news about the Pepsi contract. I'm not so sure about the Evan Harrison gig. He was creepy towards me on the Fiji shoot. I'd really rather not. Can you tell him I'm sick? Thanks, Elise." I wrote.

Elise texted back "Elise, what kind of creepy? S."

I wrote "Like rapey creepy. I won't do the gig, and warn whoever else that you send that he is slimy. E."

"Thanks for the heads up. I had actually heard rumours about him, but you've confirmed it for me. I'll only send mature girls who can handle creeps, no teenagers. S." wrote Serena.

So Serena must have to deal with this kind of person a lot. I suppose she'd feel responsible for the safety of her girls. At twenty-seven, I'd be considered one of her older girls. If they are tall and gangly, Serena will employ them as models from when they're about twelve or thirteen.

There was a text from Daniel.

He had accepted my friend's request, and wrote a message, "Hi Elise, long time no see. I haven't seen you at the pool for a bit, but I heard about Pete. I'm sorry he got done, I know you were good friends. Is that you on the Harrison Hair ad? There's a billboard near the Story Bridge, so I see it every day. Air kisses, Daniel."

I wrote back, "Daniel, darling, I miss the pool so much. I'm at the Betty Ford clinic for another two weeks, but when I'm out, I'll be there. The Harrison hair shoot was fun. Fiji! But Evan was a slime bucket. I'm going to visit Pete when I get out. Miss you too, Elise."

There was a message from Natalie Pasquale, what a surprise. "Dear Elise, of course I remember you. I did my law degree and now work as an investigator for an insurance company. Glad to see you've been sorting your life out. Love, Natalie."

I wrote back, "Dear Natalie, it has taken me some time, and a few disasters, to piece it all together. I remembered my brother Skye, and I'm going to look for him when I get out. He's not on here, or not using his proper name anyway. My shrink here is also called Natalie, she reminded me of you. Love, Elise."

Roberta and Tana had both accepted my friend's request, but not written a message.

Justin Ford hadn't accepted my friend's request.

Barnaby Jones wrote back, "Hi Elise. For a long time I blamed you for Karen's death. Then a friend asked why she was traveling in your car if you were the dealer. I realised that Karen was buying the stuff, and you were just driving her there. She was not an innocent victim, she wanted to be there. You must feel terribly guilty about it. You probably miss her as much as I do. Barnaby."

Whoa, how do I write back to that one?

"Hi Barnaby, I really miss her too. We were both drug addicts, and I should not have been driving with drugs in my system. I am going through Rehab at the moment, and trying to make amends with those who I have wronged. I can't bring Karen back, but I can apologise to her friends for my stupid behaviour. I hope you're getting heaps of work, Elise." That was about the best I could say.

Paul had also written back, "Elise, was that you on the trampoline ad? I'm working in the Casino show down in Melbs. It's fun, but I miss Brissy and the Goldy. I fly back occasionally but only for two days at a time. Hope you're well, stay in touch, Paul."

I think I needed a cigarette.

At least smoking gave me another place to go. And I even had a go on the exercise equipment. Mid-morning must be the oldies' time for a fag. I'd just had a go on the rowing machine, when Clement, Marjorie and the other old guy came down the stairs. I got up to have a smoke and be sociable.

"G'day Clement and Marjorie, are you right for smokes?" I asked.

"Yes, thanks Elise," said Clement, "it's Ernest's turn to give me one today." Marjorie had one of her Alpines, and Ernest slipped Clement a Peter Jackson from his pack. We all lit up and smoked for a bit in silence.

"So what are you in for?" asked Ernest.

"Oh, I'm a fucking mess," I said. "This time I car-jacked a man, but last time, I killed somebody."

Everyone nodded their heads.

"Yeah, I killed some people too. I was out at Wolston Park for a long time, but I calmed down and they moved me here," said Ernest.

Marjorie nodded and waved her cigarette in agreement.

Clement spoke for her, "Marjorie also killed some people. But she doesn't want to talk about it."

"I'm getting heaps better. I can remember it all now. I'm putting my life back together," I said.

"God has forgiven me for my sins," said Clement, "but he hasn't helped me to stop thinking about sinning yet."

"I wish I could forget the things that I have done. But I'm better off in here, away from everyone. I wouldn't trust myself out there," said Ernest.

"This is the best place for us, until we learn to think differently," said Clement.

As I finished my cigarette and went up stairs, I realised that I didn't know what Ernest or Marjorie had done. And I didn't really want to know.

After that break I got back into the phone session.

Instagram seemed so shallow to me now, when I used to be so in to it. But I had to look at it. Elise hasn't unleashed the beast for quite a while, but my followers have spotted me on both those ads, and tagged me in them, so they are on my page.

Oh, look, among my new followers are Russel, who calls himself "Russ and Flossie", and Carolyn, who is "CJ naughty nurse". Russel's account seems to be mostly photos of his dog, and him with his dog. There are also other dogs, but not any other people. That's fair enough. I'll follow him back. I suppose I should follow Carolyn back as well. Her girlfriend is quite pretty. She seems to mostly post photos of plants. She has heaps of gardening friends. That's something I've never really looked at before, well, not on the internet. I have always appreciated nice looking plants and trees in real life. I like the way that plants can be any size, any shape, and a variety of colours. A great garden or jungle has many different types, all growing together, some thriving in the shade, others emerging upward towards the sun.

I had mostly just looked at fashion and hair stuff on this platform. I'd really like to look at other stuff, to make my life more balanced.

I want to hand the phone in but there was something someone said that I want to follow up on. Private investigator. My Natalie, as opposed to Doctor Natalie, works as an investigator. I might just add one more message.

"Dear Natalie, I was wondering, if Skye did change his name, like if he was adopted or something, how would I find out? Where would I go and who would I ask? Love, Elise."

If anyone knew, she'd know.

160

24. Long term plans.

One question that Natalie Rosenberg had asked me was about my long term plans. If I had thought about it before, I can't remember having done so. I was always busy living one day at a time, at the most, one school term ahead was about as far as I planned.

I hadn't planned any great future with any of the men that I had seen. I never thought about having kids except for when buying contraception. I knew I'd never make enough money to buy my own place.

My thoughts on renting had been that I could move to any city in Australia, or London or LA. As a drama student, it was made clear for us that we'd have trouble getting enough work to live on in Brisbane, and that Sydney or Melbs, or London or LA were places where there was a lot more work. I had thought about as far as moving to Sydney or Melbourne. Moving overseas was a bigger step, needing more money to be saved up. I remember thinking about selling the car and moving to Sydney, after splitting up with Ray.

If I'd learnt anything from group therapy, it was that we needed a network around us, or we were lost. So I'd probably be staying in Brisbane. And I'd need a car. If I got work on the Gold Coast, I'd need to be able to drive myself there and back. I had a good agent in Serena, and work for the time being.

I would like to have a proper relationship with a man one day, maybe get married. But I'm not going to hold my breath until it happens. He's got to be easy on the eye, and close to my own age. I don't care what he does for a living. As long as he can take care of himself financially, I can probably take care of myself. I'd eventually like to live somewhere where I can swim everyday. Not just in a pool, either. I'd like to be able to swim in the ocean or a clean natural body of water. I think I was spoiled growing up near Noosa. But I'll probably have to live in a city while I'm working. Sydney and Melbourne both have city beaches.

I think that one of the things that I'd like, which would possibly be the most achievable, is to get a dog. I don't really care what breed of dog, I'll probably go to the RSPCA and find one with nice eyes. Dogs are lovely, and they love their owners. I could learn a lot about love by having a dog.

I'd like to stay clean of drugs, but it's not quite so black and white out there in the real world as it is here in rehab. I'd still like to be able to have a glass of champagne at opening night, or a quiet spliff at home on the weekend. But I don't want any more pills or powders, and that includes the pharmaceuticals that we get in here.

I'd also like to get to some big parties. I have been to the Woodford Festival, and Modifyre, and all of the big clubs in Brisbane and on the Coast, but I'd love to see Burning Man and the Glastonbury Festival. If I could get to these festivals either as a performer or a punter, I don't mind. But performing would be better. If I could work on some sort of stage act or performance art or installation, I could get paid to go and be the centre of attention too. I guess that would really be my dream. To create an act that could appear at big festivals. Something really spectacular, like that French company who make the giant puppets, or the Burners who make the weird vehicles. I'd like to run a performance production company for outrageous gigs. With amazing costumes, hair and makeup, strange vehicles, hoop skirted stilt walkers, a truck like an elephant, giant wine glasses full of bubbles, my company could do anything.

Alright! Now I had a dream. That certainly beats drifting along without one. I'll save the money I make performing, and make the contacts to help me build sets and vehicles. I could start with a weird bicycle for one, then build bigger for two or more people. Pedal power could keep the vehicles light for air freighting, and eliminate the noise of an engine and the need for fuel. I wonder if solar panels could be used for power if necessary?

But to my current plans, and a possible means to support future dreams. I needed to talk to both Russel and Anthony about their drug dealing ties, and both have sworn off drugs and people that do them. I'll have to have something else to talk to them about. For Russel, it's the dog. I'll tell him about how I'm looking for one, and ask him if he knows of any breeders or puppies.

With Anthony it's a bit harder, for a few reasons. Firstly, he's got a wife who is on to him and has put him in rehab. She won't like female friends, or druggies of any kind. I'm so not into latin dancing and have no mutual interests besides drugs. It will be harder to start up a conversation with him.

But the other thing is the drugs themselves. I will have to find them first. I think I have buried them in Cleveland cemetery. But I'm not sure exactly where. But I also know that you can't just rock up at the cemetery and start digging. I'm going to need a car and a shovel. Maybe I can be someone's loving daughter or grand-daughter, bringing in a rose bush to plant. Once I've found it, I don't want to have to hold on to it for too long. And it would be good to have a place to hide it until it's sold. I'm going to have to have a car to take it to where I sell it. And I'm going to need a gun. A real gun, not just my replica. I'm only a skinny girl, and a lot of drug dealer types might think it's easy to take the drugs or the money off me.

A real gun will stop that. But given my history, I am unlikely to be able to get a gun licence. So it will have to be an un-licensed gun. Oh, well. I'm not sure if I've got points left on my driver's licence either. Also, Anthony's contacts might be in Sydney, so that either means driving there, or forking out for air fares and a hotel. And carrying drugs through an airport. It would have to be a drive, wouldn't it?

So I've got a bit of a shopping list to be able to do this job. Or a borrowing list.

Find the coke.

Car.

Shovel.

Meet the buyer.

Contacts.

Gun.

Then I've got to think about what I do with the cash. That much cash can only be taken to a bank in instalments, otherwise it's a suspect transaction. Ten grand is the amount which will be declared suspect, no matter how valid your reason. I won't have any reason, so it's got to be deposited in multiples of nine grand. I hope that I can sell the whole lot of it it one go, or I will have to split it up and do multiple deals. That would mean another item on the shopping list.

Scales.

And I'm not doing any of it myself. Not so much as one line. I know where that leads and I'm not interested in going there again. That money is not to party on, it's to set up my production company. It's to make vehicles and to buy my own car, and make things and hire people. It's to get started on a new life, rather than plodding along, making the same mistakes as I have in my old life.

If only I had a credit rating, or could get a bank loan. I guess that borrowing is the only way I'm going to get a car, borrowing money for a car, or borrowing someone's car. Or hiring a car. That could be the solution for the time being.

And finding Skye. I've got to find out what he's calling himself, what he does for a living. If my Natalie is working as an investigator, she might be able to help me find him.

165

25. The home stretch.

I'm going to stop taking the methadone this week, I don't think I need it anymore. But the doctor probably won't let me stop taking the pharmies, so I'll have to go along with that, at least until they let me out of here.

"How are you feeling today, Elise?" asked Natalie.

"Well thanks, Doctor Rosenberg," I said. "I think I can do without the methadone now."

"Yes, I think you can too," said Natalie. "But you'll need to stay on the anti-psychotics. They have a cumulative effect, and you might have only just reached the level that you notice the results."

"Oh, I definitely feel the effects. The anti-psychotics really wake me up in the morning. I seem to do my best thinking in the morning, after these, but before as well. And I think that the anti-depressants do help me to sleep. I am feeling happier, but I think that this has more to do with thinking about my life and where it's going, than from taking the pills," I said.

"What have you been thinking about your life?" asked Natalie.

"Remember how you asked me if I had any long term goals, and I said I didn't, well, I have now," I said. "I want to continue with performing, but I want to start my own production company. I want to create acts with stilt walking and strange bicycle-driven vehicles, with fire and glow sticks, to perform at festivals and events. My ultimate goal would be to perform at Glastonbury and Burning Man. But I'd be happy to book acts where-ever, and I'd like to employ a small team for big events."

"Wow, Elise, it sounds like you've really put some thought into it. So you'd like to stay in performing, but move into production for events. That's certainly a growing business, and you'll still get to perform, if you want to," said Natalie.

"I have been involved in other people's productions, for New Years parties and Woodford Festival, but I'd like to actually design the costumes and vehicles, and learn how to build them as well. I can fix my bike, so I could learn how to build bicycle-powered vehicles. I'd like to eventually make bigger things, but start small and manageable," I said.

"I'm glad that you've been putting some thought in to it, and that you've chosen something with which you have some experience, but where you will learn new skills and run your own business. What about your relationships? How are they going?" asked Natalie.

"I've had no luck finding my brother, but my friend Natalie Pasquale is working as an investigator for an insurance company now. She might be able to help me find Skye, especially if he has changed his name. I've contacted another school friend, and a handful of my uni friends. One of then, Daniel is also a friend from Centenary pool. I'm pretty sure that none of these people take drugs, and will be suitable friends for when I get out. The drama student mob could also be people I might ask to work with me in performance productions, as I know they are all trained and professional. My group have scattered, Dustin is in London and Helen is in LA, but the rest are still local, and most still working as actors. Only one friend gave me a hard time about the accident which killed Karen. We discussed it and I apologised. Barnaby went out with her for a while, and said he blamed me for a long time. Then he discussed it with a friend, and felt we were equally to blame. I'm glad I spoke to him, or texted back and forth, anyway. I also thought that I'd visit Pete in jail. He is in jail for drugs, cocaine, but I want him to know that I'll still be his friend, and that I can help him stay clean if he is clean now. I hope he is," I said.

"It's good to see that you've been busy, and seeking out the right kind of friends. I'm not sure that I approve of you visiting your friend in jail quite yet, but if you think you should, that is up to you. Was he your boyfriend?" asked Natalie.

"No, not really," I said. "Pete and I had a casual thing going for a while, but we never had an official relationship. I made him go to the pool with me, so he would get some exercise, because he is fat. Otherwise we just took drugs and had sex together. He never told me he loved me, nor I him. I don't think I was capable at that time. Maybe I would be more capable now?"

"To be honest, that may be one relationship that I wouldn't encourage you to pursue. You're a smart, pretty woman, Elise. Don't go back to old relationships which didn't work. Unless you really can't live without him, and it doesn't sound like that. Leave yourself open to meeting someone who will fit in with your new life, and not drag you back to your old life. You must meet some interesting people working in the entertainment industry?" asked Natalie.

"I can hear what you're saying, Doctor Rosenberg," I said. "I've had poor judgement with relationships before. Pete is not someone that I'd really consider having a long-term relationship with. He had trouble seeing the real me, away from the tv ads and the magazine ads. Pete was a uni dropout who'd hardly ever worked except for dealing. He certainly never spoke about goals in life. I really want to do interesting and original work in my life, and I think I'd like a partner who also has some goals and plans in life. And not just to make money and control people, like Ray. That sugar-daddy relationship wasn't a real relationship, it was something between paedophilic grooming and prostitution. I'll bet Ray's on to his next twenty year old blonde, the dirty old perve."

"That definitely sounded like an unhealthy relationship. Possibly control obsessive? In real relationships, you discuss issues and make decisions together. I hope that you can form a good relationship. I think that your problem will be choosing the man who is good for you, rather than one who looks good and says what you want to hear," said Natalie.

"I don't know if there will be heaps of men to choose from, but I can definitely hold out until a decent guy comes along. There are always plenty of creepy broke guys who will tell you any bullshit to get you in bed. I'll meet a guy who has a life already, so I can just add to his life, and not be his life," I said.

"That is exactly the right attitude to have when it comes to finding a partner. They will come along when you are working on an interesting project together. You might be lucky and find one on the internet, but most relationships have heard about which last, start from friendships and working relationships. It's because you have interests in common in the first place, which makes you find each other interesting," said Natalie.

"Is that how you met your husband, Doctor Rosenberg?" I asked.

"Oh, I met mine ages ago, when we were both medical students. My husband is also a psychiatrist, so we have a lot in common. But we're here to talk about you. I'm glad you're getting to a point where you can analyse your life so far, and plan for your future. Do you for see any problems?" asked Natalie.

"Only smaller things like money. And I want a dog. I'm glad I've got my flat in a block which allows pets. I'm just across from Roma St Parklands, so I can take it for walks. A few of my neighbours have cats, so I hope they get on. I just want to have a normal life, and not lurch from drama to tragedy continuously. I want some certainty, a place to come home to," I said.

"I think we all want that," said Doctor Rosenberg.

Next I'd have to go to the NA meeting. I wasn't sure if Russel or Anthony would still be there. Most people stayed for the month, then took off as soon as they could. At least I had their contacts on the internet. Some of the NA crew are people who I'd never interact with in my usual life. Maybe I thought I hung out with the more glamour drug crowd, and some of them were from a more desperate crowd. The truth is that we are all druggies, whether rich or poor, alcoholics, dope-fiends, meth-heads and junkies. Some one said that drug taking was ritualised self comforting. I agree, and wonder how much the pharmaceutical drug routine is also ritualised self comforting, or even trying for the placebo effect? Taking the drugs at the same time each day might just be a way to try to make some order in a chaotic life.

There is a new young man in our ward who has been doing the yelling in the middle of the night thing. I'll bet they're trying to drug him into sleeping at nights and waking in the day. I'm glad I'm not the only screamer. Maybe we've all been there.

He was with our group as we trudged across to the Drugs Ward. The guard kept his eye on the new guy. If he made a run for it, the guard would have to leave the rest of us and chase him. He didn't.

"Hi, I'm Dave and I'm a recovering alcoholic. I'll be chairing this meeting today. This is a combined Alcoholics and Narcotics Anonymous group. We follow the twelve steps to sobriety, but without the God bits, unless you're into the God thing. These steps involve admitting we have made mistakes and accepting that, then starting a new sober life, and making amends to those we have wronged. I was a serious drinker, drinking at home, at work, even while driving. My wife confronted me and forced me to decide to change. At rehab I realised what an idiot I'd been, and started to repair my relationships with my family and co-workers. I eventually changed jobs, and have been sober for six years now," said Dave.

"Hi, I'm Linda, and I'm a recovering alcoholic, three weeks clean. My drinking wrecked my life, but I'm going to get my kids back, and study for a well-paying job. I've been studying accountancy, and am currently fascinated by all the things which are tax deductible. I like learning about money and how to make the most of it. Thanks to family members and my social worker, I will have a place to stay and a car to drive when I get out, so I'm going to make the most of my second chance. I've just got to get my kids out of the foster home before anything terrible happens to them," said Linda.

"Hi, I'm Steve and I'm a recovering drug addict. Five and a half weeks clean. This week I decided to change my phone number, and only give the number to people who need to have it. I've deleted all the people who are a bad influence on me, from my phone. That way, they can't call me, and I can't call them. Sometimes willpower alone is not enough. I'm just being practical. Also, my doctor said that I probably had Attention Deficit Hyperactivity Disorder, and gave me a script for

Ritalin. If I'm going to give that a go, I don't want to mess it up with other drugs. But I'm in two minds about it. If anyone has experience with that, I'd like to hear about it," said Steve.

Everley had sat next to Steve. Maybe it was him that she was keen on? He was tall and well built, with dark hair and eyes and a nice face. I could see why she might be attracted. Everley had taken care with her appearance today. She wore a pink and purple blouse which looked like it had been ironed, and a pair of skinny black jeans. But it was the shoes, a medium heel lace-up ankle boot that made the whole look business-like but sexy. She wasn't looking like a hooker today.

"Hi, I'm Everley and I'm a recovering addict," said Everley. "After listening to Linda talking about study, I thought about what I would study if I had the chance. I remembered making a short film at school, and thought about studying film making at Art College. So I looked online, and their admission is based on a short film and an interview, not school results. I've been writing scripts for my short film since then. I could probably even start filming bits and pieces when I get my phone. I want a proper job, and I don't want to have to go back to sex work. In answer to Steve, I had a school friend who had ADHD and took Ritalin. She said it helped her to study at home, and to concentrate in class, and she usually couldn't sit still or shut up. I think some of the boys were on it too, but I didn't know them very well," said Everley, and she smiled at Steve.

He smiled back. It was kind of cute but kind of sickening.

Next was the new guy.

"Hi, I'm Bruce, and I'm a drug addict and I'm bipolar. I work as a musician when I can keep my life together. I usually take Lithium for my bipolar disorder, but sometimes, it makes me feel like a Zomby. So I stop taking it and then I start to feel normal again. Then I can function, clean my flat, buy groceries, get to band practise and everything is cool. But after a while, I start to have these really long days that go for two or three days, and then I'll fall asleep at the post office or the bank, and someone will call an ambulance, and I'll end up in here. So I'll have to get back on my medication, or some other medication, so I can get out of here again. My dad had my cat put down the last time I was locked up, so I'll have to get out as soon as possible. I haven't taken illegal drugs for two years, but before that, I was the biggest party animal, taking lots of ecstasy, coke and smoking weed. But I stopped all that, because I think it was that lifestyle which led to my sleeping disorder in the first place. I'd probably make a good shift worker, because day time and night time don't mean much to me any more. I know I also dribble shit so I'll shut up now," said Bruce.

"Hi, I'm Elise and I'm a recovering drug addict with psychosis. I'm off the methadone now, but I've still got to take the anti-psychotics and antidepressants. I think that they wake me up and then send me to sleep a bit, but it's good to get back into that natural rhythm. I've been making amends with non-using friends on the outside, and planning for my future career. I'm going to find my brother Skye, even though I think he has changed his last name. Steve, I knew a guy who took Ritalin, and it helped him at school. Also, if he was short of tuckshop money, he's sell a pill or two to buy his lunch. The teachers thought he was dumb, but he was too shy to ask questions. Some of these drugs, you might not notice the effect straight away, as it takes a while to accumulate a noticeable dose. I reckon they're worth a try," I said.

That was about it for the NA meeting. I don't think that anyone else from our group knows any big dealers, or if they do, they're not saying it at the meeting. I get my phone every afternoon this week, so I'll have a chance to text both Russel and Anthony.

172

173

26. texting and social media.

When I got my phone, I called Judith to make sure she was alright. She was fine, and she said I'd had no further visitors. She was sounding doddery, so I told her how I was going to get another car when I got out, and I'd be able to take her shopping again.

There was another abusive text from Damien. If he's after the computer, he's not getting it.

Serena has left another text, "Hi Elise, hope you're well. I've booked you for the Myer and David Jones winter parades, and DJs will fly you to Sydney for their big one there too. Harrison said he'd double your fee, but I said no and booked another girl. Love, Serena."

That's great, I need solid work. I'll write back. "Hi Serena, thank you sooo much for booking such great gigs. It will help me buy my next car and be more independent. Elise."

Now I should check on the friends.

Daniel wrote, "Hi Elise, I heard there is an open call audition for a new Gladiators show, coming up in a few weeks. I'm going for it and you should too, though you might have to build up your arms a bit. D."

I wrote back, "Good for you, Daniel, you'd be great. I don't know about me, though, don't you have to do like fighting? E."

Natalie had written back too, "Dear Elise, that's great that you're remembering. If your brother has changed his name, you can do a search at the Registration Office in town. But you'll need his date of birth, and I think they charge a small fee. If you come in to town, we could do lunch, Nat."

I wrote back, "Hi Natalie, that is terrific news. I'm pretty sure that Skye was born on the 22 of September, 1992, cos I was the 2 of September, 1994. I know that I'll find him if I keep looking. Elise."

Serena texted back, "Hi Elise, just know that if you need a car to get to gigs before you get your own, you can borrow the company car. You have to sign for it and leave it with as much petrol as it had. S."

Wow. I'll have to text back, "Thank you Serena, that is very generous. E."

Dustin wrote from London. "Good to hear from you, Elise. I might be a bit famous, but that doesn't stop me losing money on my solo show at the Edinburgh festival. But I do make enough to live on singing and managing a cabaret, and appearing in other people's. Can you believe Justin showed up and wanted to stay in my bedsit with my boyfriend and I? I had to spell it out to him, the dumb fuck. Any work is work, at least you're working. Glad you've stopped partying so hard too, love, Dustin."

Natalie also wrote back. "Wow, Elise, you're doing well. You didn't know your own birthday at school. Tell you what, I'll go and do that search for you, since you're in hospital and can't get out. The results can take a few weeks, depending on how busy their office is. Skye Forsyth? I'll look into it. Nat."

I wrote back to her, "Thanks Natalie. I think I must be mature enough to remember now, what I had been hiding from myself in the past. My shrink has really helped too. It would mean everything to me to reconnect with my family. E."

I'll have to write back to Dustin too. "That's so cool that you did Edinburgh, even if you didn't make money from it. I want to do performance art with vehicles and one of my goals would be Glastonbury. I've mostly done ads, parades, vid clips and short films. Lots of auditions, but nothing bigger yet. Chookas, Elise."

I had to check on Russel at Instagram. He was there with his dog, brushing her hair. She was one of those high maintenance dogs, an Afghan hound or something with a long pointy nose. This would be easy. "Hi Russel, glad to see you back with your Flossy. She looks really beautiful. I'm keen to get a puppy when I get out, so ask your dog park friends if they know of any coming up? Thanks, Elise."

Anthony is going to be a bit trickier. I've got nothing to talk to him about. I'll check out his profile. Wow, his wife Lauretta is a stunner, and likes the sexy dance costumes. And there are the kids, they look like twins. Paolo and Franco, what, he named one kid after his mafia boss? Surely not. She looks like a European, and Franco's a common name in Europe. Right, exercise pics. His and hers exercise pics. Is she some sort of personal trainer or something? Okay, this is giving me something to work with.

I wrote, "Hi Anthony. Wow, you guys are both in really great shape. I think I'll have to start doing sit-ups after the good food in this place. Cute kids too! All the best, Elise." I don't want him to think I'm a home-wrecker or anything like that. And I don't want to tempt him to take drugs either. I just want him to help me set up a business deal. There's a percentage in it for him, if the deal is done. I'm not taking any, and he doesn't have to either. What he tells his wife about it is completely up to him.

I went out and had lunch with my fellow nuts and murderers, and even joined the smokers for a post-lunch ciggy. Clement and Marjorie, Jack and Steve were all out having a smoke.

"I'm very worried about him. Ernest hasn't tried something like this for a long time," said Clement.

"Did he try to top himself again?" asked Jack.

"They've transferred him to Intensive Care, I think," said Steve.

"What did he do?" I asked.

"We're not sure, just that he's hurt himself. He was in the room next to me," said Jack.

"Poor Ernest used to try it quite regularly, at least just after he first offended," said Clement.

"What exactly did he do?" I asked.

"He killed his wife and children", said Clement, looking down.

"Just like my dad," I said, "only he killed himself instead of the kids."

"Maybe Ernest had planned that too, but didn't get around to the last bit," offered Steve.

"I heard loud banging in the early morning," said Jack. "Do you think he might have been bashing his head against something?"

"That's one way to hurt yourself if there are no knives or places you can hang yourself," said Steve. "The poor bugger."

"Hopefully he's only knocked himself unconscious, and not really hurt himself," I said. We trudged back upstairs. Marjorie sat in the tv room, and gestured for me to sit next to her on the couch. She got out a little note pad and pencil and wrote on it. She passed me the note pad.

"I wanted to do that too. I killed my husband and my little girls," read the note.

"Really? You must feel terrible about that," I said.

Marjorie wrote on the pad again. She passed it to me. "I was going to kill myself as well, but the police found me before I had a chance."

"Did they come straight away?" I asked.

"No. They took a few days to arrest me," said her note.

"Did you run away?" I asked.

Marjorie wrote on her note-pad again. "No, I was just waiting for the right time to do it. And the right time never came."

I nodded my head and sat with Marjorie for a minute. Then, I asked, "Why did you do it?"

Marjorie wrote down some stuff, and handed me the book. "He had started seeing someone else. It was a friend of my daughters. They wanted me to move out, and the girl to move in with the rest of them. It was my house. I lost control of myself."

"I understand," I said. But really I didn't. I sat with her for a bit, then went back to my room. I couldn't find my lighter after that, and had to ask Clement to buy me another one.

So it seemed that family violence was a pretty common reason to be locked in the Psych Ward. Whether victims or perpetrators, it affects us all. It's almost as if mental illness was contagious, how the insane actions of the parent helps to cause insanity in the child. Is this what they mean when they say that mental illness can be hereditary?

And the paedophilia thing too. Was Clement molested as a boy too? By a priest? Did this kind of relationship become the only kind that he was capable of? At what point do you cease being the victim and start being the perpetrator? Do you really feel love in that kind of relationship?

I had another look at my phone.

Wow, there was a message from Russel already. He has sent a picture of a very pregnant black standard sized poodle. "This is my friend's dog Milly. She is expecting pups very soon. Do you want me to put your name on their list of potential owners? Milly's owner Jeremy just wants a name and number. Russel."

Oh, god, a poodle. Weren't they meant to be really stupid? Oh well, keeping focussed. "Milly is lovely. Tell Jeremy my number is 0413 413 666. That's where 'unleash the beast' came from. E." I wrote.

179

27. Wrapping it up.

The final week in rehab really was a pain. I was off the opiates, and couldn't wait to stop taking the pharmies too, but I had to while I was in here. I had to justify myself to the shrink this week, in order to be let out. So I'd have to show how sorry I was for the stupid things that I'd done, and promise not to do them again. That shouldn't take too much acting.

Importantly, I'll have to cultivate any known contacts of serious dealers, so that means Russel, Anthony, and Pete. Two fresh from rehab and one in jail. If I were making a business loan application to a bank, this would not look promising. Fortunately, the bank will only be involved as a safe place to put the money while it's not being used. I can send texts and emails to the first two, but how on earth will I contact Pete? How do I find out which jail he is in?

Who can I ask questions to about the ins and outs of jail?

Danny, he'd been inside. Steve's mate Ted was in jail, but I don't think he visited him. I'll have to ask Danny about it at the Friday night meeting this week. Also, Clement and Ernest might have been in jail, I suppose I could broach the subject at a cigarette break.

The only other person who might know a big dealer is Damien Ellis. He won't stop harassing me. Maybe I should turn it around and see if he could possibly be useful to me? Or should I just leave him totally alone? What exactly do I know about him again? I met him at a nightclub. He went out with me for a while until he got bored with me. Then he got me working as a video whore and set up the computer for me. Then he moved on to the next girl, and repeated the whole process, I'm pretty sure. So if I owe him for anything, I owe him for part of a computer which I must've been paying off. If my mental state means I can't be legally charged with an offence, I wonder if I'm still liable for some quasi-legal hire-purchase for a home computer? After I do the deal, he can have the damned computer back. But I want to wipe that whole account and history too.

There must be a way to do it on the mobile phone. I'll sit and try to work it out. Otherwise, who could I ask? Maybe Everley would know about those kind of programs and websites. I couldn't exactly ask Doctor Natalie. And I certainly don't want any of the men here to know about it.

Then there is the gun. I probably won't be able to get a gun licence with my mental health history. So I can't just go to a gun-shop and buy one. I'll have to buy an illegal one, and that means having contacts. Much as I hate to typecast people, I think that Danny the biker might be my best bet with that. Then again, Anthony might have contacts in that field too. Even Steve might have done stupid things to get his meth. People don't say everything at NA meetings, but sometimes a few clues slip out. Can I bring up guns in the NA meeting somehow?

Speaking of Steve, I think that Everley is keen to be his friend, but now I'm thinking that she has written a part for him in her film, and wants him to act in it. He would be a good actor, he has an expressive face. She'd have great fun studying at film school too.

But back to guns. What about the guys that I got my replica gun off? If he sells replicas, he might well sell active guns. Wasn't he friends with that video director Ben, who was Pete's customer? And he had a hippy name, River. That's right, River the gun guy, I remembered thinking that it was oxymoronic. He supplied guns for film and tv productions, so he had a lot of replicas. He told me that most replicas were the real guns with the active parts taken out.

When I get my phone again, I'll search Ben's friends list, he's bound to be there.

So I've basically got one more psychiatrist's appointment, and one more NA meeting to go. I'll have to convince Natalie that I've seen the error of my ways, and I'm fit to be a part of the community again. So I'd better think about having a bit to say about my plans for the future. Plans which don't include selling a shit-tun of drugs and evading the cops.

Natalie was wearing her off-white suit today, with a pastel mutli-coloured blouse and a huge white opal set in a gold pendant. I wore my jeans and pink tops. I'd finally bleached my roots, so had my hair looking a good colour, but it still desperately needed a cut.

"Hi Elise, how are you going?" asked Doctor Rosenberg.

"I'm well thanks, Doctor Rosenberg, how are you?" I said.

"I'm very well thanks," said Natalie, "and how are you going with your medications?"

"Well, they've got me on a good regular pattern of waking and sleeping. I can think clearly, and I can feel happy or sad, but not terrible, so that's great really," I said.

"That is good that you can still feel a range of emotions. This anti-psychotic doesn't work for everyone, so I'm glad it worked for you. Are you getting good sleep?" Asked the doctor.

"Yes, thanks, Doctor, very good. I've been having some weird dreams, but I guess that is to be expected. But they don't wake me up, and I'm getting full nights of sleep," I said.

"What kind of dreams?" asked Natalie.

I suppose I stepped right into that one.

"Ah, you know, like being in the jungle with heaps of wild animals creeping through the trees, and running around in the nude and stuff," I said.

"Sexual dreams?" asked Natalie.

"Ah, well, there was nudity, but it was more like Salvador Dali than some sort of porno," I said. "Nothing was on fire, but things were not as they seemed. Things would change form as I looked at them. It wasn't frightening, but things were't quite normal, I could see the trees growing, and it as a bit hallucinatory really. Maybe my usual dreams are boring and I forget them, but this one had weird aspects, so I remembered. I often don't remember my dreams at all, if I have them. I remember having scary nightmares as a child, like people running for me with a knife. Not surprising really, I suppose. I've not had dreams like that in years. I just wish I could remember more, like, was there a story, and I can only remember the sets and the props?"

"That's a very interesting way of putting it, Elise. You use theatre metaphors to express your concerns about the dream. You worry that you are only remembering aspects of your life, and not the whole picture. But I think that you have remembered the important aspects, about your parents and your brother, your foster home, the group home, and your study years. You have used your time well to concentrate on remembering things you've blocked out. I would trust my memories, if I were you. You don't seem to have created a false life history to cover up what you can't remember. And that makes it easier for you to rebuild your reality. If you had only remembered good things, I would be suspicious that these were false memories. We don't need to bury the good stuff. It's the hard, bad stuff that we hide from ourselves. Have you accepted what you have done to others?" asked the doctor.

"I feel absolutely terrible for the way I have behaved, being so focused on scoring drugs, that I'd endanger other people's lives in order to score. I lost my friend Karen, and I can never bring her back. I drove with drugs in my system, which is incredibly irresponsible and stupid. And I can't believe that I car-jacked an innocent man who was just stopped at a traffic light. I will get rid of that replica gun, it was foolish of me to keep it after being paid for a video clip with it. I want to build my career and mend my friendships, particularly with people in my industry. I'm lucky to have been given a second chance. I'll keep going to NA meetings in my area when I'm out. I've found that useful because we are all on the same journey, and the other members can understand if I do wrong, and be happy for me if I do right," I said.

"And what about setting up your own business, have you looked into that?" asked Dr Rosenberg.

"I've been looking at other artists who build similar things. In the States, there are already people making large movable artworks for Burning Man festival. In Queensland, we have the Modifyre festival, which is mostly smaller artworks and installations by local artists. I'd probably launch my work at this festival, so I'd like to be different from the other artists, and larger in scale.

Anything I build will have to be portable, and easy to assemble and dismantle, and made of light weight materials, like aluminium. I picture building the frames, and any solid looking part could be made of fabric, so I could change the colours for different events. If I need other performers, I can hire my actor friends. I've been making sketches of my vehicles, but I need to find a person to build them, and to teach me how to build them. I've been writing myself a budget, to save my money to start the business up. With my business plan, I might be able to get a business loan. Otherwise I will have to work and save for three months before I can build my first machine. But I can be doing pre-publicity work in that time, hyping up the venture for a big launch. I'm really excited about it, actually," I said.

"Well, it sounds like you've been doing a lot of planning for your new venture. And what about your brother, any luck with him?" asked Natalie.

"My friend, the other Natalie, has started a name change search for him at the Registration Office. But she said it could take three weeks or a month, depending on how busy they are. I'm sure I'll find him. It's unfortunate that I'm only famous for my face and not my name. Because I didn't change my name, and it would be easier for him to find me, than for me to find him," I said.

"I hadn't thought about it that way before," said Doctor Rosenberg, "but you're right. It would be easier for him to find you. Unless he is somewhere where he can't get online, or he has moved interstate or internationally. Even the other patients in here have seen you on the Pepsi ad, but not everyone watches tv, and how would the average person then know to contact an advertising agency or a casting agent. Plenty of creeps might call agencies, trying to get contact details for pretty girls."

"Plenty of creeps call and get us to work for them too. But my agent, Serena, is really good at filtering them out. She questioned me when I said I wouldn't work for Evan Harrison again, and then refused to book me, and said she'd send a confident older girl who knew how to defend herself to the job," I said.

"You really should press charges against that grub. It's a pity that you're a mental health patient so your testimony can be torn down. If he was responsible for leaving you looking like you did when you first came in, he is a violent psychopath. It's not bad enough that he raped you, he knew that you made your living from your looks, so he targeted your face when he bashed you. I'm really interested in psychopathic behaviour, and Evan Harrison really displays that. I've seen his egocentric advertising campaigns, he's quite the narcissist. You're right to keep away from him," said Natalie.

"Yes, he is revolting, but I don't want to get the police involved," I said. "They wouldn't believe me anyway. But hopefully I can recognise that kind of person now, and not let myself get into a dangerous situation with them. I'm actually very glad that I have an agent between myself, the clients and the general public. I hope that that Harrison creep doesn't come looking for me. But my flat is very safe, I've got bars on the windows," I said.

"I'm glad that you've got your own place, and that it's safe. But I am still worried about you. I want you to take my card, and to call me if you ever need to talk, or if you ever need help. You have messed with some dangerous people, and because of your medical history, you can be discriminated against. You can call anytime, but late at night, I prefer texts," Natalie said, as she handed me her card.

I read it and put it in my pocket. "I'll keep it in my wallet, and I'll write your number in my diary," I said.

"That's good that you have a diary," said Natalie.

"Oh, I asked Clement to go to the shop for me, he bought me hair dye too," I said.

"You do know what he's in here for, don't you?" asked the doctor.

"Well, I'm guessing he's a paedophile priest, from what he's said," I said.

"I shouldn't really breach patient confidentiality to tell you this, but he was involved in the disappearance of young boys from a home for boys, but was unable to be charged because of his mental illness. I consider him to be dangerous," said Natalie.

"I only asked him because he's a voluntary patient, so he can go out, unlike us involuntaries," I said.

"The church pays for him to be in here. They don't want to be held liable for him, to the families of his victims. He's protected in here. But he is allowed to go out. God knows what he could get up to. It's crazy," said Doctor Rosenberg.

This was the most emotional that I'd seen Doctor Rosenberg get. She clearly thought that he was a murderer who should be in jail, but was getting off lightly by being in a cushy mental hospital. She quickly regained her composure.

"Elise, I'm pleased with how you've spent your time getting off the opioids, and concentrating on remembering the various episodes of your life. You have demonstrated that you use different techniques to recall difficult memories which you had previously buried in your subconscious mind. I am pleased with your progress, and will recommend that you be released into the community on this Saturday, the 29. of February. I recommend that you continue individual or group therapy, in accordance with your mental health plan. You'll have to continue with your medication for at least the next two months, but come in for an appointment at that time to re-assess how the anti-psychotics and anti-depressants are going. Best wishes for your life in the outside world," said Doctor Rosenberg.

"Thanks, Doctor Rosenberg," I said, "you've really helped me to face and accept a lot of things. And I've got some goals in life now, and a plan. But more importantly, I know who I am, and I will find my brother. I will definitely make follow-up appointments with you, because it's hard to talk about this stuff with just anybody," I said.

28. Goodbye to Carina Private.

The last thing I had to do before I left was go to the NA Friday afternoon meeting. Steve, Jack, Bruce, Linda and I trudged over to the Drugs ward with the security Guard. Carolyn and Danny were waiting outside, and gave us a smile. They would be admitted separately. I suppose this transfer time would be the ideal time for someone to make a break for it. Our guard had a two way radio, and could call the Psych ward guard, but how many others could they call on to chase a runaway?

"Hi, I'm Dave, and I'm a recovering alcoholic. I'll be chairing the meeting today. If you have any questions, you can direct them towards myself or the whole group. Being a Friday, we've got some members who have been through Rehab, but keep coming to our support group. We talk about our efforts in our journey towards sobriety, and our challenges. If people want to ask questions, or answer, we'll do that at the end of your turn, and please keep on topic and be positive. I've been clean for six years, but I have had challenges along the way, like going to a wedding with catering and having the pressure of doing a speech. But I didn't disgrace myself, and I was still sober enough to drive home," said Dave.

"Hi, I'm Steve and I'm a recovering drug addict. I've been clean for six weeks, and I'm ready to go back to work now. I'm glad I had that extra two weeks to make some really big decisions about how I run my spare time and who I associate with. I went to my drawing class again, and I've gotten involved in another creative project as well. I'm lucky I've still got my job, I could so easily have been sacked. I'm very grateful for what I have. I'm never going to touch meth or speed or even pot, ever again. And I'm only going to drink alcohol on social occasions. Best of luck to all the rest of you too," said Steve.

I was next in the circle. I wondered if Everley's film is the project that Steve has been asked to join? I needed Everley's help for something else. And there was a new druggie here too.

"Hi, I'm Elise, and I'm a recovering drug addict and psychotic. Nearly four weeks clean, and I've just about done my time here too. I've been off the methadone for two weeks, but I have to keep taking my anti-psychotics and anti-depressants for at least another two months, maybe for a long time. But I'm so glad to have them, and a great psychiatrist in Doctor Rosenberg. She's helped me to remember the traumas in my past that I'd blocked out, and undo the cycle of alcohol and drug abuse to the point of memory loss which I had developed. I've analysed my life so far, and made changes, and goals and plans for the future. I've done heaps of stupid things to enable my drug use and partying lifestyle, which I am now really ashamed of. Including setting up a dodgy website, which I now have to wait till I get back to my computer to shut down. I'm also lucky to have a home and work to return too, and I'm going to keep building my friendships and hopefully one day have a meaningful relationship. I've never had one of those, and I think I've got a lot to learn there. Good luck to you all, if I can be rehabilitated, anyone can be. I couldn't remember what I'd done, when I first got here. My friend said I couldn't remember my birthday when I was at school. Now I can remember everything from my dead mum and murderer dad, to the dumb car-jacking that I did a month ago. Like my addiction, I accept it and I try to make retribution for my wrong-doings. Thanks Dave, and everyone for helping me to accept my failings and strive for a better life," I said.

I wondered if this was how Catholics felt when they went to confession?

"Hi, I'm Everley, and I'm a recovering addict. Two weeks clean, and I'm really getting on with my life. I've written a short film script and I'm working on a feature length film script. I'm putting together an application for Film School, and I'm really excited about it. As an ex-addict and sex-worker, I've seen a lot of the dark side of life, and I think I could represent that realistically on screen. I think that people want to see realistic television and films, and I'm prepared to put in the work, to learn how they're made properly. I've done lots of stupid things because I was desperate. But I've learned that it is wrong to keep stealing when you can afford to pay. I want to work on small projects where everybody gets credited and paid. I'm prepared to do volunteer work while I'm learning, but I want to be a professional, and make a career of it. It doesn't feel so scary once you say it," said Everley.

"Hi, I'm Jack and I'm a recovering drug addict and schizophrenic. Six weeks clean, and happy with the medication I'm on now. I've been working on my folio, and am actually applying for new jobs online. Most importantly, I'm working on my relationship with my parents and my friend Rose. I was afraid to apply for the more Commercial Art jobs before, thought they'd be boring, but I'm applying for those and even industrial design jobs, because I am qualified for those too. I am so embarrassed about my doctor-shopping past, and my pharmaceutical addiction, and how the drugs helped blur my logic to think that stealing someone's identity was a good idea. I've done what I can to make reparations to that poor bloke, and try to clean up his driving record as well. I've been meditating and doing yoga, but I'll get back to jogging when I'm out again. Might be a few more weeks," said Jack.

"Hi I'm Linda, and I'm a recovering alcoholic. I was talking to my social worker and she asked about my family. I said that I had a happy childhood until dad died and mum tried to kill herself. My brother and I stayed in a Catholic children's home while mum was locked up at Wolston Park. My brother and I were adopted, but he got into trouble at school, and was sent to live at Boys' Town. While he was there, he wrote me letters, and told me that the priest there was giving him unwanted attention. I wrote back and hoped he was alright. John died at Boys' Town when he was sixteen. I don't know if he killed himself or was killed by his abuser. The priest who abused him never came to justice. I think this is why I feel so bad about losing my children and letting them go in to care. What if someone abuses them like my brother was abused? I'm working as hard as I can to re-establish my life, with a house or flat, a job or paid study, or both, to give my kids a stable home," said Linda.

Whoa, so Linda's brother had been abused and possibly killed by someone like Clement. Possibly even by Clement. I wonder if she knows about his history? She doesn't smoke and she doesn't watch tv, and doesn't talk much at meal times either. I'll have to go and visit her in her room.

"Hi, I'm Bruce, and I'm a recovering addict with Bipolar disorder. I'm on a new medication now, because the Lithium didn't seem to work over extended periods for me. I work as a musician, so I have traveled all over Australia and the States playing with different bands, and you all know that you can't carry drugs across borders. So I got really good at recognising the places dealers went and the things they would do, so I could score weed or speed wherever I was playing. This particular skill made me popular not just with the guys in my band, but also with some guys in bigger bands than mine. Our band got a lot of big support act tours on account of that. So taking drugs just became part of work for me. It was difficult to not take drugs, and still deal, and play with a bunch of of drug-users. I'll have to really pick and choose who I play with now if I want to stay clean. Maybe more solo projects or getting into sound production. I don't know. It's terrible, because I had this great network of musicians and drug dealers all over the world, but they are pretty much all users, so I can't seek support with that network. I do have straight friends, and believe me, I've been seeking them out. One week clean," said Bruce.

Wow, Bruce might actually know somebody that I need to know. But he's such a freak, like, a long haired hippy guitarist of a certain age who very probably wears leather trousers. I'll have to be online friends with him as well as Russel and Anthony.

"Hi I'm Carolyn, and I'm a recovering drug addict and self harmer. Two years clean, after taking drugs for ten years and self harming since I was about ten years old. My partner Tracy and I have just taken in a young baby dyke who's fresh out of rehab at the PA. I've been taking her to NA meetings at Ipswich, but I'm worried that she has only given up to save money and let her tolerance go down. I'm afraid that she will score again as soon as she has some cash. It's a difficult situation for us, as her ex-girlfriend is also Tracy's ex, and I can't stand her and don't want her coming round to our place. We told Heidi that we'd only let her stay until she has money saved to get her own place. I'm finding it a bit stressful having her around, but hopefully it will only be for four to six weeks," said Carolyn. Everybody groaned.

"Hi, I'm Danny and I'm a recovering addict. I was a bad heroin addict for a long time, and it wasn't util I did rehab in the Psych Ward that I faced the real reasons why I kept going back to junk. I was seeking thrills and seeking peace in the same way. Now, I still seek thrills by riding my motorbike, in a safe, legal way. And I seek peace through meditation and positive relationships with those around me. I attend the Capalaba NA meeting as well, but that group has a pretty heavy element, and first timers often never go back because of it. So if anyone from this area wants to go there, I can be your buddy, because the place does look like a tattoo convention in a dungeon. Women, in particular, are scared off, and I totally understand why. Three years clean, many more to come," said Danny.

"This being a Friday meeting, we'll adjourn to the outdoor area so smokers can smoke, and we can have informal chats. Best wishes for those leaving rehab, and I wish you all the best," said Dave.

We trudged out to the deck, and it was just starting to get dark. The nightfall got earlier as we crept into autumn, even if the days were just as hot. I'd saved the last of my Sobranies in case Everley wanted a smoke.

"Ciggie?" I asked her.

"Thanks, mate," said Everley. "Hey, I think I could probably help with that phone app. Have you got your phone with you?"

"I do actually, just wait and I'll try to find the right page," I said.

"Are you going to smoke those things, or are you just going to wave them around?" asked Carolyn.

"Yeah, I'm going to light up, but I'll walk over the other side if you prefer," I said.

"While you're here, I just want to warn you about accepting any offers of employment from Danny," said Carolyn.

"Employment?" I asked, looking confused.

"You're psych ward aren't you? Danny is known to recruit fellow psych ward outpatients to do certain things which he knows they won't go to jail for, if they are caught," said Carolyn.

"Right," I said, "there's no way I'd do that sort of work."

"Let's hope that Steve and Jack won't either," said Everley.

"I'll go over and talk to those two," said Carolyn. She strode off towards the smokers.

"I think I've got this website sorted out. If you want to access your account information, you have to hover over the icon of yourself and click. There is a close account option at the bottom of the list. Here, I'll click on that. A box has come up and said that you have mail in your inbox. Do you want to redirect that mail to your email address?" said Everley.

"Um, no, ah, yes actually," I said.

"Ok, it's got your email. Your account on peepshow dot com is now closed," said Everley.

"Oh, thank you so much, Everley," I said. "I just couldn't work out how to do it on the phone. The computer screen is much bigger, and laid out differently."

"It's a fucking android too, my Iphone works a lot better for pages like that. But you've got to know how they lay out those little screens," said Everley.

Dave had come over and started talking to Linda, so Everley and I strolled over to where the men were smoking.

"I nearly fell over when Linda said that her brother went missing from Boys' Town. That's one of the places where the creep worked. He's in here because he thinks he can't be gotten to," said Danny.

"Yeah, but he seems pretty harmless," said Jack.

"I don't know, I've seen him checking you out Jack. I've seen him checking me out too," said Steve.

"I didn't see him checking me out," I said.

"Who?" asked Everley.

"Clement the paedo priest, in the psych ward with us," I said.

"He's a revolting old pervert," said Danny, "with a history as long as your arm."

"And he thinks no-one can get to him in here?" said Steve.

"It's probably safer than jail," said Carolyn.

"So this paedo, what did he do?" asked Bruce.

"He was a parish priest in Beaudesert, and visited the orphanage for boys, where there was a lot of corporal punishment. Some boys ran away and some disappeared. It was mentioned in the Royal Commission. The parishioners didn't like him, and accused him of groping the altar boys. The church moved him to another parish," said Danny.

"It would be such a pity if something happened to him," said Bruce.

"Actually, Danny, I was going to ask you about the jail," I said. "I want to go and visit my friend when I'm out, and I wondered how you go about that?"

"Do you know which prison he's in?" asked Danny.

"He was done two years ago, for a quantity of drugs, so I'm assuming he's at Wacol," I said.

"Yep, you're probably right there," said Danny, "You have to ring up and book a time, and you need to be an approved person. Then you turn up early for your visit, get patted down by a female guard and metal detected. You might be sniffed by a sniffer-dog, you might not. If they suspect you're carrying anything, they'll strip search you. So don't carry anything. If he doesn't want to see you, he won't approve you, but most fellows would die to have a pretty girl visit them there."

"Thanks Danny, I didn't know where to start with that," I said.

"So, can you tell us more about what Father Clement got up to?" asked Bruce.

"He was arrested and charged with numerous counts of child abuse and sexual assault, but he claimed he couldn't remember doing any of it. He started in the locked ward at Wacol, and has moved from there to here. I can't believe he's been reclassified as a voluntary patient, so he can walk down to the local public toilets if he wants to," said Danny.

"It would be terrible if something happened to him," said Steve.

196

29. Leap year day.

My last day was Saturday the 29. of February, 2020's leap year day. I packed my two small bags and presented myself at the Nurses' station. John the nurse laughed as he went to get my things out of the safe.

"You know that this is the one day of the year that a woman can ask a man to marry her?" asked John.

"Darn it, I just don't have anybody I'd like to ask," I said.

"I'm not married yet," said John.

"You couldn't marry me, I'm a patient," I said.

"Not any more," said John.

"I suppose that's true. But I'm a lot older than you. You need a young woman close to your own age," I said. This was the craziest conversation I'd had since I'd been in here.

I chatted to John as I waited for the Uber car to arrive. He handed me back my phone and the gun, still in a brown paper bag.

"Don't go shooting at anybody with that thing," said John.

"It's only a replica, so it won't shoot, and I won't point it at anyone. I'm going to get rid of it," I said.

"That's good, because I don't think I would marry a woman with a gun anyway," said John, with a sly smile.

I hopped in to the Uber, and was excited to see outside the hospital. The driver asked me to sit in the back rather than the front seat. I asked why.

"It's this new Corona virus, so I'm trying to do social distancing," said the driver.

"Oh, I'd seen it on TV in China. I didn't realise it was here now," I said.

"Yeah, it's been on the Gold Coast since the 29. of January, so it'll be here soon, if it isn't already," said the driver.

It was hot for the evening, I'd got so used to the air-conditioning in the hospital. But I didn't want to take off my cardigan in front of this man. I pushed up my sleeves. Old Cleveland Road led us through the newer suburbs full of brick houses, in to the older suburbs of quaint wooden houses, then to Spring Hill, where the cottages gave way to high-rise. The pink palace was squeezed in between two concrete towers now. As a block of twelve flats built in the 1920s, the palace had a small front and back garden, though the back was also used as a car park. The concrete towers had no gardens. Luckily we were just across the road from Roma Street Parklands, which was the old Albert Park rebranded, fenced and joined to the new rail-yard redevelopment. The Albert Park toilets had been the biggest gay beat in Brisbane for years, and probably still are.

I thanked Andrew the Uber driver, and carried my bags up the stairs to my flat. As I went to put the key in the door, Judith opened it.

"I meant to tell you on the phone. I swapped our flats. After the police going through it, and then that creepy Damien, I thought that it would be better to change the lock, then I thought of this," said Judith.

"Oh, what a surprise!" I said.

"Actually, I also exchanged our locks. Your key will work in your new door," she said, pointing to her old place. Her stuff was in my flat, heaps of pot-plants, retro furniture and a cat. I crossed the stairwell to her place, and opened the door. Judith shuffled after me. My stuff was in her flat, arranged as I had it, only neater. The flats were laid out in the mirror image of each other.

"Oh my god, how on earth did you manage that?" I asked.

"Well, you know that I worked on film sets for a long time. Continuity was my thing, and I'd take polaroids of how everything was, how open the curtain was, exactly where the chair had been. I took photos inside your flat, and I got the young men downstairs to help carry the furniture. I do laundry for some of the people here, so I can ask for favours too," said Judith.

I walked in to my bedroom. My bed and wardrobe looked great. But my desk had a gaping big space where my computer used to be.

"So this was gone?" I asked.

"I thought you'd ask about this, so I brought the photo. I think the card is in the drawer," said Judith.

The photo showed a space on my deak, with a business card sitting where the computer used to be. I opened the drawer and took out a card, which said "Detective Carol Shaw, Fortitude Valley CIB", which stood for Criminal Investigations Branch. It had boxes ticked for "Search Warrant" and "Items confiscated," and contact details.

"So the cops have got it," I said. "Do you think they'll give it back, considering they didn't press any charges on me?"

"You'd think they'd have to, wouldn't you? Otherwise it's theft," said Judith.

"I'm just so glad that Damien didn't steal it," I said.

"It's because of that young man that I went to all the trouble of moving us. He is trouble, he's been sniffing around here a few times, and he'll be back. You'll have to keep your front door closed, but at least you'll get some fresh air from your balcony. The boys downstairs know to look out for him, and so does Tiffany, the card-reader," said Judith.

"Did you have to tell the neighbours?" I asked.

"They only know that you've had some trouble, and that Damien is part of it. I showed them his photo, and Tim recognised him from his surveillance camera. He's selling pot down there, so he likes to know who's at the door before he answers it," said Judith.

"You are fucking hilarious," I said. "For a lady of advancing years, you are very turned on."

"Oh, I might be old, but I am very with it, sister," said Judith.

"Thanks for doing this for me, Judith," I said, putting my bags down, and giving her a hug.

"That's alright. You keep yourself safe, Elise," said Judith, as she headed back across the stairwell to her new place.

With the layout of our flats, all visitors with cars came from the back, and on foot or bicycle came from the front. They all had to walk past the men's flats on the ground floor before they came upstairs to our flats. The stairwell was half open to the weather, and a couple of nice tree ferns grew from the tiny courtyard at the bottom. As I closed myself back inside my new flat, I felt strangely safe, and like part of a conspiracy of other tenants. This place had been a whorehouse for American soldiers during the second world war. It must have held a lot of secrets over the years.

I unpacked my bags and made myself a pot of mint tea. I needed a plan of action, so I wrote myself a list.

CALL COP RE COMPUTER.

VIST JAIL WEBSITE

CAR

SHOVEL

GROCERIES

SKYE

It looked pretty simple when you look at it like that. I wrote "MONDAY" after the cop bit, because the desk ones only do business hours. I sat on my fluffy pink sofa, which I think Judith must have vacuumed or shampooed. I had to talk Russel into lending me his car. My bicycle was leaning against the wall in the living room, I'd move it if I wanted to do a handstand against the wall. It was pumped up and ready to go, with lights, a helmet and a big heavy lock.

I picked up my phone, and wrote a text to Russel, "Hi Russel, can I call you? I'd like to ask you about something? Elise."

He texted back, "Sure, now is a good time to talk. R."

I rang up. "Hello," said Russel.

"Hi it's Elise, they let me out today," I said.

"Hi Elise, that's great. What about this corona virus?" said Russel.

"It's not here yet, is it?" I asked.

"No, but it's down the Goldy, so it won't be long. Are you ringing about the dog?" asked Russel.

"Oh, I'm not sure if the puppy is old enough yet, and I haven't bought the supplies I'll need to look after one yet either. I was calling to ask if I could borrow your car for a couple of hours? I'll ride my bike to yours, and home again, so you won't have to go anywhere," I said.

"Why do you need my car?" asked Russel.

"I've got to pick up groceries for myself and my elderly neighbour. I'll just drive from Spring Hill to Paddington, which is the closest supermarket without paid parking. Then I'll bring it right back," I said.

"OK then, but only for a couple of hours. Are you going to get another car?" Russel asked.

"Yes, I realised I had put some money away from a big gig, and had forgotten about it till I saw an interest payment come into my account from it. I'll just get something cheap," I lied.

"Right, well I'm at 22 Langside Road in Hamilton. How long will you be?" asked Russel.

"I'll give myself about a half hour to get there, and maybe ten minutes to get ready," I said.

"Cool, I'll see you soon," I said.

I changed in to a pair of tights with a short black dress over the top, and a pair of black trainers. I carried my bike down the stairs, and set it on the footpath. Once I was down Spring Hill and past the city, it was pretty flat along the river to Hamilton. Brisbane looks great on a bicycle, I can ride on the footpath, bike track or the road, sometimes there's even a bike lane. The sky in March is still a bright strong blue, and the trees are green, no sign of autumn. The river is wide at Hamilton, and Crescent street rises steeply up Hamilton Hill, close to the castle on Toorak St. Langside Road is lined with mansions in various states of repair, looking out across the meandering river towards the city. Russel was doing well.

Russel's house needed a lick of paint, but it had river views, and an old established garden which ran for a narrow strip below his back patio. Sort of Spanish style brick with white plaster and arches, it was smallish but private. He had a white Mercedes in his open garage. I hopped off my bike, and Russel opened the metal gate on his door.

"Bring it in, there's room in the hall," he said.

The dog, Flossy, came bolting down the hall and nearly knocked me over. I patted her and made a fuss of her, who looked like an Afghan hound, but maybe crossed with something a bit chunkier.

"I can't thank you enough, Russel. I won't speed, and I'll bring it back just as it is. Nice place, by the way, and what a beautiful girl Flossy is," I said.

"Would you like to come in for a tea or something first?" asked Russel.

"Look, I'll do our shopping, then I'll stop by for tea when I bring it back, if that's alright," I said. Russel walked with me out to the patio. Shaded by flowering vines, it overlooked a formal garden with a small fountain, the flowering bushes were overgrown and the base of the fountain had fish and weeds. Flossy ran laps of the yard.

Russel's wife must have owned most of the furniture, cos the place looked a bit empty.

"This looks like a lovely spot for a cup of tea. Have you got green tea or mint?" I asked.

"I do have green tea," said Russel, smiling. He actually was not bad looking, in a really preppy kind of a way.

"Great, well, I'll look forward to it," I said, taking the keys he handed me, and heading off.

Inside the Mercedes, I could see that it was a few years old, but had been kept very well. I quickly did groceries for Judith and myself, and dropped them home. I'd taken Judith grocery shopping enough times to know what she bought. With the food in the fridge, I hooned across the river, and down Old Cleveland Road. There was a hardware shop in Carindale, so I grabbed a rose bush and a shovel. I'd brought a large shopping bag with me from home. The newer bits of Cleveland Road let me cruise along at ninety. Cycling was great, but the effortless speed of driving is something else. I climbed the gentle rise to Cleveland, then the land dropped away towards the coast, and I could see Moreton Bay across to Stradbroke Island. This was the place to turn right towards the cemetery. The cemetery was on the flat red soil, and the various religions were all clustered together in the fashion of older cemeteries. I parked the car and looked at the picture on my phone again.

There weren't many cars in the carpark. The photo had a black marble grave with the name "Samios" engraved in it in gold, and there are Russian crucifix graves behind it. I got out of Russ's car, and picked up my bag with the rose bush, and my shovel. The black dress wouldn't look so out of place in here. I scanned around the graveyard. If I had first entered it on a stolen bike, I was coming from the south east corner, near Wellington St. Sure enough, I found the Russian graves, and the Greek and other Orthodox graves. Lots of Russians had emigrated to Australia at the time of the Russian Revolution in 1917, just as heaps of Greeks and Italians came after the second World War. They're buried clustered together, a small foreign community together in death. The Russians appeared to fancy the white cross with the extra slashes through it, horizontal at the top, diagonal at the bottom. The Greeks and Italians nearby seemed to fancy the more shiny marble graves, occasionally with statues, in white, black, and a reddish marble.

There was the Samios grave. A big, altar-like box grave with three headstone engravings on the front, and space for more, and just the family name on the back. I had taken the photo from the back of it. I walked around it. There was no one around, the various fields of this graveyard were enclosed by trees, probably planted as wind-breaks, and to shade the mourners from the blistering subtropical sun. I put my bags down. On this corner of this paddock, the land dropped away a bit, and water had run this way during heavy rain, eroding the concrete foundations of these built-ip corner graves. The family grave next to the Samioses was similarly built up, in grey marble.

Under this grave, the red dirt had washed away, so that the concrete overhung a crevice, large enough for a dog or a child to get into. I dug the spade in and the soil was loose. I dug some more, making a neat pile between the gravestones. Then I hit it. I used my hands to dig out the fishing float, then I put it in my bag.

My heart was racing. The float left no room for the rose bush. I took some deep breaths. Then I took an antidepressant. I've got to keep it together right now. I turned around and saw that the foot of this grave was at the head of another. I quickly dug a hole and planted the rose bush in it, right next to the headstone, then gathered all the loose dirt and packed it around it. The empty potplant, I put over the top of the fishing float, which almost peeked out of the bag. I grabbed the shovel and walked calmly back to the car.

Now that I had it, I needed to think clearly. I needed a safe place. I needed a safe. The council worker's utility at the far end of the carpark has locked tool boxes of a decent size on the tray. I drove back to the Carindale hardware shop, and bought a large lockable metal toolbox. A nice looking man carried it to the boot for me. I dropped my things back in Spring Hill, then I drove straight to Russel's house, and felt my heartbeat returning to normal.

Russel made me a nice cup of tea, and offered to make dinner too. I stayed and chatted, but said I still needed to ride home on my bike.

"You're very easy on the eye, Elise," said Russel.

"Can't you give a better compliment that that?" I asked.

"How about you're totally hot, and I'd like show you the wonders of my bedroom?" said Russel.

"That's more like it. And though the wonders sound good, I'll have to pass this time. But give me a call. I'd love to go to your dogpark and see the dog who's had the puppies," I said.

Russel watched me ride down his street, and down the big hill to the river.

30. Safe at home.

In the carpark behind the palace, I had run in and knocked on Tim the pot dealer's door. I had put the float in the toolbox, but I figured it would be too heavy to lift by myself. Tim was stoned as, but helped me lift the toolbox out of Russ's car, and carry it up the stairs to my place.

"What have you got in here?" asked Tim.

"Please don't ask so I don't have to make up a lie. I'm trying to be good at the moment," I said.

"Okey dokey then, babe, but don't tell me it's guns," said Tim.

"It's not guns," I said.

"Cool," said Tim.

"And thanks for helping Judith move all my stuff," I said.

"No worries, Elise. You ladies have got lots of nice things," said Tim. He really was a bit sweet. He looked like he was about twenty two and went out to festivals in a Hawaiian shirt.

Back in my flat, I did a bit of a rearrange. The toolbox fit under my bed, and if I hung a draping sheet under my mattress, it couldn't be seen. I filled up the bathtub. I loved how these older flats all had claw-footed bathtubs. I put in some epsom salts and climbed in.

I've got the shit here now, and nobody knows except me. The hairdresser might suspect it was me. But he also might be worried that I could accuse him of rape, and damage his public image. Damien the video pimp is after me, but he doesn't know I've moved flats. If I was dumb enough to sign a contract with him, I could say that my signature on a document wouldn't stand up in court, because of my mental health history. If he wants the computer, he could get it off the cops.

Or I could get it off the cops. If they haven't got a case against me that needs proving, they won't need evidence. On Monday I'll ring up and find out how to get it back. I could use an Uber for that. Now I'll have to tread carefully around Russel. He's obviously keen, and I'm not. But I could really use his connection, Joe Palazzo. So I suppose I'll have to lead him on for a bit. And I've got to look into other markets too, like Anthony's dude in Sydney, Franco Panetone. And Bruce the Axeman, which is his stage-name, he is my social media friend now as well. He's still inside, but once he's out, he could be useful.

Monday, I'll also see what I have to do to visit Pete as well.

There's a couple of other things to add to the list, SCALES, BAGS, VACUUM SEALER. I can probably buy all of these things online, and have them delivered to my door. But I'm not sure I want that listed on my credit card. I'll be better to walk down to town, buy them with cash, and carry them home. I can find out which shops they are in on the internet first. I am unlikely to meet someone who can buy ten kilograms in one go. I am more likely to meet someone who might buy one kilo. Therefore, I will have to cut the block into accurate kilogram blocks. I don't want to touch it, so gloves and a mask are probably on the list too. Then I can vacuum seal the bags so they won't smell and stay the correct weight.

I think that a kilo of coke is worth about two hundred thousand. Even that is a lot of cash to have or carry around. I might need another lockable toolbox. Even getting that kind of money into a bank account is going to be a problem. The suspect transaction limit in Australia is ten thousand dollars, so that is a lot of small deposits into multiple bank accounts. At least I live near the city, so I can walk down to town and visit different bank branches to make deposits. I'll need a nice suit, a really nice suit like the ones that Natalie Rosenberg wears. They sell them in the department stores, or the boutiques near them on Queen Street.

I hopped out of the bath and dried myself, then slipped on the white fluffy towelling robe. I felt like a human again now. I cooked some spaghetti, and a little sauce with just tinned tomatoes and olives out of the jar, and anchovies. I grated some mozzarella on the top, and was so glad to have access to my own tiny kitchen again. I took the anti-depressant and went to sleep in my own bed.

I still woke up at 7am for medication time. A month of it was enough to reset my body-clock. So I got up and took my capsule and made a mint tea. I had shopping to do today. I put on my long dark grey suit which I wore for auditions and go-sees when they asked for conservative, with a white blouse, which always looks innocent. I wore flat court shoes and just some pink lipstick and brown mascara, and my driving glasses.

Town was strangely quiet, and I bought my supplies with minimal fuss. The bags came with the vacuum sealer, supposedly used for food. I got the scales from a jewellery supplies shop. The face-mask and gloves turned out to be the hardest things to buy, as everyone was buying them up for this new coronavirus, but I found some at the hardware store. So my afternoon was spent chopping up kilos of coke, and not even snorting any.

There was a text from Russel, "It was nice to see you yesterday. Thanks for returning the car. Flossy likes you too. R."

I suppose I'd have to write back. "Thank you so much for lending me the car. You've got a great set-up there on the Hill. Flossy is beautiful. E."

Not long later he wrote back, "Would you like to have dinner one day?"

So I wrote, "How about lunch?"

Russel wrote, "Ok, how is lunch on Wednesday?"

"Sounds good. Do you work in the city?" I wrote.

"Yes, and I know a nice sushi bar in the Riverside centre, if you like Japanese food?" texted Russel.

"Sounds good. One o'clock Wednesday?" I wrote back.

"See you there, Elise." texted Russel.

I was at least glad that he didn't use emojis or anything childish like that. Russel looked like he was around thirty-five, but he could have been thirty or forty. It's so hard to tell with redheads. He was divorced and didn't have kids. He probably knew how to fuck. He's had a problem with drugs, and so have I. And I'm trying to get him to introduce me to his dealer friend. I'm going to have to fuck him, aren't I?

Well, at least he's presentable and accepts a lunch date ahead of a dinner date. It could be much worse. It could even be fun. I am such a terrible person. I'll also write a personal message to Anthony. I can't put all of my eggs in one basket. I've got to try and set up a deal as soon as possible, so I have to follow all my leads, including Pete in jail.

"Hi Anthony, it's Elise. I'm out, and having lunch with Russ on Wednesday. Do you have time for a phone call anytime this week? I'm at 0413 413 666. Cheers, E." I wrote.

Now I had to work out how the vacuum sealer works, and chop up the coke. It had been compressed into a tubular shape, and I first cut it in half, using the bread knife. My other knife just wasn't sharp enough, or I wasn't strong enough to push it through cleanly. I swept up the dust I made, and put it in a little bag, weighed it and labeled the bag with "3.1g". I weighed the two halves, one was slightly over, one slightly under 5 kilograms. I took the larger half, and with my ruler and pen, marked off five equal lengths. The plastic coating of the fishing float adhered to the outside, so I left it on. It was like cutting up a giant sausage. Each time I cut, I made more powder, so I swept it up and bagged it. These bags could make up the weight of undersized slices. I cut a slice, and if it was more than a kilo, I sliced some off until the weight was correct. I bagged up those slices and weighed them too. Once I'd made five slices each, into a kilo, I started up the vacuum machine. The slices which weighed less, I wrote on the plastic "997g" and put a small snaplock with another "3g" with it, before it went through the vacuum sealer. The second five seemed easier than the first five. I put them away in the toolbox under my bed.

I took off my mask and gloves, and realise I felt a bit light-headed. I must have somehow absorbed some as I cut it and swept it up, maybe through my eyes or something. I didn't touch it with my bare hands, or have my nose or mouth uncovered. I washed down my desk with some bathroom cleaner. In the old days I probably would have licked it.

I put it away, and sat on my balcony with a cup of mint tea. The balcony was great, quite a deep room with a concrete balustrade, with wisteria vine climbing all the way up from the ground floor. I could see out over Spring Hill, at least until the high-rises blocked my view. And with no outside light, I couldn't be seen. I saw Tim drive in to our backyard carpark, and walk up to his flat. Then I saw about five other cars pull in, their drivers come up to the ground floor flats, then back again in about ten minutes. I laughed. The evening was getting chilly, and I put my cardigan on. This is how Judith knew that someone was dealing here.

I took my anti-depressant and went to bed. It has been a successful day, my plans are underway. I'll need my sleep to face the cops tomorrow, and maybe the jail too.

211

31. Dangerous Plans.

Right, today I'm going to get my computer back, and see about visiting Pete. I've got a lunch date in a couple of days with Russel, so I'll find out what I can about his friend Joe Palazzo. I actually need a haircut really badly, so I'll go to a Joe Palazzo salon in the city. I'm pretty sure there's one in the Myer Centre.

Anthony's friend Franco Panetone is also someone I'll have to find out more about. I'll do a google search on him, I'm pretty sure his name has been in the newspapers regarding various dodgy things. I'll also follow up Bruce the Axeman with some social media chat. I'm not sure that Pete could help me from jail, but I should see him anyway. He's the closest thing I've got to an ex-boyfriend.

I reviewed the literature on Franco Panetone, mostly newspaper articles. Seems he has excellent lawyers who have got him off a string of charges around prostitution, drugs and protection rackets, so I'll have to be extremely careful. I'll have to take Anthony along with me, for my own protection, and cut him in on the deal. I wonder if he would be happy with ten percent, for organising the meeting? Twenty grand is not to be sneezed at. If that's not acceptable, I can offer him more.

That raises the question of whether I should cut Russel in on the deal with Joe Palazzo. I could offer a similar deal. I just know that these kind of businessmen often have great security, and not many scruples. It can be hard for some men to watch a large amount of money walking away, especially if it's carried by a woman. I will probably need back-up. And I need to trade the replica gun in for the real thing.

I put on the suit and the wig, and took an Uber down to the Valley Criminal Investigations Branch. Luckily, Carol Shaw was at her desk, and she showed me through from the front desk into the detective's offices. A short blonde, she had those wrinkles around the mouth that heavy smokers develop in middle age. So she wore lip-liner to stop her lipstick from bleeding into the wrinkles.

"Officer Shaw, I'm Elise Forsyth. I think your officers may have taken my computer from Spring Hill? You left your card, as I was already in the Psych ward when you visited," I said, with a smile.

"Oh, hello Elise, I won't shake your hand. This virus is in Brisbane now, so we are supposed to be social distancing. Do sit down," said Officer Shaw.

We sat down on opposite sides of her desk. "Did you bring the card?" asked the cop.

"Yes, it's here," I said, as I handed it over.

She typed a case number from the card into her computer. My case file came up. She read for a bit.

"Right, so the charges against you were dropped. We are still going after Damien Ellis, but we don't think that you could be a credible witness to use against him in court. I assume you've stopped working for him?" asked officer Carol.

"I was stupid to work for him in the first place. He is a creep, he even tried to visit me in the Psych Ward. He wants the computer, but I've already paid him for it, time and again," I said.

"Ellis is a grub, we'll put him away. We've got a few people willing to testify against him. Right, your stuff is this way," said Officer Shaw.

We stood up and walked out a back door to the carpark, then into a more modern garage type building. Carol swiped the door, and we walked into a storage area of many numbered shelves.

"I'll just order an Uber, as I can't carry it far," I said.

Officer Shaw looked around, and located my computer. The screen stood separate, and the keyboard and mouse and cables had been bundled into a large cardboard envelope.

"Just check that it's all there," said the officer, as she ticked things off a form on a clipboard.

213

I looked into the envelope. There was my keyboard, mouse, internet router, the cables that connect them, and an envelope with cash in it. Five hundred dollars, in fifties. I counted it and put it away. In the Uber home, I wondered about the cash, but drew a blank. Was this money I was supposed to pay Damien Ellis? If so, for how long? A month? A week? If I had made these payments, I surely own the computer now. Or is his an endless scam?

I got home and carried my things upstairs, and got it set up on my desk. The internet came straight on, it was like a miracle. I checked my emails. There was one from Serena, with the dates and places for a few upcoming gigs. None were this week, thank God. I emailed a quick response so she knew I'd received it. There were a bunch of emails forwarded from peepshow dot com, which I'd read later. I checked my social networking sites. There were messages from Russel, Anthony and Bruce, so I was doing fine on that front.

There was a "like" from Danny the bikie. I sent him a personal message.

"Hi Danny, I would like to go along to your NA group, but would like to walk in with someone, if that's cool with you," I wrote.

Now I would negotiate the Prisons website. How many points worth of ID do I have? Can I do a gutter scan of my licence and passport? That will have to do, as I don't have a birth certificate and my bankcard doesn't have a photo or address. When I typed in "Pete Sheffield," I was given his prisoner number, and the confirmation of my suspicion that he was held at Wacol. I requested a visiting time. They would have to approve me before I could get a time.

That was not so difficult. It must have just been a mental hurdle. They will email me back.

Danny typed back, "Our NA group meets thursdays 6pm at the Scout Hall at Capalaba. Meet outside at 10 to 6 if you need an escort. Danny."

"Will do. See you there, Elise," I wrote back.

I wrote it in my diary. I was so organised now. I wrote in the gigs that Serena had booked for me. I wrote in lunch with Russel. I had a plan now. A financial plan. I would follow each lead until I came to success.

I spent some time looking at local metal-workers on the internet. I was making a list, when I cam across one guy who already worked with bicycles. Alan had made some modified bicycles for food vans, and peddle-powered fruit juice vans. He operated out of an old Woolstore warehouse in Newstead. He did commissions. Alan could be the person to make my first bicycle-driven vehicle. I'd have to draw some sketches before I go to see him.

I walked down to one of the Joe Palazzo salons in town. I noticed the Myer centre also had a Harrison hair, so I decided not to go to that one. The Queen St shop was in an older low-rise building. It was spread over the top two floors, opening onto a sweeping staircase which connected the two floors. Each hairdresser had their own station on the various levels, which must have been some sort of executive offices in times gone by. I waited in a gold-painted cane lounge to be shown to my stylist. The whole place was painted black and gold.

My Stylist today was Tony, a handsome gay man with a bit of a neat Goth look going on. I took off my wig.

"Oh, darling, I can see exactly what's been going on here. It's really damaged, and it's lost it's shape. I'm going to cut it shorter into a growing style, and give it a good protein treatment. Did you bleach this yourself?" asked Tony.

"Yes, I used Schwartzkopf, but the damage was already done. I just wanted to fix the roots, I knew I'd need help with the style," I said.

"You've come to the right place," said Tony. "I can fix that up for you."

We chatted as he did my hair. I mentioned that I had a special event coming up, and that I was looking for something to make the day more special.

Tony said, "You can always talk to me about that. We go downstairs for coffee quite a lot, and I can always meet you in the cafe on the ground floor."

So, this salon was used as a dealing spot, right on the main street of the city. This stylist would offer a complete stranger both coke and pills, at her first hair-dressing appointment. Tony gave me his card at the end of the session. My hair looked great again. A super-short bob with a big undercut, all shiny and healthy looking.

Lunch with Russel went well. The sushi bar was in a restaurant complex under a big riverside tower, so it had a view of the bike-track I rode in on. I wore a loose dusty pink outfit. Russel was already there, in a light-weight grey suit.

"Hi Elise," said Russel.

"Hi Russel," I said, with a smile.

Russel had gotten a table by the window, and a pot of green tea, and two cups. He poured me one. I sat down.

"Thanks, have you ordered?" I asked.

"No, I thought I'd wait for you to order," said Russel.

I checked the menu and we ordered. He had manners. Other women checked him out. Other men checked me out. It's a dog eat dog world.

"Russel, I've got a business proposition for you," I said.

"That's a pity, I thought you had some other kind of proposition for me," said Russel.

"Look, I'm deadly serious. I don't want you to use again and I don't want to use myself, but I've got a kilo of coke I've got to sell to get myself financially liquid again," I said.

Russel looked like he'd swallowed his chopsticks.

"I've got to do it so I can get myself another car, and set up my entertainment business. When I said I had a term deposit, I didn't mean in a bank. I buried that thing before I went to Rehab, and now I've got to sell it. There is no way I'm doing any. But I need to meet someone like Joe Palazzo in order to sell it all at once. My other contact is in jail, so I need to meet a new one," I said.

"Please tell me you're not an undercover?" asked Russel.

"As if the cops would take a fuck-up like me," I said.

"How has such a beautiful woman got herself mixed up in that kind of business?" asked Russel.

"Please don't judge me. I've come from nowhere and I've got nothing, but I want to be someone and have something. I thought that you would understand," I said.

"I'm not judging you. I think you're totally hot, but you've been lead down the wrong path. I don't want to go back down that path, Elise," said Russel.

"Look, I chopped it up into bags the other day, and I didn't touch a grain. I wore a mask so I wouldn't breathe it it, and gloves so I wouldn't absorb it," I said quietly.

"That's good, Elise," said Russel. "I've got to get back to work, but will you let me take you out to dinner on Friday?"

"Sure," I said, "Can you pick me up?"

"I'd love to, where do you live?" asked Russel.

"I'm at flat 6, 431 Wickham Terrace. I'm on the third floor, which is the top floor," I said.

"I'll pick you up at seven o'clock," said Russel, as he typed my address into his phone.

218

32. A proper date.

I hadn't been on a proper date since the Sugar-daddy. And somehow, they didn't seem like proper dates. More like some weird eating ritual between the master and his slave, really.

Russel drove the white merc into our carpark, and came up the stairs, carrying flowers. I looked around the kitchen for a vase. I had one, but it was full of pens and pencils and hair brushes and stuff. I answered the door, and Russel gave me a big bunch of pink roses. I tipped the pens into a box, and filled up the vase, for the flowers.

"Thanks, Russel, they are really beautiful," I said.

"Not as beautiful as you. I do hope you'll let me get closer to you, Elise," said Russel.

"I'm not very good at that kind of thing, but I'll try my best," I said.

"What the hell does that mean?" asked Russel, standing quite close to me now.

"I've just never had what you'd call a proper relationship," I said. "I've only had fucks and been a sugar-baby. I've never said 'I love you' to anyone, and if I did, it would have been a lie."

"Wow, I thought it was supposed to be the man who was the emotional cripple," said Russel.

I laughed. "I don't know if I'm quite that bad. Just don't expect too much of me," I said.

"Come on, I've booked us at a seafood restaurant, but it's drive away, so we've got to go," said Russel.

I let us out of the flat, and we went down to his car. He drove us up to Morgan's restaurant on the fishing wharves right up in Redcliffe, about thirty kilometres north of town. In his car, he listened to a top forty station, and sang along with all the songs. I knew one or two, and sang a bit as well. He drove smoothly, and kept taking glances at me as we sped along. I wore a long black silk dress, with a pale pink fake fur coat over the top. Russel wore a dark grey suit, over a white shirt with a patterned tie, and slip-on leather shoes. He opened the car-door for me.

The dinner was great and I felt myself relaxing. He ordered lemon, lime and bitters for us to drink, and we had oysters, mud-crab, fish and Moreton bay bugs. It was delicious.

"So when do you want to meet Joe Palazzo?" asked Russel.

"Whenever is convenient with you," I said.

"I could set up a meeting for next week?" said Russel.

"That would be perfect," I said.

"So, would you like me to take you to your house, or my house?" asked Russel.

"If we went to your house, could you drop me home tomorrow?" I asked.

"I've got gelato, lemon sorbet and chocolate at my place," said Russel.

"It's definitely your place then," I said.

He drove me back to his place, and it was immaculate. He had really cleaned up since I had dropped in for the car. He had a big vase of fragrant flowers at his place, and even the dog had been shampooed. Russel made desserts for us, and I noted his collection of alcohol bottles behind the bar.

"Have you been tempted to drink any?" I asked.

"I thought about throwing them all away, and then I just thought I could resist temptation," said Russel.

"I felt the same way about the coke," I said.

"Would you like to jump in the spa with me?" asked Russel.

"You've got a spa?" I asked.

We finished our ice-cream and Russel led me to the bathroom, which had a big oval spa-bath, warm and ready. Russel undressed in the bedroom, then walked in to the tub, naked. I went back to his room to undress, then followed him into the spa. He was in good shape. This would probably be fun. It felt a bit naughty, but fun.

"Just let me watch you climbing into the spa. You're just gorgeous, this is like a dream," said Russel.

"Ooh, it's a bit hot. I might just sit on the edge for a minute," I said.

"Take all the time you need, Elise," said Russel, and that was indicative of his attitude towards me. He let me enjoy the spa. Then he touched me softly and slowly. He kissed me very softly, and kissed my neck and my shoulders.

We moved on to his bed, and he gently dried me with a well-laundered towel. I could relax, and respond to him. He took his time, and really tried to please me.

Afterwards, he asked if I had climaxed.

I said, "No, but it can take me a while before I am comfortable enough to do that. I really liked it, and I'm sure if we did it again, I'd eventually get there," I said.

"Damn, I really wanted to do that for you," said Russel.

"Don't be frustrated, you did a great job. This is normal for me. I didn't want to have to pretend. I'd rather be honest about it," I said.

"You'll let me try again?" he said, like a keen puppy.

"Of course. The funny thing is, I can come really easily if I'm wasted on drugs. But I don't want to take any. I want to be able to do it straight," I said.

"I'll definitely help you with that," said Russel, and he looked like he was on the mission to find the Holy Grail.

222

33. Meeting the big cheese.

Russel set up a meeting with Joe Palazzo at his place. Palazzo had been there before, and Russel was comfortable at Joe's house as well. Russel told me that Joe lived in a mansion in Ascot, with an indoor/outdoor pool. So he wasn't far away. Russel still saw him at work, but he was someone else's client now.

When my Uber dropped me at Hamilton, there was a Maserati parked out the front. Flossy ran out the front gate and jumped on me as I came in the door. Russel introduced me to Joe Palazzo, and his friend, Giani. Joe was of average height, wearing a white linen suit with a white shirt, Gianni looked like a Greek god, tall and ripped, in a grey suit. He was the muscle.

We sat around the lounge room, and Russel fixed me a lemon, lime and bitters. He had mixed a cocktail for Joe, and it looked like Gianni was drinking soda water. I put my briefcase down on the floor, and sat on the couch next to Russel. I could hardly breathe. I took a sip of my drink.

Joe Palazzo said, "You're a nice looking young lady, Elise. Russel said you had a business proposition for me?"

"Thanks, yes, I've got a kilo of coke to sell," I said.

"Is it the good stuff?" asked Palazzo.

"I don't know, I haven't tried it," I said.

"Why not?" asked Palazzo.

"I don't know if Russel told you, but I am fresh out of Rehab, and I'm trying to stay clean. It's uncut, still compressed, and the weight is spot on," I said.

"I'd like to try a bit," said Palazzo. "I've got to try before I buy."

"Of course," I said, "I've got it here."

I opened the briefcase and put on my gloves. I took out the bag, which was vacuum sealed. I had a retractable knife in the briefcase, so I sliced open the end of the bag. Inside was the big block, which I had labeled "997grams" and a small snaplock with "3gs" written on it. I passed the smaller bag to Palazzo. He had been unpacking his own bag, with a small mirror, and single edged razor blade, and a small electronic scale.

"Thanks, babe," said Palazzo.

We all watched as Joe emptied the thin slice of compressed coke on to the mirror. He chopped some of it up, and it decompressed, fluffing up to pinkish white crystals. He put the majority of the slice back in the bag, and kept chopping till he had two lines cut up on the mirror. Then he took out a hundred dollar note, rolled it up and sniffed the first line.

"Whoa! That's the shit!" said Palazzo. "Anyone else having a line?"

"It looks so good, but I just can't," said Russel.

"I might just have half a line, I've got to drive," said Gianni.

Joe handed Gianni the rolled up note, and he bent over the coffee table to have a snort.

"Oh yeah, that's the good gear," said Gianni.

He had only had about a third of the line.

"Can I just have a look at the block?" said Palazzo.

"Sure, Joe, go right ahead," I said.

Joe Palazzo peeled open the bigger block of coke. He smelt it, then ran his finger along it, scraping a tiny bit on his fingernail. He then smelled his finger, and put it in his mouth.

"That looks solid, and the same as the sample," said Joe. "What is your price?"

"Two hundred thousand," I said.

"That is a fair price," said Joe.

He picked up the larger block and put it on his scales. The scales said 997 grams. Then he snorted the rest of the chopped up coke, and put the little bag on the scales. It said 3 grams. Joe was happy.

"Can you get that bag for me?" Joe asked Gianni.

Gianni walked off to the Maserati, and returned with a briefcase of his own.

"So, what did you pay for it?" asked Joe.

"I paid a high price," I said.

"How much?" asked Joe.

"I paid with my sanity. The cops handcuffed me and bashed me, but I wouldn't give it up. I spent a month locked up in the Psych Ward. I've paid and paid. It's rude to ask," I said.

"Oh, fair enough. I didn't mean to be rude, darling," said Palazzo.

He looked at me as if I was some kind of attractive insect which you'd like to touch but are worried might sting or bite you. Gianni gave him the briefcase, which he set on his lap, and flicked open. He took out a pile of hundred dollar notes, held with a rubber band, and handed it to me. Then he laid ten piles on the table, and another nine piles behind them. I counted the money. There were a hundred bills in this pile, that is ten thousand. Twenty piles of ten thousand make two hundred thousand. He had more in his briefcase, he had expected to pay more.

"This one is right, and I trust that the others are all right," I said.

"You can count them if you want to," said Palazzo.

"I'll just count another one to check," said Russel, and Joe did not seem offended. So as Russel counted another bundle, I counted a third one.

"This one is spot on," said Russel.

"Yes, so is this one," I said.

I took off my glove, and reached out to shake Palazzo's hand. He had a firm, dry grip, and made eye contact. The deal was done. I started to pack the money bundles into my briefcase, and

Joe put the coke into a large snaplock bag, into his briefcase. Just as I could see he had extra cash, about five bundles, he could see my replica gun in my case. It does look just like the real thing. I saw him clock the gun, then quickly look up at me. But I just kept packing the money away, moving the retractable knife and gun to make room. I put the used gloves back in the top pocket my bag, where I had other gloves and masks.

"People are starting to wear those masks, for this Coronavirus," said Palazzo.

"It's in Brisbane now, overseas uni students, Chinese and Americans," said Russel.

"God, what a pain, just what we don't need," I said.

"In Italy, they closed everything except food shops and pharmacies. How am I going to run my business?" said Palazzo.

"It will be just like China and Italy here. We will be shut down and locked down. Let's hope it's only for a couple of months," said Russel.

"Do you think they'll shut the airports?" I asked.

"Oh, God," said Joe.

"I wonder if they'll let me work from home?" asked Russel.

"Speaking of which, I should head home. Thanks for the hospitality, Russel. I'm pleased to meet you, Elise, it's been a pleasure doing business with you," said Joe.

"It's nice to meet you too, Joe," I said.

Joe, Gianni and Russel stood up, and Russel walked the other men to the door. Russel came back in, with an amused look on his face.

"I liked the way you told him it was rude to ask. He respects you now," said Russel.

"It was either that, or the replica in my briefcase," I said.

"Elise, was that complete bullshit what you told him, or what you told us at NA meetings?" asked Russel.

I looked at him and I was lost for words. He knew I was a liar. He knew that I was involved in some crimes. I didn't quite know how much to tell him.

"Well, I couldn't say what I was really up to at NA meetings, could I? The stuff I said there was true. I just didn't say everything. I omitted to say that I had stashed a huge block of coke and I couldn't say I was broke till I dug it up and sold it, could I?" I said.

"Where you sounding out me and Anthony and Bruce for our dealing connections? Why couldn't you sell it to your usual connection? Do you have a usual connection? Who the fuck are you, Elise?" asked Russel.

"Look, Russel, sit down here, and I'll tell you what happened. It's a long story and I feel ashamed to tell it," I said.

Russel sat down next to me, and looked at me suspiciously.

"You know how I have these psychotic episodes?" I asked, and he nodded. "I was being a hair model for Evan Harrison, on a yacht in Fiji. I knew the makeup artist, Crimson, and we did miles of coke. Evan and I had flown in and met the boat. The men talked a lot of business. Louis Primo did the photos, it was excellent, but anyway, we all sailed backed on the yacht, and I realised that it was a smuggling run. At a party after the cruise, Evan raped me, so I waited till he was asleep, then I stole a block of coke and a bicycle and I got away and hid it. But I was fully psychotic by that stage, and needing heroin, so I carjacked a man to take me to my heroin dealer's house. So he's probably really shitty with me. Evan Harrison is probably hunting me down, and I've got this video pimp called Damien Ellis following me around too. So I've got a lot on my plate at the moment and that's probably why I can't relax enough to enjoy sex properly too."

"Holy fuckballs Elise," said Russel. "Is there anything else you aren't telling me? You stole the coke? Evan raped you? Well I suppose he fucking deserved it. But I'm worried about your safety. You should stay here."

"Actually, I was going to ask you to drive me home. But could you stay at my place tonight?" I asked.

"You know I can't resist you, don't you?" said Russel. "Did you know that Joe Palazzo hates Evan Harrison?"

"No, I didn't know that. Shall we go?" I said.

I was nervous to get outside again. I collected my bags, we left Flossy to guard the house, and we took off. Russel drove me past Toorak House, to see the deer and llama they kept on their giant hilltop block. We wound our way through Ascot on the other side of the Hamilton hill, and cruised past a monster mansion.

"That's Joe Palazzo's place. You should see inside, everything money can buy," said Russel.

"He must be worth a lot," I said.

"You should see his books, I had to count the zeroes," laughed Russel.

By the time we were back in Spring Hill, we had both calmed down. Russel walked up the steps with me, and I let him in. The roses sat on my small dining table, the bunch was too big to go anywhere else.

"Come though to my bedroom," I said, walking and turning on light-switches as I went. Russel sat on my bed, and I sat at my desk's chair, and pulled a toolbox out from under my bed. As he watched, I unpacked my briefcase and put the cash and the gun into the toolbox. Then I pushed the toolbox and the briefcase under the bed. I slipped off my suit, and hung it up. I had spent the last of what was in my bank account on that suit.

"Does Evan Harrison know you live here?" asked Russel.

"No, but Damien Ellis knows I live in this block, but thinks I'm in my old flat at the front of the building, where Judith is now," I said.

"Tomorrow, I'll call in late for work, and we'll go out and get you a new car. I don't want you riding around, you're too vulnerable. And you should start to think about getting out of this flat too. How did Evan Harrison book you for the job?" asked Russel.

"He hired me through my agent Serena, he's asked her for me again, but I refused, so she refused him. He knows my phone number but that's all," I said.

"That's good too. I want you to be safe. And I want you to be able to relax enough to enjoy it," he said.

34. Following through.

I wasn't going to sit back and rest now that I had some money. I need to start up my performing arts company, contact my brother and flog the rest of the shit.

I contacted Alan the Metal Man, and went around to meet him at his workshop in Newstead. I took some sketches with me. I took the simplest ones, a set of five bicycles which could hold up a singer, guitar players and a drum-kit and drummer. Alan showed me his food vending bicycles, and a bike on stilts that he was building for a clown.

"I can build these things, but they're going to cost between five and six thousand dollars each," said Alan.

'No worries,' I said. "I can give you ten thousand to start working on them, and more as you need it."

"Really? Let me write you out a receipt," said Alan, who looked like it was Christmas.

Allan actually looked like the kind of guy I usually thought of as handsome, tall, tanned and kind of a bit bad in a tattooed, long-haired way. But it's hard to chat up guys when you have so many secrets to keep from them. And having one man interested was bad enough. Two would just be terrible.

Serena sent me a text, saying one of my gigs was cancelled because of Coronavirus. I got approved to visit Pete in jail, and I could apply for a time-slot to visit. Natalie Pasquale texted to say she had found out something and I should ring up.

"Hello," said Natalie P.

"Hi Natalie, it's Elise," I said.

"Hey, it's good to hear your voice. Guess what? I found out what your brother changed his name to!" said Natalie.

"Oh my God, what?" I said.

"I think that he must have been adopted by a family called Rider," said Natalie.

"He changed his name to Skye Rider?" I asked. That sounded weird.

"So I did a google search, and it looks like he is a Surf photographer," said Natalie.

"Did you find out where he lived?" I asked.

"That's the thing. If your brother is Skye Rider, he travels around with the professional surfing annual tour. He is secretive about where he lives, and I couldn't find a photo of him," said Natalie.

"Oh, OK. Still, that's great news, I have his name now, and I can look for him myself. He's got to have an agent or a manager or something. Thank you so much, Natalie," I said.

Of course I hopped straight on the internet, and searched the social media sites. If he had a profile, it wasn't public. He had a website full of incredible surf photos, but none of himself and no contact details. He didn't even have an instagram account. This was going to be harder than I thought.

I started four bank accounts at four different banks, and started depositing five thousand at each one, and would continue every few days. With the expensive suit and the new hair, the bank tellers just smiled and asked about my day. I had to legitimise the cash, and this was the only way to do it. I didn't feel safe with that much cash at home. It was too risky. And if the police found it, I'd have no legitimate excuse for having it.

I got a message on Instagram from Bruce, saying he was out of Rehab. I texted him congratulations, and asked if he wanted to meet for a coffee. What I had to ask him couldn't be said on the phone. Bruce wanted to meet at a cafe with good music. I told him the way things were shutting down, we'd be lucky to find any cafe where we could actually sit down, most were only doing take-away due to Covid restrictions. We arranged to meet next week.

The jail trip was not so difficult. I was approved and given a time, on Friday the thirteenth of march, at ten in the morning. I could drive there in my new car. Though I'd wanted to get a red one, Russel had talked me into a silver Mazda three, because it wouldn't stand out so much.

The Arthur Gorrie Correctional Centre was busy this morning. I brought a mask, but didn't wear it, as nobody else was either. I waited in the waiting room with my ticket until my number was called. Then I went through the ominous doorway, got patted down by a female officer and had my bag searched. A different prison officer led me to the meeting room, where many prisoners were meeting family or friends. Four rows of picnic tables were close enough to supervise, but offered some privacy, if we talked quietly. Pete was already there.

"Hi Elise," said Pete.

"Hi Pete, I'm sorry I took so long to visit," I said.

"It's cool," said Pete, "If you had rocked up how you used to be, they wouldn't have let you in anyway."

"Yeah, you're right," I laughed, "I just got out of rehab two weeks ago. While I was in there, I thought about you, and thought that a proper friend would visit."

"I'm so glad you went to rehab, Elise. I just had to go cold turkey in the watch-house and here, it was ugly. But I'm good now, and we even have an NA group in here," said Pete.

"Well you're looking good, actually, you've lost weight," I said. He was still a little overweight, but he had been really huge before. And he'd had his hair cut, he was actually looking quite respectable, in his prison track suit.

"We don't get much to eat, and the food is not great, but I have been doing some exercise for fitness and boredom," said Pete.

"I've been riding my bike, and I bought a new car. I got a Mazda three. I went to Centenary, and I saw Daniel, but I could only manage about three hundred metres. I've been out of the pool too long. Daniel is still acting, and said he'd be keen to perform with my company, and learn how to ride the bicycle machine. I'm so happy to be starting this company, and taking artistic control, instead of always working for other people. But I needed to straighten out, and have time to think about what I was doing with my life," I said.

"You're starting a performing company? That's great! What kind of stuff?" asked Pete.

"You've been to Woodford Festival, haven't you?" I asked. "You know how the best performance art is the stuff that roves through the crowds, the bigger the better, many on stilts, or those giant puppets as well? I've seen footage of bicycle driven vehicles at Burning Man, some of which have many drivers and riders dancing and doing circus tricks. I thought I would start with five small vehicles, to carry around members of a band, as they played, so with space for amplifiers and batteries, one has room for a drum kit. If I can get three big gigs this year, the business can pay for itself. So I've been reaching out to my actor friends, who I can trust to perform. And also to my other friends."

"Why did you come to see me today, Elise?" asked Pete.

"I've got a big pile of lollies to sell. I was wondering who you used to buy yours off?" I said.

"I used to score from a guy called Sinclair who worked at the Harrison Hair in the Valley. That's why my hair always looked good. He wouldn't let me walk out of the salon with bad hair," said Pete.

"Is he a hairdresser?" I asked.

"No, darling, he's a stylist and colourist," said Pete, in a very gay way.

"Right, so I might be able to get my hair cut there," I said. There was no way on earth I'd be going in there.

"I'm not going back to dealing when I get out, Elise. And I hope you are very careful if you are doing that," said Pete.

"I just have a certain amount to get rid of, then I'm done for good. But I'm starting my new life, and that's what I'm focusing on. I had this crap before I went away. It's my ticket to a new life, my own home, my own business. It's one bad thing I've got to do to gain financial independence. And it's better than sex-work. I'm never doing that again. How could I have been so desperate?"

"You were just doing what you had to do to get by. And so was I. But I'm going to go straight too, and do a job I enjoy. I was thinking about selling real estate, it's got to be easy. The people are all there wanting to buy, you're just helping them to choose and doing the paperwork. I'd make similar commission to selling drugs, but it's all legal," said Pete.

"That's great, Pete, you'd be good at that," I said. "I also remembered my schoolfriend, who has the same name as my psychiatrist. She's an insurance investigator now, and she's been helping me to track down my brother," I said.

"I didn't know you had a brother?" said Pete.

"The shrink helped me to remember that my dad killed my mum, and then himself. My brother must have been fostered and adopted by a different family. He was Skye Forsyth, but he is Skye Rider now," I said.

"That surf guy?" asked Pete, and I nodded. "He came in here and gave us a motivational speech. He said he was a juvenile offender, but went on to build a career and take control of his life. He spoke at the kids' jail too," said Pete.

"Fuck, you're kidding. He was in here? He was a juvenile offender? What did he do?" I asked.

"He didn't say. You don't say. Jail's not like an NA meeting. It's enough to admit you've been inside. Most men won't ask. But the fact that he came to visit made an impression. He looked a lot like you, when I think about it. He said he lives on Straddie, when he's not touring, he's on Minjerribah, that's what he called it. Must be the Murri name. I think he's down with the Native Hawaiians and stuff too," said Pete.

235

"I've been trying to contact him, but I was having trouble. This kind of explains it. I had blocked out all that childhood stuff. If he was in jail, there was no way he could contact me. I'm famous here, but only my face, not my name. If he's touring a lot, he probably hasn't seen the Pepsi ad or the trampoline ad, or any of that shit. He's not on facebook. I'd so like to see him, it's been twenty years," I said.

"Elise, I hope you find him. It's good to have family. Only my family have really visited me here. And I'm sorry that I never told you that I loved you, when we were together. I knew you were hooking it, and I thought you'd laugh at me," said Pete.

"I was so fucked up then I probably wasn't capable of love. I don't know if I'm capable now. But I did love you as much as I could, at the time, as a total fuck up," I said.

I gave him a hug before I left.

237

35. Capalaba NA.

I was working though my list of both things to do and people to see. Anthony rang, and he agreed to meet Russel and I for a coffee on the weekend. But before that, I had a NA meeting to attend. I had texted Danny, and we arranged to meet outside and go in together. I met Danny having a cigarette by his motorcycle. Then one by one more motorbikes rocked up. I felt like I should have been wearing leather, but I just had jeans and a cardigan on.

"How have you been keeping, darlin'?" said Danny.

"Great, I've been straight, though I've had temptation," I said. "How are you, Danny?"

"Flat out like a lizard drinking," said Danny. "Have you caught up with anyone?"

"Only Russel," I said. "He leant me his car till I could buy another one."

"That looks new," said Danny.

"It is new, and I'm going to try to keep it really nice," I said. "Danny, I need your help."

"What kind of help do you need?" asked Danny.

"I need to cash my replica gun in for a real one," I said, with a smile.

"I knew you were a smart girl. After the meeting, we can go to my place at Carina Heights. Handgun, is it?" asked Danny.

"Yeah, thanks heaps," I said, as the others got closer and we walked in to the Scout Hall. How had Danny described it? Like a medieval biker's conference? There was a big biker contingent, and some goths, as well as the flannelette shirted bogans typical of the outer suburbs. I was glad to have Danny to walk in with.

I won't describe all the members and their habits, but let's just say that there had been a lot of meth, smack, and even crack blowing through the suburbs and it sounded like there still was. And there's obviously a lot of things people aren't saying either, like what I didn't say. If I sit there and say that I'm just out of rehab, and staying straight, and I've just flogged a kilo of coke, what is everybody else not saying? There could have been a major league drug dealer in the room, but for all I could tell, it could have been anyone.

After the meeting, Danny stood around chatting for a bit, and introduced me to a biker called 'Skidmarks,' and he invited him back for 'coffee' as well. Danny gave me the address in case I got lost, but we drove in convoy through the southern suburbs to Danny's house.

It was a quiet brick place which backed on to the White's Hill reserve. The men left their motorbikes on the driveway, and I parked out the front of the house. In through the garage, where another bike was partially dismantled, in to Danny's man-cave. He had a Guns'n'Roses pinball machine, a jukebox and a small pool table. On the bar was a coffee percolator, which Danny put on.

"Are you both having coffee?" asked Danny.

"Yeah mate, milk no sugar," said Skidmarks.

"I'll just have a tea or a herb tea," I said.

"Yeah, I've got green tea, will that do?" asked Danny.

"Perfect, thanks Danny," I said.

"Skidmarks, Elise has a replica that she'd like to replace with the real thing," said Danny.

"Well let's have a look at it then?" said Skidmarks.

I took the gun out of my handbag and laid it on the table. Skidmarks picked it up and had a look at it.

"It's a Beretta," said Skidmarks, "nice work, worth about three hundred. Would you like the same handgun, or are you ok with any type?"

"The same, if possible, but really any type would do," I said.

Danny came over with our hot drinks, and sat down.

"We've got one of those, don't we, but it's a bit old. We've got a couple of Glocks and a Browning which are in better condition. Have you got your key?" asked Danny.

Skidmarks stood up and reached into his pocket for his keyring. He handed it to Danny, who walked over to a metal gun-locker in the corner of the room.

"In our chapter, we have two arsenal officers who both have a key to the locker. That way no-one borrows or drops off without at least two other members knowing," explained Danny.

He brought three guns over to the small table between the couches. One did look like mine, but older. All three guns were compact, black, and would fit in my handbag.

"Pick them up and have a feel, they each are a slightly different weight and balance," said Skidmarks. I picked them up, one at a time and felt the weight of them.

"I think I like the Glock, though the Baretta 96 is a very nice gun," I said.

"Well, either of them will set you back twelve hundred with the trade-in," said Danny.

"Actually, I'll take the Baretta. It feels a bit lighter. I don't mind that it's old, as long as it works. Do you have ammo too?" I asked.

"Can't just drop in to the gun shop?" asked Skidmarks.

"With my mental health record, they won't give me a gun licence," I said.

"Elise is my friend from the Carina Private rehab group. We're actually looking for someone to do a job in there at the moment," said Danny.

"This Beretta has a 15 round magazine, I'll show you how to load and release it," said Skidmarks.

Skidmarks showed me how the gun worked, and made sure I did it right.

"What kind of a job are you talking about, Danny?" I asked.

"Oh, a vendetta job against that old priest," said Danny.

"Clement, the kiddy fiddler?" I asked.

"Yes, one of the boys he targeted is a man now, and wants him dead. There's ten grand in it for whoever does it, but they've got to be able to get into that locked ward," said Danny.

"Are Steve and Jack still in there?" I asked.

"I thought I had talked Jack into it, but he's a mess," said Danny.

"Linda would be into it too, but wouldn't risk her record, she's got her kids to think of," I said. "It's always good to have a lookout, or a distraction, or something," I wondered aloud.

"Linda and Jack could be lookouts or a diversion, but we need someone more solid to do the actual deed," said Danny.

"Did you know that Bruce just got out? He'd be a more likely candidate. He could always get committed again," I said.

"If he could be persuaded," said Danny.

"I'm actually meeting him for coffee next week," I said.

"Tell him that the contract is ten thousand, not bad for a month's work," said Danny.

"I'll tell him, and I'll tell him about your Thursday meetings here," I said

"You can always come along to the NA meeting at Carina," said Danny.

"There's no way I'd risk going back in there. I'm putting myself in enough danger. But good luck with that job, I can totally understand it. I'll see what I can do to talk Bruce into doing the contract. I think he'd be up for it," I said.

"See, people in your legal position, Elise, or Bruce's legal position, for that matter, can get away with a lot of things. They'll never put you in jail, just in a ward. The length of time you'll stay there depends on how good an actor you are. I'm sure you're a good actress, because you got out in the minimum time. But Clement's a good actor too, and he doesn't want to get out," said Danny.

"Steve's a tradesman, and he's in there voluntarily. Offer him the contract. He's already extended his stay once, it seems pretty standard. If he can make it look like suicide, he could get away with it," I said.

"Come along for a Friday meeting and help me?" asked Danny.

"I'll think about it," I said. "Thanks for the gun and ammo. I've got to go, but I know where you are now, Danny. I'll do what I can to talk Bruce into taking the contract, and re-admitting himself. I think he'd do it for the money, and maybe the challenge as well."

"Cheers, darling," said Danny.

"Lovely to meet you, Elise," said Skidmarks.

The guys put their arsenal away, and showed me to my car.

243

36. One step closer.

I've been ticking things off my list. I've had lunch with Natalie, and caught up on her world. She is going to get married, and wants me to go to her wedding. That will be fun. She said I could bring Russel, or come by myself, whichever I preferred. Natalie doesn't think she'll be able to have bridesmaids because of Covid restrictions, otherwise, she said, she'd have asked me to be one! Anthony came over for coffee, and he has agreed to introduce me to Franco Panetone, for ten percent of the action. Panetone's going to drive up from Sydney, he's got some flash new car. I'm planning a weekend on Stradbroke with Russel, to see if I can track down Skye. I've got a coffee date with Bruce that I'm quite looking forward to.

But the worst thing is this damned Coronavirus. On the 19., a ship called the Ruby Princess docked in Sydney, full of the virus, and they just fucking let the passengers out, to fly across Australia and infect everyone. So the politicians are going mental, and they're shutting everything down. First the gym on top of the pool closed, it's in a crazy modernist curved building that sticks out over the kiddies' pool. Then, the pool closed. Cycling is the only exercise I've got now, and Russel thinks it's dangerous for me in case I get followed from my place.

Serena texted to say another of my gigs in cancelled because of the virus, as it was a big parade. At least the other job is in a studio, and should still go ahead.

Alan had made a start on my vehicles, he had borrowed a drum kit and stool to work on the hardest one first. The seat would be part of the bike, but had to be at the right height for the drummer. He'd made the rider higher than the drummer, so they could see over the musician's head.

"I've got some friends in a band that practise in the next wool-store. They leant me the drums, and they are advising me of comfortable seating for playing guitars, and where to place the amplifier," said Alan.

"Wow," I said, "I'm going to need a band to give the vehicles a test run. Are they any good?"

"They were a well known band, but they've kind of split up, but some of the guys are practising with some others now, so I think it might be a new band, I'm not sure," said Alan.

"No worries, Alan, I can always get my agent to help me hire a good band, but ask your friends as well," I said.

Alan was good. He bought what he needed and worked quickly, he didn't mess around. These machines were going to look excellent. I've been looking at the websites for Woodford Festival, Glastonbury and Burning Man, and I realised I'd need great photos and video to apply. I wrote the various deadlines in my diary, and set about planning which actors would ride the things, and possible bands as well. I was actually liking the look of a local band who had three female singers and two male musicians, and the girls played various instruments too. They all dressed well, and looked the part. I didn't really want to have an all-blokes band.

Daniel told me his regular gig as a kid's party superhero had canned all his bookings. Barnaby and Roberta had similar stories, and both said they'd be keen to perform on the bicycles, and happy to rehearse. I needed another actor who was reasonably strong, and I thought of Steve, and if he'd acted in Everley's film yet. I sent him a message, and he said that he had, and that Everley wanted me to act in her film too. I told him to get her to send me the script. I didn't act in just anything. If Everley was good with a camera, she might be good for filming our initial performance, to use as publicity material.

I met Bruce at Jimmy's on the Mall. But they would only serve us take-away drinks. Bruce didn't have a mask, so I gave him a spare one. We got our coffee and mint tea in take-away cups, and took them down to King George Square to sit and talk.

"You got out quick," I said.

"Oh, I've been in there enough times to know what I have to say," said Bruce.

"Bruce, I asked to meet you today for a couple of reasons. And they are both a bit dodgy," I said.

"Well, luckily 'Dodgy' is my middle name," said Bruce.

"Bruce, the Dodgy Axeman?" I asked.

"That's why it's a silent middle name," joked Bruce.

"Bruce, I've got a kilo of coke to sell, and I'k looking for a buyer," I said.

Bruce nearly spat out his coffee. "Oh, Elise, you sweet little lamb, Rehab must have been hell for you," laughed Bruce.

"Get fucked," I said. "I haven't been doing any myself. And neither has Russel. He helped me move another one, and we didn't even have a taste."

"Oh, okay then, good on you both," said Bruce.

"It was definitely tempting," I said.

"I don't know if I could be that strong," said Bruce. "But I do know someone. Clayton used to be in that band, the Goat-herders, and now he runs a venue called the Sailing Ship."

"I remember the Goat-herders," I said.

"He's in a business partnership with some rich builder dude. The Ship has part of an actual tall ship built into it, under a big old aircraft hangar. It must have cost a bomb to build. I'll have to make an appointment to go and see him, but I'm pretty sure he deals in a large way and could want to buy what you're selling. I'll make an appointment to see Clayton. He's got an office backstage at the Ship, but he's a busy man, a business man," said Bruce.

"That would be excellent, thanks, Bruce," I said. "There is no big rush. You approach him how he likes to be approached. Now, the other matter."

Bruce nodded and looked at me. So I continued, "You remember the paedo priest, Clement, in the ward?"

"Fucking creep," said Bruce.

"I went to a Capalaba NA meeting with Danny the other day, and he told me that there's a contract out on the priest," I said.

"To knock him off?" asked Bruce.

"And it's got to look like suicide. And it's got to be done by someone inside," I said.

Bruce nodded as the implications of the contract settled in his mind.

"So I'd have to do something to get myself committed again?" asked Bruce.

"It's either that, or you can go back as a voluntary patient, like Steve and Jack did. All that takes is a shrink's appointment, talk about your meds not being effective, feeling anxious or depressed, need some time out. You seem to be able to do a week by week extension on your original month of rehab or assessment. But the Involuntary Assessment Order means a full month, at least. I suppose it depend on if your health insurance will cover it too, I don't know?" I said

"I'd rather go back for a week or two than a month," said Bruce, warming to the idea.

"Danny said the contract's worth ten grand," I said.

"That's not a bad little earner," said Bruce. "The most difficult thing is going to be the actual method. Everything is restricted in there."

"Clement wears a belt," I said.

Bruce looked at me and nodded.

"Ten grand for a couple of weeks, or a month's work?" asked Bruce.

"If Jack and Linda are still inside, they are prepared to help by being lookout or creating a diversion," I said.

"Fair dinkum?" asked Bruce.

"Danny offered Jack the contract, but he didn't think he could do it. But he said he'd help someone else to do it," I said.

"OK. I think I can do it. But I'll need a bit of time to plan things," said Bruce.

"Here is Danny's number. He's near White's Hill reserve. And if you could see that Clayton guy for me, there would be a percentage of any deal going your way as well," I said.

"So nice catching up with you, Elise," said Bruce the Axeman.

The deal with Anthony kept changing. Since Covid19 affected the states differently, there were heaps more cases in Sydney and Melbourne, and talk of closing the borders. Anthony told me that Panetone was afraid of being stopped at the border in either direction, and was planning another way in.

Now, Franco Panetone was driving to Grafton, then flying on a private plane to Stanthorpe. I was to drive out and meet him in a farmhouse in Rivertree, which had it's own airstrip. It sounded a little bit suss, so I decided to take Danny with me instead of Russel.

We met at my place, and Anthony wanted to take his car.

"Can we take mine?", I said, "it's new and I want to give it a good run, and besides, the stuff is already in my boot."

"Have you got a sat-nav?" asked Anthony.

"It's built in, in this model. It's terrific, almost like a space-ship, compared to my old car," I said.

"OK, well let's hop in the space ship and fly to Rivertree. I can key in the address for you," said Anthony.

"Cool, I was going to sit in the back anyway," said Danny.

Danny was dressed quite conservatively for him. Anthony was in a good shirt and trousers, and I had on a grey coat-dress, and charcoal slacks. I liked dressing to match the car now. As a pale blonde, grey was a colour I could get away with. The drive was easy, out past Ipswich and Toowoomba, then out through the rolling Downs. Anthony told me when to slow down for the gate, and we stopped to open and shut the gate. There were a few cows roaming the property. We drove over a slight hill to the homesite, where two old Queenslanders say side by side, looking down to a small dam, an airstrip and a big shed. We parked in the gravelled area in front of the houses. There were two four wheel drives already parked there, the lower parts covered in dust. Anthony had been texting while I was driving.

"We're going to the house on the left. The owners are in the house on the right, and they've left it open for us. Franco said he's nearly here too," said Anthony.

"It's a nice place, heaps of privacy," I said.

"Pop the boot, Elise, and we can grab our bags," said Danny.

He'd brought a man-bag to go with his leather coat and "good" jeans. I had my briefcase. We walked into the empty house to wait for Franco's arrival. A simple wooden house, it had wide verandas, and big rooms with white curtained windows. We walked through the french doors to the back verandah, which had the view. We sat on squatter's chairs, canvas deck chairs designed for the heat. There was a jug of iced water and glasses on the veranda table.

"That's them, now," pointed out Anthony.

We saw a small white Cessna coming down towards the far end of the runway. The pilot landed smoothly, and cruised down the runway, to stop next to the shed. The pilot hopped out, and opened the shed. Franco and another man climbed out. These two were in middle grey and chocolatey brown suits, and waved up at Anthony, as they walked up the path to the house.

Anthony made the introductions, "Franco and Massimo, I'd like you to meet Elise and Danny."

'I suppose we shouldn't shake hands, because of this coronavirus," said Franco, "It's weird, isn't it.

"I'm pleased to meet you," I said. "I'm just glad you could still travel across the border."

"So are we, to be quite honest," said Massimo, in a deep, resonant voice. I liked his brown suit too. I've got to stop looking at the mafia muscle and concentrate on the deal. Franco Panetone was hot for an older man too. I'll bet he had plenty of women to choose from before he got married.

"Our pilot, Hal, is writing the flight up today. But we were just discussing writing this flight as a non-stop, sight-seeing trip in the future, if things should change," said Franco.

"So it's like a practise flight for possible future trips?" asked Anthony.

"Exactly," said Franco.

So they were doing a dry run ahead of illegal border crossings, come the closure. They were smart guys. This was why our plans had kept changing.

"So forgive us if we do this quickly, Miss Elise. The pilot wants to make the Grafton landing in time that it might look like one continuous flight," said Massimo.

We walked inside the house to the dining table, where the five of us could sit together. I had my two guys on one side of the table, Franco and Massimo across from us. I put the briefcase on the table, opened it, and took out the mask and gloves, and put them on.

"I'm fresh out of rehab, and I don't want to risk exposure," I said, and the men nodded.

Then I took out the vacuum packed kilo. I opened the retractable knife and slit open the vacuum sealed bag. Inside, I found the oval slice in one bag labeled "998" and a tiny snaplock labeled "2g". I handed them both to Franco Panetone. Massimo opened his briefcase, and took out an electronic scales. He weighed the small bag first, then threw it to Franco. Franco had one of those large flat mobile phones, and he chopped up some lines on it. Again I watched the compressed coke fluff up into glittering crystals. Franco hoovered one up, then passed the phone to Massimo, who did the same. Massimo then passed the phone over to me, but I waved it away. Anthony also waved it away, but Danny took the phone. Offered the rolled up note, Danny shook his hand at it.

"I'll just have a little dab," said Danny, as he pressed his finger over the end of one line. He put his finger in his mouth, and appeared to rub his front teeth.

"It's good gear," said Franco, as he took the phone back from Danny, and had another line. Massimo refused a second line, so Franco scraped the remaining coke, and tipped it back into the bag.

"The weight is right," said Massimo.

"Was it two hundred?" asked Franco.

"Yes, thank you," I said.

Franco took bundles of hundred dollar notes from his briefcase, and laid them out before me.

"I hope you're not offended if I count them?" I asked is a girly voice.

"Not at all, young lady," said Franco.

"If you guys help, it will be quicker. Chuck them in the briefcase, once you've counted," I said. It didn't take us too long, and Franco looked happy with the coke and the deal.

"So, you bought a new car?" asked Anthony, "What kind?"

"Oh, let me show you a picture," said Franco, tapping his phone and scrolling to find a picture. It was a gold Maserati. What is it about these guys and Maseratis?

"Brother that is one nice ride," said Anthony.

"We did Sydney to Grafton in five and a half hours," said Franco.

"I hope you weren't exceeding the speed limit," said Danny, and we all laughed.

"We won't be on the way home, because I'm driving," said Massimo. "It might be more like six and a half hours."

"Drive safely," I said, looking at his big brown eyes. God, stop it, stop it, you've seen handsome guys before.

We watched them walk back down to where the pilot had turned the plane around. But they didn't climb in.

"The pilot's still doing his checklist!" Franco called out.

"Right, we'll be off then!" yelled Anthony.

We stopped in the living room, and I handed Anthony two bundles of hundreds, and I gave Danny a grand for being security for the day.

"I thought you were six years clean, Danny," said Anthony.

"One of us had to try the gear, or it would have looked funny. Like we were trying to poison them or something. People don't expect the rehab gang to supply the gear. It was strong, too, my whole mouth is numb. Am I speaking funny?" asked Danny.

We all laughed and headed towards the car.

"You can drive, if you like, Anthony," I said, and I handed him the keys.

I relaxed in the passenger seat on the way home.

The border between Queensland and New South Wales closed on the 25ᵗʰ of March 2020, for the first time in 101 years.

253

37. Taking care of Damien.

I was in the bath when Russel came over, and I greeted him in my robe.

"I think I saw that Damien guy in the carpark. Have a look and tell me if that is him," said Russel.

I switched off my bedroom light, and stepped onto the balcony. Russel had parked the Mercedes next to my Mazda, and there, peering into it, was Damien Ellis.

"Yeah, that's him, alright, the scum," I said.

"Where is you gun?" asked Russel.

"It's under the bed," I said, grabbing my keys from my handbag.

I unlocked the toolbox and handed the Beretta to Russel.

"This is a real gun, is't it?" asked Russel.

"Yes," I said. He was't stupid.

"Loaded?" Russel asked.

"Yes," I said.

He went to my front door.

"Be careful," I said.

I closed the door and went to watch from the darkness of my balcony. Russel approached him quietly with his hand in his jacket pocket.

He said something like, "That's my car you're leaning on, buddy."

Damien said something like, "My car is here too."

Russel said, "You don't live here, mate, but you've been hanging around here stalking someone who does. I want you to get in your car and fuck off and stop coming around here."

"Who's going to make me?" asked Damien.

Russel took his hand and the gun out of his pocket, and just pointed it at Damien. Damien backed off, fumbling for his keys, and he ran down the carpark to the street outside, jumped in his commodore and sped away. Russel came back upstairs to my place.

"Thanks so much for that," I said.

"I needed to tell him to leave you alone. I want to protect you from men like that, Elise," said Russel, and his eyes were blazing.

"I'm so glad you did. It's been making me feel on edge," I said.

"We've also got to get you out of this place, to somewhere that's at least got a lockup garage," said Russel. "Hey, is that bathwater still warm?"

"Yes, I only just ran the bath. Hop in, we'll have to get delivery food tonight, because the restaurants are all closing for dine-in," I said.

"Bloody coronavirus. How's a man supposed to impress a woman if he can't take her out?" asked Russel.

"Oh, you've impressed me very well," I said, "Very well."

I carried a chair from my room to the bathroom and sat with Russel while he bathed. I was getting kind of used to him now. He was smart and he was well behaved. And he was brave too.

"When I first saw you at the meeting, I thought, 'What a knock-out! I hope she's smart', then, when you talked about yourself, I thought you were too fucked up. But then I thought that I was still making value judgements, that I was clearly as bad an addict as you. You had just survived trauma, and were still in survival mode. I really like you a lot, Elise, and I'm prepared to do whatever I have to, to be your partner. And I can wait, too, until you're ready, or whatever. I don't want to scare you away," said Russel.

"Oh, you really are so sweet," I said. "You won't scare me away. I'd like to be your partner. I could handle that. You treat me like much more than a pretty face. I've looked at some hot guys recently, and thought, 'How would I even start to introduce myself, without having to lie, or lie by omission?' But you know the real me, and accept me, which means a lot. You've been through the rehab thing like me, so we can support each other with that. Most importantly, you've shown me that you're willing to risk yourself to protect me. That means an awful lot."

"Because no one has ever protected you before, have they?" asked Russel.

"No one except my brother Skye. I've had to look after myself," I said.

"How's the hunt going? Did you arrange to meet?" Russel asked.

"My plan is just to go over to Straddie, and hang out and watch the surfers. I can't find a phone or email, and Serena has left messages with his agent, but no luck," I said.

"Oh, well, the island is a great place to hang out. And the pub is a great place to stay. We can walk to all the beaches, or drive if we're feeling lazy," said Russel.

"At least the island's not shut for the virus, but I suppose that's coming too, is't it?" I said.

257

38. Bruce and the Contract.

There was a super full moon Wednesday the eighth of April. Russel and I got fish and chips and ate it in the park at Kangaroo Point. All the restaurants are closed now. Our little Crab House is making hampers in baskets to be carried to the park.

We found a picnic table with a view up to the Story bridge, and down to the river, across to the high-rises of the CBD. There was no-one around, it seemed weird. The tide had come right in, covering the sandy beach which formed a crescent around the meander of the river here at low tide. The swing set was taped off with yellow and black plastic tape from the Health department. There was hardly any traffic on the bridge.

"My boss asked me if I wanted to work from home for the next two months," said Russel.

"Really?" I asked. "I wouldn't have thought your office would be that crowded?"

"He wants to rearrange the whole floor, and just keep the Admin women who deal with mail and document filing there in town. They'll spread out into the Accountants' offices, while the central typing pool area gets reconfigured. Their desks were too close in there, and raising desk-dividers was just going to make it look like some sort of prison camp. We'll come back when the new fit-out is done," said Russel.

"Yeah, town is pretty dead now anyway," I said. "I've been riding through the Botanic Gardens, and Southbank's dead too since they fenced off the beach."

"I'll still worried about you riding by yourself," said Russel.

"I thought about what you said," I said. "And I bought these sunglasses. My helmet covers my hair now, and with these on, it's hard to tell it's me."

I took the glasses with the reflective lenses out of my handbag, and passed them to him.

"Not exactly your style," said Russel, as they were a bit 'Top Gun' and not my style at all. He handed them back to me and I put them on.

"This is only part of the look," I said. "Picture me wearing a baggy polo and a big pair of boardshorts, with running shoes. I look like I could be a self-conscious skinny guy out trying to bulk up."

Russel laughed and smiled. "You don't look like a guy to me. You look stunning. I like your long red dress and your boots are very sexy. But I can picture you in your incognito exercise wear," he said.

"I would have slipped the boots off and walked around on the sand, if the high tide wasn't covering it up," I said.

"It must be a king tide. It's a super full moon tonight," said Russel.

"Yes, it is a big moon. This is always a busy night in the Psych Ward, it's when all of the lunatics go off," I said.

"We should go back to mine. It looks like there's a storm brewing tonight too," said Russel. "Flossy will be scared." He was a very thoughtful guy.

Next day we woke up at Russel's house, and he was flicking through his social media for the morning news.

"Guess what?" said Russel. "There's been a fire overnight at Carina Private Hospital. One dead. Two burned, seven treated for smoke inhalation. Fuck!"

"One dead? I wonder if that was Father Clement, by any chance?" I said.

"Do you think so? God! How will we find out?"

"I can try texting Bruce or Linda. I think they're both still in there," I said.

"But their phones could be locked in the safe. And they'd have to watch what they say on their phones. We could go to tomorrow's evening NA meeting?" suggested Russel.

"Oh God, do we really have to?" I said.

"We could find out what happened a lot easier than some journalist from the Courier Mail could," said Russel.

"We could. Or we could leave that place the hell alone. Curiosity killed the cat, Russel," I said.

"It's lucky that I'm a dog person. I'm dying to find out what happened. Aren't you?" asked Russel.

"I've just got such bad memories of being dragged in there the first time. Going back will be hard," I said.

"I'll be with you. Or if you like, I'll go alone," said Russel.

"No, I'll come too," I said, "I'm very curious too, and with two of us, we have double the chance of finding out what happened."

Danny told me that we had to ring the hospital on the day to say we were attending an NA meeting. Russel drove us, we made sure we had masks, and we talked about strategies.

"The best times will be when we're lining up to go in, or during smoking time at the end," said Russel.

"If it becomes a men here, women there thing like it can, you ask the guys and I'll ask the girls," I said.

"God, it's boring like that isn't it?" laughed Russel.

We parked and walked past the Psych Ward to get to the Drugs Ward. There was a big blue tarpaulin covering the rear part of the roof of the Psych Ward. There was a skip full of burnt building materials and a backhoe parked on the lawn.

Carolyn was already waiting outside, and Danny arrived at the same time as us. The guards let us in. The Psych Ward people must have been put into spare beds in the Drugs Ward. When we walked into the conference room, two large concentric circles of chairs greeted us, all spaced 1.5 metres apart from each other. The other patients were already there.

"Hi, I'm Dave and I'm a recovering alcoholic, I'll be chairing this meeting today," said Dave. "I'm not going to lie, it's been a terrible week. We've had the fire, and the cops coming through this place like a ton of bricks. And with all this Covid 19 stuff, it's all pretty stressful and I totally understand if people have been tempted to drink or use drugs again. All of the inpatients have been questioned by the police, and that's set a few people back a bit, we've had a couple of people who applied for and were granted early release. Feel free to vent about the whole episode. I know it's pushed me to the door of the bottle shop. Um, six years and three months clean."

"Hi, I'm Linda and I'm a recovering alcoholic," said Linda. "I've been clean for seven weeks now, and I'm never drinking again. I'm studying for my Certificate Four in Accounting, and I'm already applying for jobs. I was pretty shocked by what happened on Wednesday night. Why did she have to do it on the deck? She must have known that the deck was our marshalling area in case of fire, and that we were all locked in. I breathed in heaps of smoke and had to breath with an oxygen mask for a day. The cops gave me the third degree, and asked me a lot about my brother who died almost thirty years ago, which was really weird. And moving from there to here was a pain too. But I'm glad we've got somewhere to go. And I feel sorry for Marjorie. She's in the Burns Unit and apparently is looking pretty bad."

"G'day, I'm Jack, I'm a recovering drug addict and schizophrenic," said Jack. "Ten weeks clean, and still dealing with issues. I'm a bit pissed off at Marjorie because the treadmill is one of the things she set fire too. I really miss running, and feel really antsy if I can't have a run everyday.

I waited a week when I first got in before the treadmill got here, and it was new. I guess she didn't have a lot of stuff to burn. She stacked up the chair cushions from the TV room, and the chair frames, just whatever she could pull out there. The nurse must have been doing something somewhere else to not notice. It was fucking chaos, and the guards not letting us out was fucked. I went to help Bruce carry Clement out. We had no knife to cut him down with, so we chewed through his belt and the electric lead. We both breathed in heaps of smoke and Bruce got burnt too. We all got out eventually but we had to drag Clement. He was fucked up, but we couldn't leave him there," said Jack.

"Hi, I'm Elise and I'm a recovering psychotic substance abuser," I said. "I've been clean for two months, and out of rehab for five weeks. I've had a lot of temptation since I've been out, but I've been really strong. I started with a few acting jobs, but now most of my bookings have been canceled because of Covid. But I've started building my own performance company, for when this whole thing passes. I'm sorry to hear about the fire and how people got injured. I was anxious about coming here today, but I wanted to make sure everybody was OK," I said.

"Hi, I'm Russel, I'm a recovering substance abuser. Two and a half months clean. I've also had a lot of temptation, but I've been strong and I've had support. I've been asked to work from home because of Covid, and I've still got a nice collection of spirits on the bar at home. But I only offer them to guests, I'm not touching it. I heard about the fire on the radio news, and was so worried and concerned for everyone. How did Marjorie start the fire? Did she use the stove or toaster or did she have a lighter? Burns at her age can be really serious, the poor dear. Had Clement already hung himself, and you guys went to find him to evacuate? That's so traumatic for you to have found him and dragged him out of there. That was brave, guys, to make sure everybody got out," said Russel.

"Hi I'm Max, I'm a recovering drug addict, three weeks clean," said a youngish blond man in a band t-shirt and jeans. "I've been making real progress with the cravings until the fire, and now I've got intense cravings again, and a feeling of general unease as if something terrible could happen at any minute. I know it's illogical, but it's just an overpowering feeling. I woke up on Wednesday night when the smoke alarm went off, and I tried going to the deck, but there were flames up to the ceiling and the roof when I looked. People were screaming, gathering at the door and running all over the place, and the smoke was filling the building from the ceiling down. None of the windows open, and the sprinkler system started going off, and Nurse John was calling for help from Linda's room and then from Clement's room. I went to look for something to help cut Clement down with, and smashed a window to try to get a bit of broken glass to use. Ernest tried jumping out the window, and I held him back, but then he just ran at the security guard at the door and ripped his swipe card off him. John had pulled Marjorie out of the fire, and was screaming for help, so I got a wet towel and went over to help carry her out too. John got burnt but I was lucky. Ernest made a run for it. We haven't seen him again, so I suppose he got away," said Max.

Whoa. So a number of plots became entangled on the night. Ernest escaped! Clement died. Marjorie lit a fire. Holy fuck-balls!

"Hi, I'm Carolyn, I'm a recovering alcoholic and two years clean," said Carolyn. Tracy and I have been through a stressful month with our young friend Heidi, but she's got a new place and has moved out. Yay! It wasn't all bad, though. Heidi encouraged us to have some friends over on Saturday nights, and we all invited just a couple of people. It wasn't any huge party, I know they're banned. It was more like a dinner party. But it was great to just talk and see each other face to face, especially if all the clubs and cafes are shut, and we can't go anywhere. There's quite a bit of Covid at my work at the Ipswich hospital, but we all do the drill with our PPE, and hardly any staff have caught it. So sorry to hear about you guys getting injured, and poor Clement. Hope you all get well soon," said Carolyn.

"Hi, I'm Bruce and I've got Bipolar and substance addiction," said Bruce. "Six weeks clean this time. I got out, but the pressure to use was too great so I came back in for a bit more time. It's all the musicians I work with, someone's always lighting a joint in the rehearsal room and offering it to me. I didn't smoke it, but I think I got high just passive smoking. Wednesday night was a big blur to me. Linda had dropped her computer and broken the glass, and cut her hand when she picked it up. John was helping her, and called out for anyone who was awake to bring him some bandages. On my way down the hall, I saw the fire and I went looking for an extinguisher. The guard was outside and wouldn't come in. Then he was inside and wouldn't let us out. Everyone was at the door except Clement, so I went to look for him. He was hanging and he looked pretty dead. He was hanging from the shower rail, it wasn't very high. We couldn't cut him down and the rooms were all filling up with smoke. Jack came to help and we bit through the extension cord and belt that he had used and dragged him out of there. The worst bit was the cops. The firemen came and just got straight in there, put it out, and went, but the cops hung around questioning us all until the sun came up. It totally fucked up my sleeping patterns. And my hand is burnt. Marjorie's much worse though," said Bruce.

"Hi, I'm Kath and I'm an alcoholic," said a pretty overweight brunette, about twenty-five. "Thirteen days clean. I drank until I gave myself liver disease. Both of my parents are alcoholics. But I'm going to break the tradition. I was so worried about Marjorie. I'd already stopped Clement from smashing his head on the ground one night, I didn't know that Marjorie was suicidal too. Poor Nurse John was overwhelmed by himself. My room is next to Clement's, well it was, and I'd hear him praying and talking to himself all night long. He was a tormented soul. Hopefully he has found peace now. The doctor told me that Marjorie would probably come back to our ward, when she's out of intensive care," said Kath. I'd have to try and chat with her at smoko break.

"Hi, I'm Danny, I'm a recovering drug addict," said Danny. "Seven years clean, since I lost my wife. Sometimes it takes something like that to shock you out of your habit. I'm sorry to hear about Clement, though I never met him. It sounds like you guys did everything you could to evacuate everybody. Good on you. It's easy to only think about yourself in an emergency. There has already been one character assassination of Clement in the Courier Mail, and I'm sure we'll see plenty more. It's better not to read that stuff sometimes. If the cops try to frame any of you for anything, get legal advice. I go to Capalaba NA on Friday nights, if any of you are on the south east side when you come out," said Danny.

Then it was back to Dave. "Being a friday night, we'll have a chat on the deck, but we have to practise social distancing. It's mostly the walk through to the deck area, we'll form a line and walk in spaced out single file. Someone has marked out Xes on the deck with chalk, so stand on an ex and talk loudly. It's a wank, I know, but I had to work out a 'Covid plan' to be able to keep having meetings. Thanks everyone," said Dave.

We filed out in a Covid-safe way, and stood on our exes. Russel stood on an ex near Bruce and Jack. I stood on an ex near Linda and Kath. Carolyn came to stand near the girls. I had brought a packet of extra-light ciggies, or 'air-darts' as they're called in here.

"Anyone want a ciggie, they're air-darts?" I said.

Kath said, "I'd kill for one, actually. I'm doing it hard right now."

"Here you go," I said, handing her one and lighting up my own, and handing over the lighter.

"Thanks, Elise, is it?" said Kath.

"Yeah, I'm only a month out of here, and I started seeing Russel, who I met in here," I said.

"I thought you guys came in together," said Linda. "You don't waste any time, Elise."

"He lent me his Mercedes to go on a grocery run, so I knew he must be keen," I said.

"He could never take his eyes off you," said Carolyn. "I notice that stuff."

"Well, he has been really supportive," I said. "My work has been all over the fucking show, but Russel has been a rock. He's pissed off about the lock-down because he can't take me to nice restaurants."

"You deserve a good man, Elise," said Linda. "I think that Everley asked Steve to make a film with her."

"Yeah, I got that vibe too," I said.

"So is rehab a big pick-up joint then?" asked Kath.

"Only if you want it to be," said Carolyn.

"I can't believe it about Clement and Marjorie," I said.

"Oh, that Clement,' said Kath. "With him, it was only a matter of time."

"What do you mean?" asked Linda.

"He was always trying to harm himself," said Kath. "I'd hear him praying really loudly, late at night, saying stuff like, 'forgive me Lord' and 'I'm a sinner' and shit. And he would bash his head against the wall or the floor, repeatedly."

"Shit," was all that Carolyn said. We were all thinking it.

"He must have had a lot on his conscience," said Linda.

"You didn't hear anything unusual on the night?" I asked.

"No, mate, I sleep like a log. It's got to be loud to wake me up. I didn't get up till the fire alarm," said Kath.

Perfect. Unless the cops had something on Bruce, it sounds like he's gotten away with it.

"Did the cops hassle you a lot?" asked Carolyn to Linda.

"I just couldn't understand it," said Linda. "I never left my room till we evacuated. I dropped my tablet and tried to catch it before it hit the ground, but the glass broke and cut my hand. John came in but needed band-aids and a bandage. Then Marjorie lit the fire, and it was chaos."

"What did the cops ask you?" I said.

"At first they just took a report, the same as they did from everyone. Then they came back, and started hammering me about my brother. It was like 1992 when he died, I could hardly remember him."

"Did he live in that orphanage where the priest worked – Boystown?" asked Carolyn.

"He used to steal food for us, so they put him in that place, we called it Reform School."

"Clement killed himself, didn't he? There's no way they could blame you for that," I said.

"We're in the locked ward of a mental hospital, there's no way they're pinning any crime on anybody, for fuck's sake," said Kath.

We all laughed.

Meanwhile, Russel had been over chatting with the blokes. In the car on the way home, he told me how their conversation had gone.

"Did you get to talk to Bruce?" I asked.

"Oh, Bruce is a mess. Apparently Linda was supposed to do the diversion, but Marjorie decided to choose that night to create her own diversion. Bruce was still helping Clement commit suicide when the fire broke out, and Jack was standing guard. Jack told Bruce to lock the door, and he'd come back when it was safe to leave. When they gathered at the door, Jack said Bruce was just behind him, they couldn't see much for the smoke. Jack ran back to help 'find Clement', he was dead by then, so Jack kicked the door in and found Clement dead. Others including the nurse ran in and saw Clement hanging, and in the confusion of shouting and running, they decided to try to bring the body with them. But there was nothing to cut the cord and belt with. Bruce had nicked the extension cord from behind the nurses' station, where it plugged the fridge in. Jack had smashed the surveillance camera just before he pinched it. So the new guy, smashed a window to try to make a piece of broken glass, then old Ernest tries to jump out of it," said Russel.

"It sounds like a total fucking nightmare. That Clement was a big guy. Bruce did well to get him strung up by himself," I said.

"That's the weird thing," said Russel, looking me in the eye for a moment, "Bruce said that he got in there with the cord, and the priest actually wanted to die, Bruce set up the cord with the belt as a noose, and Clement put his own head through it. Bruce said he helped weigh him down, as his knees still touched the floor, like he was praying."

"Oh, that's terrible. Still, if Bruce was one of the ones dragging him out of there, any evidence of Bruce touching him could be from the dragging out bit. That was quick thinking on their part," I said.

"A coroner would find Clement died of hanging, and other injuries might have occurred as he was cut down and dragged out. The cops couldn't pin anything on anyone, as they're all mental patients," said Russel.

"They had a big go with Linda. They drilled her about her dead brother, and asked the others if they'd seen her go to his room that night. But Linda said she could hardly remember her brother. And she had Nurse John with her when the whole thing happened," I said.

"Danny was well pleased with Bruce and the whole lot of them," said Russel.

"Well, he should be pleased. It's like he's got his own headcase hit-squad, who the law can't touch. That's quite an achievement," I said.

"Are we accomplices?" asked Russel.

"No, we're the cheer squad, I mean, the support group," I said.

270

39. Seeing Skye.

We took the last car-ferry on the Friday evening, and it was quiet. There were still some commuters in their city cars, but more four wheel drives with families, heading to weekenders. It's a pleasant forty minutes of smooth sailing to Stradbroke Island, we walked on the deck to get fresh air. Russel had taken off his suit coat, and put on a zip-up navy parker. I had a nice duffle-coat, lined with fake fur, to protect me from the wind over the bay. It was only a barge, but it felt like leaving all the worries of the big city behind us.

We drove to the pub, and checked in to our room, then lost our shoes and went for a beach walk. The restaurant downstairs was closed to diners, only doing take-away and room service, and there were Covid notices everywhere. Stradbroke island has a string of white sandy beaches between rocky headlands, with deep gorges cut into the rocks as well. Our walk was stunning, and I could see that the wind was coming up from the south that day. The Main beach had big waves, and it was gentler swell around at Cylinder beach, near our pub. We found fish and chips on the way home, some things were still open. We slept well in the solid brick luxury of the hotel, hearing the waves break on the beach.

In the morning, after a swim together, I left Russel for a walk around the beaches. I saw that the wind was more easterly, and checked out a few surfers, but no Skye. In the afternoon, I did the same thing, but this time, was more lucky. The wind had moved around to the north, and all the surfers were on Cylinder beach, lining up for positions in the waves. I phoned Russel, and got him down to wait on the beach with me.

Skye did look like me. He was tall and blond, skinny and tanned, with only a couple of tattoos. He could really surf, but was happy to wait while the younger boys and even some girls had their turns on the waves. When he came in, I let him pick up his towel, then I walked over to him.

"Skye, I'm Elise Forsyth," I said, "I think you are my brother."

"Jesus Christ! Elise, it really is you, isn't it?" said Skye, looking confused.

"Yes, it's me. I'm sorry, I had blocked you out, but in rehab I remembered. So I thought I'd try to find you," I said.

"I've tried to find you, when I was at school, and later, but I spend so much time traveling now, I just zone in on work. I thought you might not want to know me. I even tried to get my parents to adopt you too, but they said you'd already been adopted by someone else," said Skye.

"Oh, Skye, I got adopted by abusers, and then I went to a group home that was run by abusers too. But I'm glad you got a good home, and built a great career," I said.

"Oh, I've had my ups and downs. But what about you? What have you done with your life?" asked Skye.

"Me? I've done a drama degree, and a lot of modelling and acting, but now I'm forming a production company, making moving art for festivals. I just came over for the weekend with my partner, Russel," I said.

"Oh, man, I would love to take you guys to the Whale Watch, but I think it's closed, but would you like to come over to my place for diner?" said Skye. "I'm at 16 Bambara St, near Deadman's beach."

"Oh, great, we're just staying at the pub. I'll drive over, we don't really drink," I said.

"I heard the bar was closed anyway, but they couldn't shut the bottle shop, or there'd be a riot," said Skye.

"We'll come over around seven," I said.

I was excited to tell Russel, and get ready for dinner. I put on a long white dress with my grey knitted hoodie, and Russel put on his comfy jeans and a big blue jumper. We drove along the East Coast Road, all the way to the Point and back, just because it was so beautiful. We could see over the cliffs down to Frenchman's beach, and caught a glimpse of the Bather's Gorge on our long cut to Skye's place. Skye's house was the small bungalow with a brick wall on the side where the storms came in, and lots of windows around the other sides.

"Come inside, you must be Russel, it's good to meet you," said Skye.

"Nice place you've got Skye, I love the island," I said.

"Well, you can tell you two are siblings, you look like twins," said Russel.

"No, I'm the older by two years," said Skye. "If you guys want to help yourselves to drinks, I'm busy cooking, and it's nearly ready. I've got juice and tea and soda water."

Russel went to the fridge to fix drinks. Skye, in the kitchen, looked over the lounge, so it was easy to talk. On the brick wall, Skye had put up his photographs, huge curling waves, with men or women sailing across them, some just the waves, turtles and dolphins. I walked around in front of them.

"Great pictures, Skye, you really capture the movement and the clarity of the water," I said.

"It's what I always wanted to do. I love surfing, but you can't take everyone there physically, but I can show them the picture. Or the film. I do a bit of film work now too," said Skye.

"How did you get into it?" asked Russel.

"I was always into surfing, and when I was fifteen, my mum gave me an underwater camera, and I started taking photos. I got published in the surf mags, and then one of them decided to employ me, to follow the surf tour. Now I freelance, and it's great. What do you do Russel? And how did you meet Elise?" asked Skye.

"I started as an accountant, and now I manage and invest rich people's money for them. I had played in a band when I was a uni student, but we never got anywhere. I did too much coke with one of my business associates, and sent myself to Rehab. I met Elise in there, at a NA meeting. I couldn't believe my luck," said Russel.

"So you guys had a rehab romance?" asked Skye.

"When you put it like that, it sounds so tacky," I said. "We met there, but Russel didn't ask me out till later. I was so fucked up, Skye. I couldn't remember anything about myself," I said, looking down.

"Elise was in the Psych Ward, and I was in the Drugs Ward, we only met at group therapy. Elise had a lot to deal with, mentally. I was so happy to see her improve, and when she shared what she was remembering, I understood why she made herself forget. She's had no-one, for so long," said Russel.

"How did you find me, Elise? I try to keep to myself," said Skye, as he brought the plates to the table. He'd cooked mudcrabs and fish, and made a salad.

"My friend Natalie did a name change search, and found your new name. Then I visited a friend in jail, and he said you'd given them a motivational speech. You told the inmates that you lived here when you weren't on the surf tour," I said.

"Oh, right," said Skye, "I usually just say I live near a great Australia beach. I've had a stalker before, so I value my privacy. Straddie is a great place if you like to get away from it all. It's pretty quiet. Great seafood."

"This is terrific food, thanks Skye," said Russel.

"Why were you in juvenile detention, Skye?" I asked.

"It was that whole mum and dad thing. Do you remember?" asked Skye.

"I thought that dad killed mum, and then himself?" I asked, confused now.

"We couldn't very well say that when he had twenty stab wounds in his back," said Skye.

"If you killed him, you were only trying to save mum," I said.

Skye took my hand across the table, and said, "You don't quite remember it all, do you Elise?"

I shook my head.

"I tried to pull dad off mum, but she was already dead, then he started strangling me, and you picked up the knife I dropped, and got him off me. You wouldn't stop stabbing him, even after he stopped moving. I had to take the knife away and tell you to go and have a shower. The neighbours had called the cops. The cops took us to the station together, but then they separated us. They told me that one of us would have to go to jail, you or me. They took me to juvie, and initially I got seven years, but reduced to two years on appeal. Then I was lucky to get fostered, then adopted by the Riders. You had already been adopted by another family," said Skye.

"I did it?" I said. I clenched my hand. Holding the gun was just like holding a knife, if you're cutting downwards. How did I even reach him? He was grabbing Skye, who was small too, already bending down. I could see it now, feel myself doing it in my muscle memory. There was blood everywhere. Mum's face was blue, and she was covered in dad's blood. So was I. Skye grabbed my hand and dragged me to the shower, and stood under it with me. He left me there and went out to meet the police when they came in. Skye spent years in kid's jail because I did it?

"Are you alright, Elise?" Russel was saying.

"Yeah, I'm alright. I guess I'm alright. I'm as alright as anyone who killed their dad when they were eight. No wonder I blocked it out," I said.

"Sorry, I thought you had remembered," said Skye.

"Not quite every last detail," I said.

Acknowledgements.

Thanks to my Psychology lecturers at UQ, as well as Richard Fotheringham, Veronica Kelly, Adrian Kiernander RIP, Carole Ferrier and Cliff Watego RIP. Thanks to Paul Hourigan, Thomas Sidey, Anthony Richmond, Jason Kuimans, Stephen Dimmick, Andrew Druery, Tiffany Beckwith-Skinner, Mark Wilson from Hairy Dog RIP and Louis Girardi RIP. Thanks to my friends from Narcotics Anonymous. Thanks to the doctors, nurses, ambulance staff and paramedics at the Children's Hospital, Brisbane. Thanks to my fellow security guards and trainers. Thanks to my fellow writers, Dirk Flinthart, Aiki Flinthart, John Birmingham, Karen Thurecht, Jo Beresford, Krissy Kneen, Des Partridge. Thanks to the Sisters In Crime, Brisbane Writers Centre and the ASA. Thanks to my husband Edward, and my daughters Veronica and Jessica. Thanks to my dog Gypsy and my dogpark friends. Thanks to Langlands Pool, Centenary, Spring Hill Baths, Vulcana Circus, 4ZZZ FM and Spencer Howson from 4BC. Thanks to my readers and reviewers on Goodreads and Amazon Author Central.

About The Author.

Mandy Curties Partridge.

Mandy Partridge is a Brisbane writer who has done time in Perth and London. Mandy wrote "Long Pork: Behind the Bamboo Curtain" in 2020, and "Acrobalances", a nonfiction book, in 2015. Mandy is the official Brisbane Town Crier, and represents her city nationally and internationally. Mandy has written for stage and film, "Mistress Mandarella's New Boots", "The Mermaid's Necklace", "Death wears a Red Nose" and "Alice's Excellent Adventure."

Books By This Author.

"Long Pork: behind the Bamboo Curtain: A political adventure."

"Long Pork" follows expat Doctor Liza, working at the Freeport gold and copper mine in West

Papua, as she tangles with gun-runner Arthur and Konia from the Free Papua Organisation. Aurora

House. ISBN paperback 9781922403155, ebook 1922 403156. ASIN BO8SLP11R

"Acrobalances" by Mandy Partridge.

A nonfiction book about Acrobatics in Circus, Sport and Physical Theatre. Hudson Publishing.

Photographs by George Caddy, Pandora Karavan, Ponch Hawkes and others from Australia and

around the World.

ISBN 9780949873903.

www.ingramcontent.com/pod-product-compliance
Lightning Source LLC
Chambersburg PA
CBHW030529030726
47495CB00004B/915